EDGE OF EXTINCTION

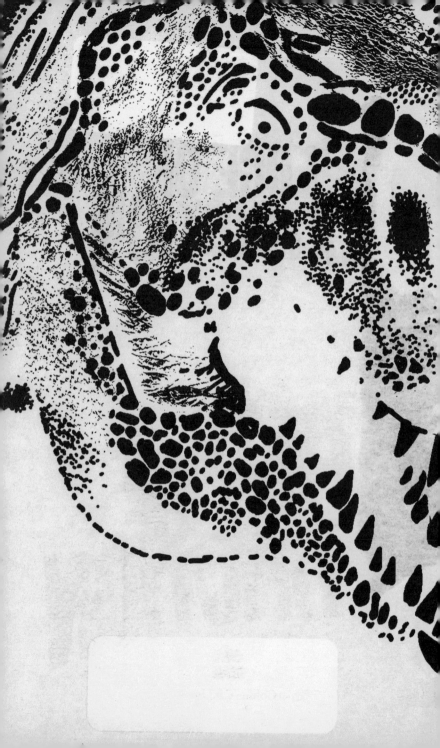

LAURA MARTIN

EDGE OF EXTINCTION

HarperCollins *Children's Books*

First published in Great Britain by HarperCollins *Children's Books* in 2016
HarperCollins *Children's Books* is a division of HarperCollins*Publishers* Ltd,
HarperCollins Publishers
1 London Bridge Street
London SE1 9GF
The HarperCollins *Children's Books* website address is
www.harpercollins.co.uk

1
EDGE OF EXTINCTION
Text copyright © Laura Martin 2016
Laura Martin asserts the moral right to be identified as
the author of this work.

ISBN 978-0-00-815289-5

Printed and bound in England by
Clays Ltd, St Ives plc

For all the kids with their nose in a book.
You are my favourite kind of dreamer.

CHAPTER 1

I needed two minutes. Just enough time to get to the maildrop and back, but I had to time it perfectly. Dying wasn't an option today, just like it hadn't been an option the last ten times I'd done this. I'd thought it would get easier after the first time. It hadn't.

I gritted my teeth and scanned the holoscreen again. The mail was due to arrive in less than a minute, and although the forest above me looked harmless, I knew better. The shadows between the trees were too silent, too watchful. I hit the refresh button. The drill was simple – refresh the screen, scan for a full minute, refresh again and scan the opposite direction. I imagined it was similar to what parents used to teach their kids about crossing the street, back when there were still streets to cross and cars to drive on them.

The thumping whirr of the plane crackled out of the holoscreen's speakers and I glanced at my watch.

6:59 a.m. Right on time. My nerves tingled with a dizzying mix of excitement and terror as I watched the small black aeroplane come into view on the holoscreen. It whipped the surrounding forest into a frenzy as it glided just above tree level. I bounced on the balls of my feet, rolling my head back and forth to stretch out my neck as I gave myself a mental pep talk. *Be smart. Be aware. Be fast,* I commanded myself. Every second counted. A small hatch at the bottom of the plane opened and a large bundle fell the remaining thirty feet to the maildrop's landing pad. The plane quickly regained altitude and zipped away over the trees towards the other side of the compound, where it would pick up the outgoing mail.

With one last look to confirm the coast was clear, I clambered up the ladder, unlatched the thick metal plate that served as the compound's entrance, and launched myself from the hatch. It was like entering another world. After the silence of the tunnel, the buzz of insects was almost deafening. My feet dug into soft, damp earth as I ran, and the humidity made the air heavy in my lungs. I felt alive. I felt exposed.

The maildrop was located one hundred yards to my left and I reached it just as the lid was starting to close. The maildrops had been designed back when our founding fathers had believed that the human race would be able to live at least part of their lives topside. They'd been wrong. The drops had all been re-engineered over fifty years ago so that no one had to risk their life venturing aboveground. But there was a thirty-second delay before the mail shot underground to be sorted and searched. Thirty seconds was all that I needed.

There were at least forty packages and letters, and I pawed through them looking for the marines' official seal. My breath caught in my throat when I finally spotted a large bundle with the black circle and golden ark on the side. Jackpot. I grabbed the package by each end and ripped it right down the middle, hoping the marines would think it had broken open when the plane dropped it. Inside I found a jumble of uniforms, regulation grey socks and port-screen batteries. I was starting to worry that this whole trip was going to be a bust when I saw the small black box. I scooped it up, feeling an almost painful surge of hope in my chest.

The tiny devices were used to pass information and messages between the compounds. This one's rubberised case was roughly the size of a deck of cards and was made to protect the data plugs on the inside from the jarring airdrop. I was already pushing it on time, but I jerked the scan plug out of my pocket and jammed it into the side of the box anyway. Maybe this time the box would have something.

Five seconds later, I'd downloaded everything the information box could tell me. Pulling out my plug, I wiped the box on my grey uniform to remove any traces of my fingerprints before pushing it back inside the half-open package. In a community where resources meant the difference between life and death, theft was not tolerated. Although, I reasoned, I hadn't *really* stolen the information. I'd just made a copy of it. Still, if the marines even suspected the information box had been breached, there would be an investigation. I double-checked the package to make sure I'd left no trace of my tampering. My double-checking nearly cost me my hands, but I managed to yank them out before the steel lid of the drop clicked shut. Seconds later the packages plummeted down the three storeys to the mailroom below.

I heard the sound of a tree branch snap and I jerked my head up, scanning the surrounding trees. My feeling of elated hope from just moments before fizzled in my chest, replaced with a cold familiar knot of fear. I'd been above for only a minute, but that was more than enough time for them to get my scent. I'd taken too long at the maildrop. Double-checking the package had been a stupid mistake. And my survival depended on not making stupid mistakes.

Turning on my heel, I sprinted for the compound entrance. I spotted the disturbance to my left when I was still fifty yards from safety. The ground began to tremble under my feet, and I willed myself not to panic. Panicking could happen later, when I was safely underground with two feet of concrete above my head.

I spotted the first one out of the corner of my eye as it burst from the trees. Blood-red scales winked in the dawn light as its opaque eyes focussed on me. It was just over ten feet and moved with the quick, sharp movements of a striking snake.

My stomach lurched sickeningly as I recognised the sharp, arrow-shaped head, powerful hindquarters and massive back claw of this particular dinosaur. It was a deinonychus. Those monsters hunted in packs. Sure enough, I heard a screech to my left, but I didn't bother to look. Looking took time I didn't have. I hit the twenty-yard mark with my heart trying to claw its way up my throat. The deinonychus was gaining on me.

Fifteen yards.

Ten yards.

Five.

Two.

Like a baseball player sliding into home base, I dropped neatly down the compound hatch and locked it in one practised movement before plummeting the remaining few feet to the floor. Two seconds later, too close for comfort, I heard its claws tear at the metal lid. A heartbeat after that, the rest of its hunting mates joined it in an attempt to flush me out of my hole. I was lucky I was fast, but then again, you didn't last long topside if you weren't.

I leaned over the small holoscreen monitor on the wall and typed in the anonymous user code my best friend, Shawn, had shown me when I was seven. Almost five years later and it still worked. The screen beeped and chirped happily at me, completely at odds with the crunching, scratching and mewling screams coming from five feet above.

The creatures would dig around the concrete-enforced entrance for another ten minutes or so before they moved on, and I didn't want anyone else to run into them. Not that many people ventured topside besides me. It wasn't exactly legal. The compound marines would be furious if they knew that an eleven-year-old girl had dared to stick her head above the ground. I bit my lip and typed in the message that would be delivered across North Compound. *"Pack of deinonychus at entrance C. 7:01 a.m. – Anonymous User."* I had my own code, but there would be too many questions if I used it. Questions I had no intention of answering.

I glanced up at the only security camera in this tunnel. It had been disabled for exactly two days and eleven hours. They weren't as hard to break as you'd think. The fact that it was *still* broken was a little amazing, though. I'd thought I'd have to break it again this morning. Compound security must be slipping with all of the extra manpower they'd been throwing at tunnel reinforcements.

I sank down against the wall and took a deep breath, readjusting my lungs to the filtered, weightless air of the compound. I always felt like my senses were somehow dulled and muted after surviving a trip topside. Things down here just weren't as bright, smells weren't as strong, and sounds weren't as crisp. Not that

I could really complain. The topside world was amazing, but the compound had one thing going for it the topside world never could. It was safe.

I pulled the scan plug out of my pocket and stared at it for a second, wondering what information I'd managed to copy this time. It was probably nothing, I warned myself. Just the same old messages about supply drops and regulation enforcements. But a stubbornly hopeful part of me couldn't help but think that maybe, just maybe, this time it would have information on it about my dad. I tucked the plug into my bag, careful to conceal it inside the lining. I would hide it properly later, but this would have to do for now. Getting the information almost made up for the fact that I was going to be late to class. Again. But at that moment, after almost becoming a dinosaur's breakfast, I couldn't make myself care.

Deciding that I was going to be late no matter what I did, I reached in my pack and pulled out my journal. Its leather cover was soft and familiar under my hands as I opened it to the entry I'd made about *Deinonychus*. I looked at my rough sketch of the dinosaur that still screeched above me and shook my head in disgust. The dusty volume I'd found on this particular dinosaur had apparently been riddled with errors. For one, that back claw was way longer than I had drawn it, and I'd had no idea just how fast they really were. I quickly sketched in the claw and added in the few facts I'd been able to gather while running for my life. Satisfied, I put it away to work on at another time. Even though the camera in this tunnel was disabled, it made me nervous having my journal out in the open. It wasn't exactly legal either.

As I shut my pack, I realised that my hands were still trembling and I flexed my fingers in irritation. I was safe, but my hammering heart and tingling nerves hadn't got the message yet. *Nothing like a good dinosaur attack to wake you up in the morning*, I thought wryly.

My dad used to tell me stories about life before the dinosaurs, before the Ark Plan had been enacted, but it was hard to believe them. I couldn't imagine a world where people lived with all that sun and sky and freedom, three things sadly lacking in North Compound. I glanced up and felt a reluctant gratitude for the thick concrete above my head. Without it, the human race wouldn't exist. And I guess when you thought of it that way, sun, sky and freedom weren't that high a price to pay.

The holoscreen beside me chirped, and I squinted at it. Someone had responded to my alert. It flashed twice and then a message scrolled across the screen. *"Sector 24 reinforcements postponed due to deinonychus report. Reminder – no resident in North Compound is authorised to have an anonymous account."* I rolled my eyes. Our government's quest to abolish the anonymous accounts had failed time and time again. But I was glad to see that tunnel reinforcements had been moved. The compound's marines occasionally had to go topside to check that the reinforcements were being installed properly, and even with their stun guns, it was often deadly. My anonymous account had potentially saved someone from getting eaten today.

One of the deinonychus's claws screeched across the metal hatch that separated their world from mine, forcing me to clap my hands over my ears. The creatures were still scrabbling and roaring, furious at their lost meal. And I wished, for the millionth time, that I could feed them the idiot scientists who had brought them out of extinction in the first place. Although being ripped to pieces might be too kind for the people who had almost wiped out the entire human race.

CHAPTER 2

I needed to get away from the compound entrance before someone came to investigate my report. As I got to my feet, I eyed my reflection in the glossy surface of the holoscreen. Sweat dripped down my face, my grey eyes looked a bit wild and my curly red hair had broken free from its ponytail. As I battled to get it back under control, I remembered my dad standing behind me, a look of pure bafflement on his face as he tried to force my hair into some sort of order. At times like that, I think both of us had thought about my mum and how, if she hadn't died giving birth to me, it probably would have been her teaching me about hairstyles. He'd actually got pretty good at it before he'd disappeared, but I'd never developed the knack. Now I scraped it back into its ponytail. It would have to do. I set out at a jog.

The floor of the tunnel slanted downwards as I

wound my way through the cement maze that made up North Compound. Of the four compounds in the United States, North was the smallest. Sometimes I loved that, but most of the time I didn't. It meant that I knew everyone in the compound and everyone knew me. Which would be fine, if everyone also didn't hate me.

I'd played around with the idea of asking for a voluntary transfer to East Compound or West Compound, but I'd never been able to bring myself to do it. The clues to my dad's disappearance were here. So here was where I had to stay. I turned a corner and ran past countless doors embedded in the tunnel wall but ignored them. They were empty by now anyway – everyone needed to report to work by seven fifteen sharp if they wanted to avoid a late penalty. That thought had me picking up my pace. Goose bumps broke out on my arms as the temperature dropped the further down into the compound I went, the walls alternating between the smooth concrete of man and the rough rock of nature.

The North Compound, like the other three compounds, had originally been built as a bunker in case of nuclear decimation or something like that. Almost two hundred years ago, engineers had sat around discussing how to turn an abandoned rock quarry into an underground city where people could survive for months or even years. They had no way of knowing that what they built would protect the human race, not from nuclear fallout but from animals that had been extinct for thousands of years. I wondered if they would have designed things differently if they'd known.

Five minutes later I was out of the habitation sector and entering the main labyrinth. Here the tunnels bustled with activity as men and women, wearing the same faded grey as myself, hurried off to their various occupations. I weaved my way through the crowd, avoiding eye contact. Five years had taken the edge off most of the residents' general dislike for me but hadn't dulled it completely. I did my best to stay off their radar, and in return they didn't go out of their way to give me dirty looks. It wasn't a foolproof system, but it worked.

I made it through the crowd and jogged down the side tunnel towards the school sector and my homeroom. Right before I rounded the last turn, a muffled sob brought me to a halt. *Not again.* I groaned as I backtracked down the tunnel. Stopping outside the third storage door, I lifted the latch and flicked on the light.

Shamus was sitting in the corner of the small stone

room, wedged between two stacks of broken desks, just like I knew he would be. His big blue eyes blinked up at me, and I sighed. Shamus Clark was five and, like me, a social outcast. His father was the allotment manager, the most hated job in the NC. No one liked to be told that their food ration had been cut. Unfortunately, the other kindergarteners in Shamus's class had inherited their parents' prejudices. I knew how that felt all too well.

"Toby again?" I asked, wiping a tear off his chubby cheek with my thumb.

Shamus nodded, scrubbing at his snotty nose with his sleeve. "He… he pushed me down, and he took my lunch ticket. I scraped my knee. See!" Tears momentarily forgotten, he proudly showed me a small scrape.

Lunch tickets were given out to each family as part of their weekly allotment and were the first thing taken away if a job was shirked or done poorly. Knowing your child would go hungry was enough to keep people reporting to work every day. It was a harsh system, but it was fair. Although that could be said about every aspect of compound life. I frowned. No matter how good the system was, it hadn't prevented Shamus from being bullied. Toby's parents didn't seem to care that

Toby stole Shamus's lunch tickets because they failed to provide them for him.

"You are going to have to start standing up for yourself," I explained gently, pulling Shamus to his feet and brushing dirt off his uniform. He wiped his eyes and looked unconvinced. "You know he only takes it because he's hungry, right?" I sighed. "Let's go. We need to get you to class." Shamus trudged along beside me, his hot little hand grasping mine, and I felt a flash of guilt. If I'd got eaten this morning, who would have found Shamus in the broom closet?

I knocked on the door of Schoolroom A, and the kindergarten teacher, Mrs Shapiro, answered looking annoyed. With a wide smile I didn't really mean, I ushered Shamus into the room.

"I'm sorry he's late. It's completely my fault."

Mrs Shapiro huffed in exasperation, slamming the door in my face. Lovely.

Two minutes later, I slid through my classroom door and to my desk in one seamless motion, keeping my eyes down in the hopes that Professor Lloyd wouldn't see me if I couldn't see him. Slipping my port out of my backpack, I laid it on my desk and finally looked up. Luckily, his back was to me as he scrawled out an agenda on the board.

"Not bad," quipped a familiar voice at my elbow. I flicked my eyes up to see Shawn Reilly grinning at me from across the aisle. I rolled my eyes and bit back a smile.

"Shamus," I mouthed in explanation as I turned on my port. Its screen flashed blue and then green.

Shawn held up three fingers, wordlessly asking if it was the third time in the last few weeks that I'd had to help out Shamus.

I shook my head and held up four. He nodded. The PA system hissed and crackled, and we all fell silent as we waited for the day's announcements.

"Good morning," barked the voice of our head marine, First General Ron Kennedy. I wrinkled my nose in dislike. Each compound had ten marines stationed to keep the peace and assist in brief forays topside for things like tunnel reinforcements. They were the Noah's eyes and ears at each of the compounds, reporting back problems that arose. Of those ten, General Kennedy was my least favourite. "Today is Monday, September 1. Day number 54,351 here in North Compound." Kennedy went on. "Please rise for the pledge." As one, the class rose and turned to face the black flag with the Noah's symbol of a golden boat positioned in the corner of the classroom.

"We pledge obedience to the cause," the class chanted in unison, "of the survival of the human race. And we give thanks for our Noah, who saved us from extinction. One people, underground, indivisible, with equality and life for all." We took our seats.

"Tunnel repairs are continuing," General Kennedy's voice went on, "so please avoid using the southern tunnels in sections twenty-nine to thirty-four unless absolutely necessary. Mail was delivered today," he said, and then he paused as though he could hear the excited murmur that had greeted this news. Mail was delivered only four times a year between compounds, and sometimes less than that due to the danger of sharing the skies with the flying dinosaurs. Although I was pretty sure the ones that flew and swam weren't technically considered dinosaurs. I remembered a science lesson where we'd learned they were really just flying and swimming reptiles, but I didn't see what the difference was.

"As always, the mail will be searched and sorted before being delivered. We appreciate your patience as we work to ensure the safety of all citizens here in North."

When I glanced up, Shawn was studying me suspiciously, his brow furrowed over dark blue eyes.

I tried to keep my face blank, like the mail being delivered and my being late had absolutely nothing to do with each other. But I was a horrible liar.

"It wasn't just Shamus, was it?" Shawn hissed, pointing an accusing finger at me. "You were checking the maildrop again."

"Shhhh," I hissed back, as General Kennedy went on to discuss the upcoming compound-wide assembly scheduled for later this week.

"You are going to get killed," Shawn frowned. "And all for some stupid hunch."

"I won't." I huffed into my still-wet fringe in exasperation, wishing that I'd chosen a best friend who wasn't so nosey. "And it isn't a hunch."

Shawn raised an eyebrow at me. "OK," I conceded. "It's a hunch." But just because year after year there'd been no mention of the disappearance of the compound's lead scientist didn't mean there never would be, I thought stubbornly. How could I explain to Shawn the pull I felt to find out what had happened to my dad? I imagined it was similar to what it felt like to lose a limb, a constant nagging sense of something missing, a dull ache that wouldn't go away.

"It's been almost five years," Shawn pointed out. "The odds that you are going to find out anything at this point are low."

"Does that mean you don't want to see the information I got?" I asked, trying hard to keep a straight face.

"I didn't say that," he grumbled, and I grinned, knowing I'd won.

"You should have at least told me you were going topside so I knew to send the marines' body crew out for you if you didn't make it back," Shawn grouched. I made a face at him. The marines' body crew was a standing joke between us. There was no such thing as a body crew in North Compound, because what lived above us didn't leave bodies behind. The crackling of the PA system signalled that announcements were over and I turned my attention back to the front of the classroom.

"Miss Mundy," Professor Lloyd called out, and I jumped. "I can only assume you were late because you were spending your time studying for our literary analysis today. Please stand," he said, not bothering to look up from his port.

"Busted," Shawn hissed.

"You too, Mr Reilly," Professor Lloyd said. Someone

25

sniggered, and my face turned bright red as I stood. Shawn grumbled something incoherent, but he stood as well.

"All right, Miss Mundy," Professor Lloyd said, glancing down at the port screen in front of him. "If you wouldn't mind giving the class an explanation of the similarities between the events that transpired in Michael Crichton's ancient classic *Jurassic Park* and the events that have transpired in our own history."

"Similarities?" I asked, swallowing hard. I'd just finished reading the novel the night before, so I knew the answer, but I hated speaking in public. Facing the pack of deinonychus again would have been preferable. I wasn't sure what that said about me.

"Yes," Professor Lloyd said, a hint of annoyance creeping into his voice. "Quickly, please. We are wasting time that I'm sure your classmates would appreciate having to work on their analyses."

"Well," I said, keeping my eyes on my desk, "in Mr Crichton's book, the dinosaurs were also brought out of extinction." I glanced up to see Professor Lloyd staring at me pointedly. He wasn't going to let me get away with just that. Clenching sweaty hands, I ploughed ahead. "The scientists in the book used dinosaur DNA, just like our scientists did a hundred and fifty years ago. And just like in the book, our ancestors initially thought dinosaurs were amazing. So once they had mastered the technology involved, they started bringing back as many species as they could get their hands on."

"Thank you, Miss Mundy," Professor Lloyd said. He turned to Shawn, who had propped one hip on his desk while he was listening to me, the picture of unconcerned boredom. Professor Lloyd noticed too and frowned. "Mr Reilly, if you wouldn't mind explaining the differences between Crichton's fiction and our own reality?"

"Sure," Shawn said, with a wide grin. "Well, the obvious one is the size of the dinosaurs, right? I mean, ours are gigantic. Almost twice the size of the ones that Crichton guy talks about."

"That's correct," Professor Lloyd said, addressing the room. "As Mr Reilly so eloquently put it, that Crichton guy based his dinosaurs on the bones displayed in museums and pictured in Old World biology books. What Crichton didn't take into account was how different our world was compared with the dinosaurs' original harsh habitat. Chemically enhanced crops, gentler climate and steroid-riddled livestock made them grow much larger than their ancient counterparts."

"You can say that again," Shawn said, and the class chuckled. I didn't laugh. The memory of my close call with the pack of deinonychus was still too fresh. They'd seemed massive, and they weren't even one of the bigger dinosaurs. The compound entrances were set in a small clearing bordered by fairly thick forest, which made it impossible for the larger dinosaurs to get too close.

"Anything else, Mr Reilly?" Professor Lloyd asked, a hint of annoyance back in his voice.

"Yeah," Shawn said. "The people in the book didn't have them as pets, on farms, in zoos, or in wildlife preserves like we did before the pandemic hit. They were mostly kept to that island amusement park thing."

"And why is that important?" Professor Lloyd prompted.

Shawn rolled his eyes. "Because when the Dinosauria Pandemic hit our world and wiped out 99.9 per cent of the human population, it was really easy for the dinosaurs to take over. Which is why we now live in underground compounds, and they live up there." He pointed at the ceiling.

"For now," Professor Lloyd corrected. "Our esteemed Noah assures us that we will be migrating aboveground as soon as the dinosaur issue has been resolved."

"They've been saying that for the last hundred and fifty years," I muttered under my breath, just loud enough for Shawn to hear. He flashed a quick grin at me. The different plans to move humanity back aboveground had spanned from the overly complicated to the downright ridiculous, but each time a new plan was brought up, the danger of the dinosaurs was always too great to risk it.

"So in summary," Professor Lloyd said, motioning for us to have a seat, "the scientists of a hundred and fifty years ago were unaware that by bringing back the dinosaurs, they were also bringing back the bacteria and viruses that died with them. And as you all know about the disastrous devastation of the Dinosauria Pandemic, I will stop talking to give you as much time as possible to complete your literary analysis. You may access the original text on your port screens."

I glanced down at my port screen, where the text had just appeared. Professor Lloyd was right – we all did know about the disastrous effects of the Dinosauria Pandemic; we lived with them every day. I tried to imagine what it had been like back then. The excitement as scientists brought back new dinosaur species daily. The age of the dinosaur had seemed like such a brilliant advance for mankind. How shocked everyone must have been when it all fell apart so horribly and so quickly.

The Dinosauria Pandemic had hit hard, killing its victims in hours instead of days like other pandemics. It had spread at lightning speed, not discriminating against any race, age or gender. I could just imagine how shell-shocked the few survivors must have been, those who'd been blessed with immunity to a disease that should have been extinct for millions of years. They must have thought the world was ending. And I guess, to some degree, it was.

One by one, the countries of the world had gone dark as news stations went off air and communication broke down in the panic that followed. I wondered if anywhere else had fared better than the United States. Were there underground compounds sprinkled throughout Europe? Asia? Africa? Were people thousands of miles away huddled together thinking they were the last of the human race just like us? I hoped so, but I doubted it.

The United States had got lucky to avoid extinction. With no formal government left standing, one man had stepped up to rally what was left of humanity. He'd called himself the Noah after some biblical story about a man saving the human race in a big boat called an ark. He'd arranged for the survivors to flee into the four underground nuclear bomb shelters located in each corner of the United States. And once we were out of the way, the dinosaurs quickly reclaimed the world, and we'd never been able to get it back.

I pulled up my copy of *Jurassic Park* on my port and flipped through the pages, looking for something I could use in my analysis. I'd hated reading Crichton's book, and I doubly hated having to write about it. His descriptions of life topside made my insides burn with jealousy. It wasn't fair that one generation's colossal mistake could ruin things for every generation to come.

CHAPTER 3

I was the first one to finish the analysis. I was always the first one to finish an analysis. Poor Shawn was sweating, his tongue protruding from compressed lips as he scribbled furiously. When the bell rang ten minutes later, he finally walked up to plug in his port and I could tell from the look on his face that it hadn't gone well.

"Miss Mundy," Professor Lloyd called out just as I was slinging my bag over my shoulder to leave, "a moment, please."

My heart sank, but I dutifully filed up to wait by the side of his desk as the last few students plugged in their ports and left. He gazed at his own port, moving his finger down the list of students, ensuring that all of our assignments had been uploaded for him to grade before turning to me with a frown.

"It didn't go unnoticed that this was your third

tardy in three weeks, Sky."

"I'm sorry, sir." I hung my head.

"I believe you know what to do with this," he said, pressing a button on his port screen. Immediately my own port vibrated and I glanced down to see a work detail form filling my screen. There was a place at the bottom for a parent's digital signature, but Professor Lloyd had crossed out the word *Parent* and instead typed the word *Guardian*.

"Yes, sir." I slipped the paper into my pocket. It would get signed for the following day, but I would be the one doing the signing.

I bolted for the door, and almost ran headfirst into Shawn.

"Whoa!" he exclaimed, catching my port screen deftly before it could hit the concrete and shatter, again. "Where's the fire?"

"No fire," I scowled, taking back my port. "Just another stupid work detail."

"Work detail is a character-building experience," he said sarcastically.

"Then why don't you serve it for me if they're so great?" I asked.

"Because my character is already flawless," he

grinned. "It would be a waste of our compound's precious resources."

I gave him an elbow to the ribs as we headed towards science class. We paused in the hallway to let the kindergarteners totter past us on their way back from the library. Shamus waved at us shyly and I noticed Toby Lant slumped at the back of the line, his head down. He had the greasy, unwashed appearance of a kid whose parents didn't keep track of how often he bathed and a hollow look that I'd seen in the mirror a bit too often. My heart hurt for him, even if he had been bullying Shamus.

"Do you have a lunch ticket?" I asked Shawn as we watched the kids' progress down the hall.

"I have my pack for the whole week. Why?" I snatched the entire pack from him before he had them halfway out of his pocket and hurried over to crouch by Shamus. Tucking the lunch tickets into his hand, I whispered in his ear. He smiled nervously at me but nodded. After a quick ruffle of his hair, I hustled back to join Shawn.

"Why did you just give Shamus my lunch tickets? Not that I'm complaining, but I was planning on eating at some point this week."

"I don't think you'll starve to death," I grinned. When Shawn had stopped growing at five feet one inch, he'd decided that what he lacked in height he could make up for in bulky muscle. I doubted that a few missed meals would affect him. "Besides, you know your aunt could get you more. Just tell her you lost them. Shamus needed to buy lunch for his new friend, Toby."

"Does Toby know he's Shamus's new friend?" Shawn asked. I shrugged. I would have given Shamus my lunch tickets, but I had lost those last week for not reporting to work detail on time.

Shawn must have understood, because he didn't say anything else about it as we ducked into our science classroom. This was my favourite class of the day because the room had a domed skylight ceiling. Of course, the Plexiglas of the skylight had been patched, repaired, barred over and reinforced in so many places that it didn't really afford much of a view of the outside world any more, but the natural light still managed to filter through, and it was a relief after the harsh fluorescents. Humans weren't meant to live their lives underground, and sometimes my skin practically itched for the sunlight.

Soon, though, even this little piece of the outside world would be taken away when the workers began concreting over the glass. Noah had insisted that we fortify all topside surfaces. This new decree seemed silly to me. The dinosaurs had never penetrated the barrier that separated our world from theirs, so why waste the resources? Unfortunately, no one asked my opinion on the matter, especially not the most powerful man in the world.

I glanced around at the rows of plants lining the walls and frowned. They would all be dead soon unless we brought some grow lights up from the farming plots. The rest of my class filed in, all eight of them. Professor Murphy moved to the front of the room to begin trimming back a fern whose leaves reminded me of Shawn's hair – floppy and out of control. Shawn sat down beside me and slid a bag of crackers on to my desk. He knew that I'd have skipped breakfast in order to make it out to the maildrop. When I went to thank him, I saw that he was working furiously on the homework from the day before. The crackers had the slightly chemical taste that most compound food had, but I savoured every one, especially now that Shawn's lunch tickets were gone. As the class began, I couldn't help but wonder if I would have resorted to stealing lunch tickets if I hadn't had a best friend who was willing to share.

Shawn and I once joked that the entirety of our education in North Compound could be summed up into two lessons. Lesson one was some variation of a history lesson about how the human race had found itself living in underground compounds. Today's English lesson with Professor Lloyd had fallen under that heading. Lesson two was how to actually survive in the compound. Professor Murphy's lecture landed squarely in the second category. She started discussing the finer points of artificial turnip germination and I zoned out immediately. Since the majority of the supplies and food for the compound were generated within the compound, lessons like this were common, but I just couldn't get excited about turnips. From the way Professor Murphy kept stifling yawns, I had a feeling that she felt the same way.

Seven hours later, when the last bell of the day finally rang, I made my way through the crowded south tunnel to find Shawn. Being crowded was a good thing. North Compound had started off with just twenty survivors. Luckily the immunity that had saved those original twenty from the Dinosauria Pandemic seemed to pass on genetically in most cases, so our population levels were slowly climbing. I think we were at ninety-five last I'd heard. After years of teetering on the edge of extinction, the human race was making a slow but steady comeback.

I tried to ignore the fact that none of my classmates felt the need to include me in their easygoing conversations. I was an island in a sea of chatter and laughter that I wasn't allowed to be a part of. Some of these kids' parents had written petitions to have me banned from attending school altogether. Luckily for me, all those petitions failed. In a community grounded on principles of collaboration and equality, even the daughter of a traitor was owed an education. *I wouldn't want to be part of their stupid conversation anyway,* I thought as I ducked my head and made my way into the library to find Shawn.

A library hadn't been on the original engineer's design plans for the compound, although they'd thought of almost everything else. There were huge spaces on the bottom level equipped with water lines and grow lights to cultivate plants, a water and electrical system that could function without any outside power or input, and even a livestock area for animals like cows or pigs. But those stalls had long ago been turned into offices and storage units since, in the chaos of fleeing the topside world, no one had thought to grab any. Now the poor creatures were extinct. A cow didn't stand a chance against a dinosaur. Which wasn't saying much. Most things didn't stand a chance against a dinosaur.

I found Shawn near the back of the library. A bench seat had been chiselled out of the concrete, and he sat in the nook, his port screen in hand, brow furrowed in concentration.

Sitting down beside him, I peered over his shoulder. "What are you working on?"

"My written analysis from this morning." Shawn grimaced. "It was apparently so terrible that Professor Lloyd said he'd let me take it home to fix."

"He posted the grades already?" I pulled out my own port screen, but before I could access the grade account, Shawn was shaking his head.

"Not yet," he said, his face flushing a little.

"Oh." I nodded, understanding. Shawn lived with his aunt, who was a council member in North Compound. And even though the law stated that no citizen should have more than another, that we share every resource available, somehow government officials still ended up with the best apartments, extra allotment tickets for food, and the most opportunities.

"I didn't ask him to." Shawn shrugged sheepishly.

"But he wants to get on your aunt's good side, right?"

"Pretty much," Shawn said. "I think he's petitioning for funding for the library or something at the next council meeting."

I leaned my head back against the cool concrete of the wall and stared up at the ceiling of the tunnel.

"I wouldn't take the help," Shawn said, "but if I don't get my grades up, I'm going to be stuck with a work assignment in sewer detail." He was right. Our grades weighed heavily in the final decision on work assignments when we turned fifteen. It wasn't like better jobs got better pay. We all worked for free because it was our responsibility to do so, and because if you didn't work, you didn't eat. But the better your grades, the better the job you were likely to be assigned. Shawn really had nothing to worry about. With an aunt as high up the chain as his was, I doubted sewer detail was in his future. However, even with my good grades, I was disliked enough that it was a possibility for mine.

"It's fine," I said, turning to smile at him. "It's not your fault everyone likes to suck up to your aunt."

"I wish *your* aunt had transferred to North Compound instead of mine."

"Shawn Reilly," I said, "stop wishing fictional relatives on me. I'm fine."

"I asked her again last night about getting you out of there, but she brushed me off and gave me the same old story about rules and regulations. It's not fair." I agreed, but telling Shawn that would just make him feel worse than he already did.

"It's OK," I said. "You deserve good things." I'd never met anyone with a bigger heart than Shawn Reilly, and without his friendship my life in the compound would be worse than miserable.

"So do you," he scowled, and the way it wrinkled his forehead and made his mouth pull down at the corners was so familiar that I had to smile.

"I can think of a way you could make it up to me," I said slyly, glancing at him from the corner of my eye, "if the guilt is *really* eating you up inside."

"So I take it your mail run this morning was a success?" he asked drily, putting his port screen away.

Shawn knew the purpose of my mail runs, and he knew full well what I needed him to do for me. But he liked to be asked. It was small payment for asking him to break the law for me on a routine basis.

I grinned wickedly. "My best friend gave me this great scan plug, and I put it to good use."

"How long did it take to upload?" Shawn asked.

"About five seconds," I said.

He nodded. "Not bad."

"Any longer and you might have had to send the body crew out after me," I admitted.

Shawn froze. "What happened?"

"A deinonychus pack."

"What kind are those again?" he asked, his forehead wrinkling in confusion.

I groaned in exasperation. For someone who lived in an underground compound because of the millions of dinosaurs stomping around overhead, Shawn knew next to nothing about them. He preferred to spend his time tinkering with anything and everything mechanical.

"They travel in packs, and have huge claws on their hind feet for ripping their prey open."

"They sound like loads of fun," Shawn drawled. "I

can see why you'd want to go running around with them."

I rolled my eyes. "You're impossible."

"No," Shawn countered, "I'm just not obsessive about researching the ugly things like some people I know. Let me guess, you already updated your journal?"

I kicked him hard in the shin, glancing around the library shelves to make sure they were deserted.

"Youch," he grimaced, rubbing his shin. "That wasn't really necessary."

"I disagree," I snapped. Shawn knew I had a strict rule about never mentioning my journal where we could be overheard. "Now are you going to help me or not?"

"Of course," he grumbled, standing up and slinging his bag over his shoulder. "I can't come tonight, though; my aunt needs my help with the new baby while she goes to a meeting."

"Tomorrow, then?" I asked.

"Sure." He nodded. "We'd better get going. Your work detail starts in fifteen minutes."

"Right," I said. Shawn turned towards the tunnel that would take me home, even though it was out of his way. After leaving the library, we turned left and walked for about five minutes before we came to a hub tunnel that split off in five different directions. Once upon a time there had been signs marking which way things were, but they had long ago broken and worn away and no one had bothered to fix them. These tunnels were our entire world, and we knew them well.

"See you tomorrow," Shawn said, heading down the tunnel second to the left, while I took the tunnel straight ahead. "Be on time!" he called over his shoulder.

I broke into a jog and didn't slow down until I hit the entryway to the Guardian Wing. Unlike the habitation sector, the Guardian Wing was built in the part of the compound that had originally been the rock quarry; its walls and rooms were cut out of granite instead of crafted out of smooth, man-made concrete. I still remembered that scary night five years ago when I'd first seen this section of the compound.

"This is your new home," General Kennedy had told my seven-year-old self after escorting me past the guardian on duty to a tiny room where a small bed and mattress sat along the back wall. "Lights go off at nine o'clock sharp, and you will be locked in at night."

"Locked in?" I'd asked.

"The Guardian Wing is for those who don't have

a place with the rest of the community. The doors are locked for safety purposes. Show some gratitude that the Noah allows you to stay here. You are a burden on our society." He'd turned and walked out, locking the door behind him. I'd looked around the tiny room and my chest had ached with homesickness for the little apartment in the seventh sector my dad and I had shared. And then the lights had gone out. I'd sat down on the icy floor, too exhausted to attempt to find the bed, and cried myself to sleep.

The sound of something scratching at my door had woken me, and I'd sat bolt upright in a panic. Before I could scream, my door had opened, and a short, stocky boy had been silhouetted in my doorway, an odd flashlight clutched in his hand. Holding a finger to his lips to keep me quiet, he'd eased the door shut behind him. He'd tiptoed over and looked down at me, sitting among the meagre supplies Kennedy had given me.

"How did you get in?" I asked, blinking tear-swollen eyes.

"Lock picks," he said, holding up two small metal sticks. "I'm Shawn."

"I'm Sky," I said, wiping my eyes on the sleeve of my grey compound jumpsuit. "Why are you here?"

I'd meant my room, but he misunderstood, dropping down to sit opposite me on the cold stone floor.

"Same reason you are," he said. "Orphaned when my parents died in the tunnel collapse two months ago."

I'd wrapped my arms protectively around myself and felt my chin jut out defiantly. "My dad isn't dead."

"Is so," Shawn argued. "Otherwise you wouldn't be in the Guardian Wing."

"Is not," I said, swallowing a lump in my throat. "There is going to be a mandatory assembly about it tomorrow."

That assembly had been awful.

His picture had been projected up on the wall while government officials explained how one person's selfishness could jeopardise the entire compound's survival. They'd itemised the things my dad had apparently stolen from the marines' barracks before he fled, explaining how the loss of those items put the survival of every inhabitant of North Compound at risk. They'd called him a traitor to the human race, worse than a criminal. There had been rewards offered for information leading to his capture. I'd watched the entire thing from the front row, feeling the disapproving glare of every citizen of North Compound digging into my back. Guilt and confusion had gnawed at my guts, almost overshadowing the feeling of loss and betrayal that made it hard to breathe. Needless to say, after that assembly, sympathies for the recently orphaned Sky Mundy had hit a record low for everyone – everyone except Shawn Reilly.

"It's not so bad here," Shawn promised. "You'll get used to it."

"I hate it here." I sniffed.

"Well," Shawn said, holding out a hand to pull me to my feet, "that's probably because you're sleeping on the floor." And he'd helped me make my bed by the light of the flashlight. A flashlight I found out he'd made from broken pieces of machinery he'd found sorting trash during work details.

Shawn had made life bearable. For two years, we lived in the Guardian Wing, breaking into each other's rooms to talk and laugh. I told him about how I was determined to find out what really happened to my dad, and he told me how he felt guilty that his parents had died in that cave-in. Apparently he'd made them late that day, putting them in the wrong place at the wrong time. Sometimes I thought he saw looking out for me as his way of making up for that, but I didn't mind. I needed a friend desperately.

I'd been almost happy. But then Shawn's aunt had been transferred to North Compound, and she'd insisted that he come to live with her. He'd wanted to refuse the offer, too worried about leaving me behind. But in the end he'd gone, while I remained with the handful of unwanted misfits our society didn't quite know what to do with.

Now I slowed my jog to a walk as River, the guardian on duty, narrowed her eyes at me in warning before going back to tapping on her port.

"Five minutes until work detail," she said without looking up. "General Kennedy is on duty tonight."

"He would be," I muttered before hurrying back to my room. I threw open my door and let it slam behind me before peeling off the grey starch of my school uniform and pulling on loose grey overalls. Everything in the compound was grey. The walls, the clothing, even the people were starting to look a little grey after so many years without sunlight. I yanked my hair out of its ponytail and jammed my hard hat on my head. I was about to bolt out of my door when I spotted my schoolbag. My heart squeezed painfully as I realised what I'd almost just done.

Grabbing it, I pulled out the scan plug and my journal. The metal springs of my bed groaned and creaked as I climbed on to it. Standing on my tiptoes, I stretched to reach the large recessed light in my ceiling. I usually avoided doing this when the lights were on, but I didn't have a choice. Using the sleeve of my jumpsuit to protect my skin from the hot bulb, I unscrewed the entire thing from the ceiling. The light canister hung down by its wires as I shoved my plug and journal inside. Shawn had shown me this trick shortly after I'd moved in. It had been too time-consuming for the compound engineers to drill through the solid rock of the original rock quarry to install lights, so they had created false ceilings instead to run their wires behind. It was the perfect hiding spot for things you didn't want found. I replaced the light and jumped off my bed just as the whistle blew to let me know I was late. I groaned and ran for the door.

CHAPTER 4

I dashed out of the Guardian Wing. Two minutes later I rounded the last corner and ploughed full force into a body. My feet went out from under me and I landed hard on my butt. I gazed up into the disapproving eyes of General Ron Kennedy.

"Late again?" he asked, pulling out his port to make a quick notation. "That makes the fourth time in three weeks." He glanced down at his port and then raised an eyebrow in amusement. "Maybe a full week of work detail will make you be more punctual."

I just stood up silently and brushed myself off. The six other people standing behind Kennedy wore overalls that matched mine and were studiously ignoring me, although I saw one woman smirk. Most of the time, I was proud of being a member of North Compound. Even though I was held at arm's length by almost everyone, it didn't change the fact that we were survivors – the scrappiest and toughest of the human race. But at times like this, I wished there was somewhere else I could be. My mind flashed to the few minutes I'd spent topside just that morning: the way the sun had felt on my skin, the smell of earth and pine in the air. A traitorous part of me wondered what it would be like to leave the grey compound tunnels behind. But I shook off the thought. Life topside might seem wonderful, but I knew all too well that it was deadly. I wiped a hand across my face and discovered I'd got a bloody nose from the impact.

"Don't get blood on your overalls," Kennedy snapped. "Or you'll have work detail for the rest of the month."

"Yes, sir," I said. As he turned and walked up the tunnel, it took everything in me not to make a face at him. Instead, I followed as he led us towards our work assignment for that evening. During the day, all the adults in North Compound reported to their various day tasks — tending the farming plots, fortifying the tunnels, cleaning the public areas, or teaching. In the evenings, those who had the misfortune of earning work detail reported for duty.

Work detail could be assigned for anything — being late, not putting enough effort into your job, offending a government official, being found with contraband in your apartment, not taking care of the compound resources. It usually lasted around three hours and was led by one of the compound's marines. The job could be something simple, like searching one of your fellow citizen's quarters, or something harder, like moving rock or chiselling out a new bench for public use. Everything was done for the common good. It was one of the things that Shawn and I both valued about compound life. It could be brutally hard, but everything was done to ensure that the human race survived another day.

For the last two weeks, my work detail had been rock removal. There had been a tunnel collapse in the southern corner of the compound and all of the fallen rock needed to be carried up the tunnels to a removal site. I usually didn't mind work detail. It gave me time to think, to use my muscles, and I liked the feeling of accomplishment that came from a job well done. But I knew that with General Kennedy overseeing us this particular detail would be anything but enjoyable.

I grabbed one of the wheelbarrows leaning against the wall and made my way over to the mound of rock and rubble blocking the tunnel. Luckily, this one had been empty when it collapsed. Without the ceiling above, I was able to look up through three levels of tunnels. It was an eerie sight. This tunnel had been one of the newest additions to North Compound, built to create a shortcut from the business section to the residential tunnels. Unfortunately, many of the engineering skills for constructing tunnels like this had been lost over the years. Grabbing a rock the size of my fist, I threw it into my wheelbarrow. It rang hollowly against the metal, sending echoes up and down the tunnel. Mine was the first one filled, and I turned it around, careful not to bump into anyone, and began the arduous task of pushing it back up the tunnel.

"Hold it," General Kennedy said, coming over to inspect the contents of my wheelbarrow. "That's only half full. Fill it the rest of the way before you head up to the drop site."

I thought about telling him that if I filled it any more it would be too heavy to push. But I knew a hopeless case when I saw one. So instead, I rolled it back around and headed down to retrieve more rocks. I felt his eyes on me as I worked. General Kennedy had been the one who led the search of our apartment on the night my dad disappeared. I was the daughter of a traitor, and he wasn't going to let me forget it.

When I returned to my room two hours later, my muscles burned and my hands were covered in blisters. I was about to flop down on my bed when I noticed that it wasn't made. A prickle of unease raced up my spine as I looked around my room. My school uniform was no longer in a pile by the foot of my bed but rather shoved haphazardly into the corner. My dresser drawers stood open, their contents spilling out. Thankfully my light was still screwed tightly into the ceiling. Sighing in relief, I sank down on to my bed. I'd been searched, again. Just then the lights blinked out and the lock on my door clicked.

"Well," I grumbled. "That's just perfect." I spent the next half hour struggling to put my things back where they belonged. Compound searches were done randomly, but I got the feeling my room was searched more often than most. No one trusted the offspring of a traitor. I finally climbed into bed, too exhausted to even change out of my work overalls, and fell asleep almost instantly.

When I woke up the next morning, I stared at the ceiling of my room, trying to ignore the fact that every movement sent pain radiating down my arms and legs.

I stood up and unscrewed my light. I pulled out my journal and plunked back down on my bed. It was time to finish updating my information on *Deinonychus*.

The journal had been a gift from my dad for my seventh birthday, three days before he had disappeared. I'd woken up that morning to the sound of him singing. He had this big booming voice that always seemed at odds with his tall, slim build. That morning, it had been a rendition of 'Happy Birthday' in French. I'd smiled and rolled over, pretending to be asleep as he switched to singing 'Happy Birthday' in Russian. My dad collected languages. In a society where we owned nothing and shared everything, knowledge was one of the few things left to collect. He spent all his free time away from the lab, where he worked as a technology expert, studying any language he could get his hands on. He was fluent in ten of them and knew five others well enough to sing 'Happy Birthday'. A fact he demonstrated as he switched from Russian to Chinese. This was too much, and I giggled.

"Is the birthday girl awake?" he'd asked, and I felt the soft bristle of his beard brush my cheek as he bent to give me a kiss. I giggled, and he flung my covers on to the floor, laughing when I squealed in protest.

"She can't sleep the day away! Up! Up! Or you won't have time to open your birthday present." He started another round of 'Happy Birthday' in German, and handed me a small package wrapped in one of his grey lab coats.

"What is it?" I asked, sitting up.

"A gigantic spider," he teased. "I found it wandering around the lab, and thought, I know who'd love this. Sky!"

I rolled my eyes. My dad knew how much I hated bugs. "What is it really?"

"Open it and find out," he laughed.

I carefully unfolded each of the corners of the lab coat, revealing the soft leather cover of a book.

"But, Dad," I said, stroking the cover reverently, "we aren't allowed to own books."

"Which is why it's not a book," he smiled, and lifted the cover to reveal thick ivory pages, each one blank. "It's a journal."

"A journal." I'd repeated the unfamiliar word, trying to hide my disappointment. I'd hoped it was a book. There was nothing better than the feel of a real book. It was so much better than a port screen, but North Compound had strict rules requiring that all books stay in the library for safekeeping. It made sense: just like everything else in the compound, we had no way to replace them, so we had to preserve and protect them.

"You must never show anyone that you have this," my dad cautioned. "It's very valuable, and just like the books, individual citizens aren't allowed to own them."

"Is it like your compass?" I asked.

"It's exactly like my compass," my dad said, pulling it out of its hiding place inside his jacket. "We don't show anyone or tell anyone that we have it." I looked down at the journal with newfound appreciation. I'd always been a little jealous of my dad's compass. It was broken, but it was his. Now I had something that was mine. I liked the feeling.

"How did you get it?" I asked.

"I have my ways." He winked. "And it's even more valuable than a book in our library."

"Really? Why?"

"Because it's going to contain the great and wonderful thoughts of Sky Mundy," he smiled.

I studied it for a moment, flipping through its blank pages as though they might shatter if handled too roughly. "Thank you," I said.

"Anything for you, my dear," my dad said, hugging

my shoulders. "Anything for you."

Three days later, my dad disappeared. He'd tucked me into bed, and the next thing I knew I was waking up to the marines searching our apartment. One of them had taken my compound-issued backpack and stuffed some of my clothes into it before making me sit outside in the tunnel. I must have been a sorry sight: seven years old, terrified and crying so hard my eyes had practically swollen shut as everything in our apartment was confiscated. No one searched my bag, though. It went unnoticed in the chaos. If they had, they'd have found the journal, cleverly concealed within the lining at the bottom of the bag. My dad had managed to hide it for me in the one place the marines wouldn't think to look. It had been so well hidden that I hadn't found it until weeks later when I noticed that my bag was heavier than it should be. I could still remember how excited I'd been.

I'd opened the journal eagerly, expecting a letter from my dad explaining why he'd left the way he had, and when he was going to come back for me. But as I paged through and found it blank, my heart sank. He had left me nothing.

It wasn't until I reached the back half of the journal

that I discovered its secret, and I gasped at what my dad had done to my birthday present. A rough circle had been cut out of the back half-inch of pages, creating the perfect hiding spot for his worn brass compass. I gingerly pulled it out of its paper nest, rubbing my fingers across the worn brass. The lid of the compass had long ago broken off and the small dial inside that was supposed to point north was stuck halfway between south and west. I'd flipped through the remaining pages, each with a gaping hole in its centre, but every single one was blank. No note. No explanation. What good were hundreds of blank pages if he couldn't even fill one?

I felt like someone had punched me in the gut, and for a moment I almost believed the marines. Maybe my dad really was just a selfish criminal. Maybe he didn't have a reason for leaving the compound, and me, behind. I'd squeezed my eyes shut and let the pain and anger roar through me until all that was left was a hollow pinched feeling in my chest.

But then I'd opened my eyes, set the compass back inside the journal for safekeeping and pushed away my doubts. Although I'd still been bitter that he'd had time to hide his precious compass but not to write even one word to me, I knew my dad. He wouldn't have left me unless he absolutely had to.

After that day, I'd begun researching dinosaurs and putting my findings on to those empty pages. We knew about the dinosaurs of a hundred and fifty years ago, but no one was brave enough to do any kind of extended study on the dinosaurs that roamed our world now. So I read the few books we had in our library, trying to understand what my dad might have faced when he left the compound to survive topside.

Surviving topside. The statement alone was one of those oxymorons, like friendly takeover or loud whisper. No one could survive topside. The human race was no longer at the top of the food chain. In fact, we were somewhere near the bottom these days. And after centuries of being the predator, we weren't very good at being the prey. The thought of what my dad had encountered up there terrified me. If I was brutally honest with myself, I knew the odds were against him surviving very long, but part of me was unwilling to give up the hope that he was out there somewhere. So while I waited underground, desperate for answers, I researched the creatures that made the topside world so deadly.

I opened my journal to the beginning and looked at my early sketches. I couldn't help but notice that my drawing skills had really improved. The first dinosaur I'd drawn was weirdly disproportional, and a little froglike. The compound buzzer sounded, and I jumped guiltily. School, I'd forgotten all about school. I ran a hand through my dishevelled curls, making them stand up and frizz out alarmingly. I was still wearing my grimy overalls from the night before, and I looked awful and smelled worse. A shower was not optional this morning. Grabbing my towel, I threw open my door, and yelped in surprise to find Shawn standing there, his hand poised to knock.

"What are you doing here?" I asked, putting my hand to my pounding heart.

"Hello to you too," Shawn said. He looked me up and down, an eyebrow raised. "Although I have to admit, you've looked better. Trying out a new unshowered-crazy-person look I should know about?"

"I was just heading to the shower," I said.

"I thought you said that you needed my help?" He glanced up and down the tunnel to make sure it was clear and then leaned in conspiratorially. "A certain scan plug you wanted looked at?"

"Right!" I said, feeling excitement bubble up in my chest. "Did you bring it with you?"

Shawn nodded and came inside holding up the port screen. Unlike our standard-issue port screen, his was one of the bigger, older models that had been retired years ago. I jumped on my bed to retrieve the scan plug, but no sooner had I unscrewed my light than it flickered and died. Sending us into darkness.

"Not again," I groaned, reaching for the flashlight by my bed.

Shawn looked up at my light and shrugged. "It's probably just one of the wires coming loose. It wasn't really meant to have someone pulling it out of the ceiling every day."

"Says the boy who showed me how to do it," I said, feeling indignant.

"That wasn't my point," Shawn said, climbing on my bed to remove the metal panel on the side of the light. "All I'm saying is that none of the compound systems was built to last as long as they have. It's really pretty impressive when you think about it."

"What I don't get," I grumbled, interrupting him before he could get any momentum in his admiration of the Noah's ingenuity in shared resources or compound sustainability, two of his favourite topics, "is how we get new port screens and holoscreens every few years, but we can't get new lights?"

"Well," Shawn said, inspecting the guts of the light, "our government values port screens and holoscreens. They are small, and West Compound has the equipment to manufacture them. The Noah's plane can deliver them. They are what you call portable." He began pawing through the inside of the light, twisting here and tightening there. "Industrial-sized lights," he went on, "aren't exactly portable. And since updating them isn't vital to our survival, no one is spending precious time and energy making new ones."

He was right. I hated the technology disconnect in North Compound. So many of the things we used were just patched-up versions of what the original survivors had brought with them.

Shawn twisted something inside the light and it flashed back to life. Grinning broadly, he jumped off my bed and took the massive port screen from my hand. Shawn had found it during one of his work details sorting for recyclable materials in the compound's trash heap and, after months of work and scavenging parts, had managed to get it up and running. I hadn't really understood the point when we each had working ports, but I'd quickly changed my tune when I realised that, unlike our ports, his was off the grid.

I handed the scan plug to Shawn.

"Can you get it uploaded while I shower?" I asked.

He grunted absentmindedly, perching on my bed to tap at the screen. Shawn loved these behind-the-scenes glimpses of the inner working of the compounds, the coming and going of supplies, the nitty-gritty details that went into keeping the remains of the human race alive. After I'd had a chance to look it over for any information about my dad, he would spend days poring over the files. I could picture him as a top compound official someday, or maybe even the Noah. The thought filled me with pride.

Trying not to get my hopes up, I grabbed my towel and dashed out of the door for the bathroom. Three minutes later I was back, and I found Shawn frowning at the screen of his makeshift port.

"Found anything?" I asked, plopping down beside him. I ran my fingers through my wet curls, and he made a face at me as the motion sent droplets of water over his screen. He gingerly wiped them away with his sleeve.

"It looks like the mandatory assembly in a couple of days will be about the compound entrances."

I waved my hand impatiently. "I meant anything about my dad."

"Nope," Shawn said.

I sagged in disappointment. "Are you sure?"

"Positive," he nodded, shutting down the port. He glanced at me, taking in the disappointment on my face, and frowned. "Don't look so down," he said.

"But I am," I whined, flopping backwards on the bed to stare glumly at the ceiling. "It's been five years. I'm never going to know what happened to him. He left me a stupid blank journal and a stupid broken compass, and I was stupid for thinking I could find out anything from the compound's stupid information boxes."

"That's a whole lot of stupid you're slinging around," Shawn quipped.

"I feel like a whole lot of stupid."

Shawn reached over to snatch my journal off my bed. He opened it and paged through as I stared moodily at my ceiling. My rusted light still hung garishly from it, like an eyeball loose in its socket. Shawn had known about my journal for years. I'd thought my journal was so special, but he'd informed me that most people in the compound owned at least one thing. He had his recycled port and an old music box from his mum, and I'd been shocked to hear that even his aunt had a silver wristwatch. I guess it was human nature to want something to be yours and no one else's. When I finally sat up and peered over Shawn's shoulder, he was looking at a drawing of *Stegosaurus* I'd done a few weeks ago. It was one of my better drawings. I'd even drawn a person standing next to it for scale.

"Is that me?" Shawn asked, pointing at the tiny figure.

"No," I said, but then I paused. There was something about the nonchalant way the figure was standing, with the shaggy hair and arm positioning that was vaguely Shawn.

"Oh," Shawn said. "It looked a little like me."

"I should just throw it away," I groaned, throwing myself back on my bed.

"Let me guess," Shawn laughed. "Because it's stupid?"

"Yes," I frowned, as the bell rang, signalling we needed to be on our way to school.

"Well," Shawn said, "let's get going to that stupid school of ours."

"You aren't funny," I grumbled.

He stuffed my journal, the scan plug and the flashlight back into their hiding spot before screwing the light back in place. "I am, actually," he countered. "You're just in a bad mood."

"You can say that again," I said, sighing as I followed him out of the door for another day in North Compound.

CHAPTER 5

I woke up a few days later to the sound of a lock pick working at my door.

I got out of bed and shivered in the damp chill of the room as I hurried to let Shawn in.

"Go away," I moaned, when I opened the door to see him standing on my doorstep, way too alert and happy for this time of the morning. "I'm going to tell the guardians I'm sick today and skip school."

"And give up spending your birthday with me?" he asked, pretending to be hurt. "Never. Besides, we don't even have first period this morning." When I just stared at him blankly, he sighed in exasperation. "Why are you giving me that look? Because you forgot it was your birthday or because you forgot about the compound-wide assembly?"

I smacked my head.

"So both," Shawn said. "Impressive. Even for you."

"You are the only one who cares about birthdays,"

I grumbled. "I do my best to forget about mine."

Shawn grinned crookedly. "Congratulations. You succeeded."

"But I can't believe I forgot about the assembly," I groaned as I hunted around my room for my towel and soap. "They've been announcing it for days!"

I bolted for the bathroom. Five minutes later I was showered and dressed and back in my room. Shawn sat on my bed staring at his feet like they were the most interesting things in the world, and I paused for a second in my doorway, studying him. There was something off about his expression, and in my fog of sleepy shock over the forgotten assembly I hadn't noticed before. Shawn had always been horrible at secrets, and it was obvious in the worried lines of his forehead and crooked set of his mouth that he was hiding something.

"OK, spill it," I commanded. "You're hiding something. What is it?" He looked back down, nervously pulling at the fraying edge of his grey uniform sleeve. Finally he sighed and looked up at me with worried blue eyes. "It's big." He glanced back down at his sleeve, and I gritted my teeth impatiently, wishing I could yank the truth from him. "I just wanted to do something nice for your birthday, and then I found something."

Hope surged in my chest. "Did you find something about my dad on the scan plug after all?"

He shook his head. "No." A frown twisted his lips, and I knew he was lying. When I just stared at him, he looked down at his hands guiltily. "And yes," he mumbled.

"Yes?" My heart slammed to a startled stop in my chest. Had he really just said yes?

"But it wasn't on the scan plug," Shawn added quickly. "It was in this." He held up my dad's compass, and I snatched it from his hands.

"How did you get this?" I searched my memory, trying to remember the last time I'd looked at it. I'd assumed it was resting in its hiding place above my head, safe and sound in my journal.

"Remember when I was looking at your journal the other day? Well, I kind of borrowed it. I had this idea that I would fix it for your birthday."

I glanced down at the face of the compass and gaped in surprise to see that the little arm was no longer stuck; now it swung back and forth, finally settling to point north.

"Shawn," I gasped, "this is incredible." I looked up at

him in confusion. "But I don't understand. Why did you think you could fix it? You've tried before. Remember? Right after I moved into the Guardian Wing."

He nodded in agreement. "Right. But I've learned a lot since then. So I thought I'd take another crack at it. And, well, I managed to get the back off it this time. That's what stopped me the last time, remember?"

I nodded, recalling a seven-year-old Shawn sweating as he tried to unscrew the back of the compass. I'd finally stopped him, afraid he would break it.

"You said you found information about my dad?" I prompted.

"I did." He sighed. "And to be honest, I kind of thought about throwing it away and not showing you."

"Shawn!"

He held up his hands in defence. "I didn't throw it away."

I clenched my teeth so hard my jaw popped. "You need to explain, and explain quickly."

"I got the back off, and this was inside," Shawn said, pulling two small pieces of folded paper out of his pocket. My hands shook as I took them from him. Not really believing that this was happening, I unfolded the first one to reveal my dad's handwriting.

Sky,

It is my greatest hope that you never find what I've hidden inside my compass. That I will have fixed things and returned to North Compound to be with you long before your eleventh birthday, which is when I've programmed the port plug to reveal itself. Even at eleven, you will be young to do what I need you to do. But time is running out, and there is no one else I can trust.

If you are reading this, I've failed, and you need to deliver the port plug I've hidden in my compass to another member of the Colombe. Ivan is the closest to you, but I don't know where he is these days. The other member is further away, but I know his location. I have marked it for you on the map. The plug is an exact copy of the one I carry with me. The Noah's people haven't yet discovered the security breach that allowed me to steal the information contained on these plugs. Information that could forever change the fate of the human race. When they do, I'm going to have to flee, and it will be too dangerous to take you with me. I always thought that I wouldn't put you in danger for the world, but it turns out that, for the world, I will. Good luck, Sky. Know that I will love you always.

Dad

I put the paper down and stared at Shawn for a second, feeling numb. Then I lurched to my feet, ran for the waste bin in the corner, and puked. My head pounded as I emptied what little I had in my stomach. When I was done, I wiped my mouth and walked over to pick the paper back up. It was circular, its edges roughly cut, and I would bet anything that it fit perfectly into the missing circle of my journal.

Shawn looked at me in concern. "Well," he said after a minute, "that wasn't exactly the reaction I expected. Are you OK?" I didn't say anything as tears started sliding silently down my cheeks.

"Hey," Shawn said, sounding a little alarmed as he put an arm around my shoulders and squeezed. "It's OK." And then I punched him. Hard.

"You were going to throw this away?" I cried. "How could you even think about doing something like that to me?" He alone knew how many hours I'd dedicated to discovering just what had happened to my dad.

Shawn winced and rubbed the shoulder I'd punched. "There it is."

"There what is?" I snapped.

"The reaction I expected. Actually –" he rolled his shoulder – "I thought you'd go for my face."

"Don't tempt me," I muttered as I reread the letter. I was confused. After five years, I'd hoped for more than a few hastily scrawled sentences. I read it a third time. And then a fourth. My dad had put some kind of timed mechanism inside the compass, but the mechanism hadn't sprung open on my eleventh birthday like he intended it to. And today was my twelfth birthday. If Shawn hadn't decided to tinker with my compass, I wouldn't have found the letter at all.

"Why didn't the timer work?" I asked, looking up at Shawn.

He shrugged. "Something had to have come unlatched on the inside for me to be able to open it now."

I glanced back at the note and then up at Shawn. "Who do you think the *they* is he talks about? Who was after him?"

"Your guess is as good as mine. He didn't make them sound very friendly."

I nodded, considering. Then I waved the piece of paper in his face. "Do you know what this means?"

"I have a feeling you're going to tell me," Shawn said, and there was something odd about his expression. I ignored it as a heavy weight eased off my aching heart.

"It means he left for a reason," I whispered, brushing away the tears that clouded my vision. "He *had* to leave me behind."

"You thought he wanted to leave you behind?" Shawn asked.

I shrugged. After five years of thinking and rethinking, dissecting every memory of my dad I could recall, of sitting through an assembly where he'd been declared a traitor, I wasn't sure what I had thought any more.

I carefully unfolded the map. My dad had drawn a meandering path from the compound up to a small red circle located in the middle of Lake Michigan. North Compound was located in what used to be Indiana. I studied the route curiously. I knew the places on the map by name only. There had been a few history lessons in school on the surrounding topside landscape, but they were nothing but fuzzy memories now. What was the Colombe he'd mentioned? And what was a member of it doing in the middle of Lake Michigan? The note created way more questions than it answered, and I felt a surge of frustration.

I glanced at Shawn. "What port plug is he talking about?" Shawn took the working compass off the bed where I'd dropped it in my haste to read the notes. Pulling out a small screwdriver, he opened the back. I watched in amazement. I'd tried that same manoeuvre about a hundred times with no success. He handed me the back of the compass, and I looked inside.

My dad had used a piece of waterproof tape to adhere a port plug to the inside. Info plugs were used to store data outside of a port, and most of them were cylindrical, much like old-fashioned pills used to be. But this one was exceptionally tiny, no bigger than my thumbnail, and much too small to fit in a regular port screen. It seemed so fragile I was afraid to pry it off the cover.

After I examined the plug, I turned my attention back to Shawn. His face was pale and drawn.

"He wants me to leave North Compound," I said, feeling stunned as this piece of information finally got past the pure adrenaline of reading my dad's note.

Shawn shook his head. "You can't do that. No way, no how."

"That's why you didn't want to show it to me?" I realised. "Because you knew I'd want to leave?"

"No," Shawn said carefully, as though he were explaining this to someone Shamus's age, "because I didn't want my best friend to get eaten alive. No one survives topside, Sky. You know that. What your dad asked you to do is crazy."

I didn't want to admit it to Shawn, but I thought it was crazy too. I picked the note back up and read it again. Why couldn't he have included more details? Would it have killed him to tell me what I was up against?

I looked at Shawn. "Whether I go topside or not really isn't your decision."

A strange expression crossed his face, and he stared at the wall, deliberately avoiding eye contact. "You can't leave."

"I can." I was already thinking of all the supplies I'd need to get my hands on in order to survive topside. There it was, that oxymoron again: surviving topside. I swallowed hard. Could I really leave the safety of North? I glanced back down at my dad's familiar handwriting and squared my shoulders stubbornly. I'd spent the last five years of my life wishing for answers to my dad's disappearance. Now that I had them, there was no way I was going to let my dad down just because I was scared of living without two feet of concrete above my head.

"Your dad's not there, you know," Shawn said, and I snapped my head up to look at him.

"What?"

"You think your dad's there," Shawn accused. "In the middle of Lake Michigan." I stared at him a moment, stunned. I'd almost given up on the idea of ever seeing my dad again, and had told myself that I would be content if I just found out why he'd left. I realised now that I'd been lying to myself. Shawn had just called me out on a hope so deeply rooted in my soul that even I hadn't realised it was there.

"It's possible," I whispered.

"That's where you're wrong." Shawn snatched my dad's letter from my hands. "If he'd made it, he'd have come back for you. It says so right here," he said pointing.

"Even if my dad's not there, whoever is there might have answers or an explanation for why he left." I snatched the map and the note back from him. "If you want me to admit that my dad's probably dead, you're wasting your time," I muttered.

"No," Shawn said slowly, "I'm not trying to do that. You've been in orphan denial since the day we met. It's just that, if he couldn't do it, what makes you think you can?"

"Because I'm not going to let him down. Whatever is on that plug was worth abandoning me for, and I want to know – I need to know," I corrected, "what's on there." When he didn't say anything, I folded up the map and note and placed them in the back compartment of the compass, using my fingernail to screw it shut again. Realising that there was no way I was going to let this thing ride around in my journal any more, I looped one of my old shoelaces through the small ring at the top of the compass, creating a makeshift necklace.

"What you are suggesting is insane," Shawn said, sounding a little defeated.

I slipped my compass over my head and tucked it in the front of my shirt. "I'm going, Shawn."

"We'll see," Shawn said, and there was something about his tone that made me look at him sharply.

"Shawn, what do you know that I don't?" Just then the bell rang, signalling that we were going to be late if we didn't hurry.

"We need to go," Shawn said, grabbing his bag and standing up. Everything in me wanted to skip the assembly. To stay back and reread my dad's note again, to plan out how I was going to get my hands on the supplies I would need. It was going to take weeks of careful planning, a thought that made me itch with impatience. According to my dad's note, I was already a year late delivering whatever was on that plug. But I dutifully picked up my own bag and followed Shawn out of the door. If I wasn't at the assembly, a marine would investigate to find out why. And the last thing I needed right now was an investigation. As we hurried towards the assembly, I couldn't help but replay Shawn's words in my head. No one survived topside. I could only hope that I was about to prove him wrong.

CHAPTER 6

I f you cut North Compound right down the middle and pulled it apart so you could see its guts, I think it would look a lot like an anthill. At least, that's how it had looked when I'd sketched it in my journal. Tunnels and small rooms made up most of the structure, but in the centre of North Compound was the assembly hall. A small stage stood at one end of the room, but instead of chairs, the floor sloped upwards so that the citizens could stand and still see the platform. Shawn and I made it to the assembly doorway just as the last and final bell rang out throughout the compound. The marine at the door, Sergeant Novak, gave us a disapproving look, but I saw that he checked us in as present on his port. We flashed him grateful smiles and slipped inside to stand at the back of the crowd.

"If that had been Kennedy," Shawn whispered, "we would have had work detail for a month."

I nodded, my mind still preoccupied with my dad's note. Everyone fell silent as the microphone at the front crackled and screeched.

The five compound council members filed on to the podium and sat down on the low metal bench. Shawn's aunt was one of three women on the council, and I saw her scanning the crowd. She smiled when she saw Shawn, but that smile slipped a little when she spotted me standing next to him. Council member Wilkins, a short, compact man with greying hair and a wide, soft face, stood up and walked to the microphone, his port screen in hand.

"Good morning, citizens," he said.

Everyone chorused back their own 'good morning' and he smiled at us like we were a pet that had just performed a trick perfectly. "We have gathered you all together to pass on the latest news from our esteemed Noah." I watched him talk, wishing I was anywhere else. This Noah was just like the other three Noahs that had come before him, and at that moment, I couldn't have cared less what he wanted us to know. Besides, all the information he was going to tell us had been uploaded to Shawn's port a few days ago. If there had been anything important, he would have told me.

I tuned back in to council member Wilkins as he smiled broadly in my direction.

"Our Noah believes that it is his duty to ensure our safety no matter what the cost or inconvenience. As such, he is requiring that all four compounds begin the process of laying up extra supplies in the coming months." This news was met by a nervous murmur. "No need to be alarmed. We have had supply shortages in the past when the plane hasn't been able to make it, and our Noah believes it's vital to our continued survival for each of the compounds to be capable of functioning independently for periods lasting up to a year." The decree made sense. I could still remember a few winters ago when the supply plane had missed two drops in a row. We'd lost half our crop because the key valve replacement we'd needed for the watering system hadn't been delivered, and everyone had developed a lean look as we shared and conserved what little we had until the plane finally made it through.

"Here at North, we plan to do our part to help in this endeavour. As we are the primary producers of grow lights, our Noah has asked that we step up production. He has given us two months to complete this task. I am sure that none of our loyal citizens will mind putting in the extra hours in support of mankind's continued survival." This was met with more muttering, but no one protested. No one ever did. If the Noah said it, it was law.

I glanced over at Shawn to see his reaction to this, but he was studiously ignoring me. It made me feel uneasy. Shawn never ignored me, and he had an almost guilty look on his face. I made a note to pin him to a tunnel wall and force the rest of the story out of him as soon as this meeting was over. I wasn't done being mad at him for not showing me my dad's note as soon as he'd found it, but I understood why he hadn't. The compound was all he knew or ever wanted to know. Going topside was almost equal to suicide in his book. He'd been trying to protect me, just like he'd done so long ago on my first night in the Guardian Wing.

I thought again about the note. Despite Shawn's arguments against it, I hadn't given up on the idea that my dad was at Lake Michigan. Maybe he'd made it there but something had happened to keep him from coming back for me. At the very least, someone there would know what had happened to him. *Answers*, I thought, almost giddily. I was finally going to get my answers.

"Our Noah also has concerns for our safety," Wilkins went on. "He believes that compound entrance hatches present a weakness." My head snapped up, and for the first time, I really paid attention to what he was saying, feeling uneasy. "In order to ensure our compound's continued safety, we are going to be installing lock mechanisms on all compound exit hatches. General Kennedy assures me that this can be accomplished within the next day or so." Icy dread washed over me, and I turned tortured eyes to Shawn. He gazed down at his feet, guilt written all over his features. He had known this was happening. It was why he'd given me my dad's note instead of throwing it away. He knew that I wouldn't be able to leave anyway. A cold sense of betrayal slid down my spine as I stared at my friend.

"This brings our assembly to a close," Wilkins said. "Those of you involved in grow light production, please remain so we can discuss your altered work schedules."

I followed Shawn and the rest of the crowd out of the assembly hall and into the tunnels.

I knew my face was a thundercloud, but I didn't care. Shawn Reilly was going to get a piece of my mind, and possibly a black eye. They were locking the compound entrances. I hadn't even had time to wrap my head around this mission my dad had given me, let alone collect supplies I needed. I was out of time before I'd even begun. If I wanted to leave the compound, I should have done it a year ago. Now I might be trapped. I grabbed Shawn's arm to pull him down a side tunnel. From the resigned look on his face, he knew he was in for it.

"Shawn." A voice rang out through the tunnels, and we both turned to see Shawn's aunt weaving her way through the crowd. She had white-blonde hair like Shawn's, pulled back in a neat bun at the base of her neck. Her compound uniform was perfectly pressed, and she glanced at my frizzy hair and rumpled appearance with disapproval.

She turned to Shawn. "I need your help for a moment."

"Is everything OK?" Shawn asked.

"Fine," she smiled. "One of the microphones is malfunctioning and I volunteered you to take a look at it. I've already alerted your teachers, so don't worry about being late." I shot Shawn a look that made it clear that we were going to be having a very serious discussion in the near future before he turned and followed his aunt back through the crowd.

I whirled and strode down the south tunnel towards school. I wanted to skip it with every fibre of my being, but my absence would be investigated and a work detail handed out as punishment. I would get through the day, I told myself, feeling my resolve solidify, then I would get ready to leave. If I had less than twenty-four hours to prepare myself, then I would just have to make it work. I was still going to make a run for it, taking my chances that the locks hadn't been installed yet. I sat down in my first class of the day and swallowed hard. I was going topside.

Shawn's words echoed in my head: *no one survives topside.*

I spent the first few minutes of class thinking up the many ways I was going to make Shawn pay for what he'd done, but he never showed. By fourth period, I'd given up, assuming his aunt had let him take the rest of the day off for being so helpful. She had the power to do that. It wasn't until I was walking home from school alone that I realised that I might never see him again. I was still angry enough that the thought didn't bother me.

When I got back to my room, I shoved my chair under the doorknob and climbed on to my bed to empty out my hiding spot. I spread my meagre belongings out on my bed. There wasn't much. The flashlight Sean had made me sat forlornly next to my journal, scan plug and my set of lock picks. I carefully placed each item into my backpack. Opening my journal, I flipped to one of the damaged pages at the back. I had to write small and squish my words around the hole, but I made a list of supplies I would need to survive topside. It was a long list and the only place to get everything on it was the marines' barracks. My stomach flopped sickeningly at the thought. Turning a few pages, I found my meticulous accounting of the marines' schedule. I'd written it down ages ago when I first started my runs to the maildrop.

I bit my lip as I planned how I was going to get in and out of the barracks undetected. My dad had stolen his supplies from the marines when he'd disappeared, so I knew it was possible. Difficult. Deadly. But possible. I glanced at my supply list again. If I could get my hands on one of the marines' specialised camouflage body-armour suits and a stun gun, I might just have a chance. *Might* being the key word. Going topside was crazy, but I knew I'd never be able to live the rest of my life locked underground, knowing I'd passed up my one shot at finding out what had happened to my dad.

I sat back and looked around. Tonight was the last night I would spend in the compound. The thought was bittersweet, and I unscrewed my compass to read my dad's note again. Just holding it made me feel tougher, more confident than ever that I could do this. And maybe, just maybe, I would find out what had happened to my dad.

CHAPTER 7

I woke up at 4 a.m. when my alarm began vibrating. Turning it off, I crept out of my bed for the last time. My nerves were buzzing. I pulled on the grey leggings of the compound and an old long-sleeved grey thermal before grabbing my backpack. I looked around my room one last time. My compound blanket was coming with me, but everything else given to me upon my arrival at the Guardian Wing sat in a neat stack on my bed. Years of conserving and caring for our resources wouldn't allow me to leave my things in a mess. I glanced at my clock. Time to go.

I eased out of my room and closed the door behind me quietly. The tunnel was deserted and I could just make out the faint light of the guardian's desk at the end of it. My heart hammered as I crept down the dark tunnel, staying close to the wall. The last door before the lobby was the supply closet and I pulled out my lock picks. Shawn had trained me well and it took only seconds to get the door open. I slid the padlock into my pocket.

The supply closet was pretty pathetic, with only a few of the bare essentials sitting limply on almost empty shelves. After surveying the soap, extra towels, bedding and various cleaning products, I seized a bar of the compound-made soap and slipped it in my bag. I may not be able to shower topside, but if I survived longer than a few days, I was going to need to get clean somehow. That mission accomplished, I picked up one of the large metal buckets used to mop the floor and eased the door back open. I could see the guardian on duty. It was River, and she was awake, scrolling through her port screen. I took a deep breath, and with as much force as I could muster, I threw the metal bucket back down the tunnel towards my room.

I shut the supply door as the bucket clattered and banged loudly against the stone floors. The sound of River scooting her chair back echoed off the stone floor, and I held my breath, praying I wouldn't get caught. As soon as I heard her run past the supply closet to investigate, I slipped out and ran. I waited to hear my name called, but I reached the end of the tunnel undetected and turned left, pelting towards the marines' barracks. I slid to a stop outside door number twelve and stood in the shadows, chest heaving. Two minutes later a buzzer sounded, and five marines trotted out just like I knew they would. I slipped inside before the doors could slide shut again.

My eyes scanned the room; I was interested despite having only minutes to get what I needed and get out before the night shift came in. By compound standards it was luxurious. One wall held supplies, while the other had what looked like lockers flanked by thickly cushioned couches. It had a clean, bleached smell and the overhead lights were so bright they hurt my eyes.

Dashing across the room, I snatched a coil of rope, a camouflage body armour suit, a large canteen and a ration pack from the wall of supplies. The stun guns were locked inside a large glass-fronted case and I rattled the handles hopelessly, knowing my lock picks didn't have a chance against a fingerprint-coded lock. I'd just have to make do without one. Along one wall was a long, low table, and I stopped when I saw that three of the marines' ports were plugged in to charge. The marines' ports were more high-tech than the average citizen's. I picked one up so I could see if any of the holes in the side would fit my dad's port plug. I unscrewed the back cover of the compass and held it up to the port screen, but the plug inside was much too small for any of the available holes. It wasn't until I'd tucked the compass back inside my shirt that I noticed the small security camera in the corner of the room, its red light flashing. Recording. I'd only ever seen cameras at the compound entrances. This wasn't good. I bolted for the door.

Slipping out of the barracks was surprisingly easy and I took off towards the topside entrance. Running uphill was a lot harder than running down and my laboured breath echoed eerily in the silent tunnels. I had an hour before North Compound awoke, but only five minutes before the night-shift marines discovered my theft and the compound went into full lockdown. If I was still inside when that happened, it was all over. I was young, so I probably wouldn't be executed – the usual punishment for jeopardising the survival of the human race – but I wasn't positive on that.

I was almost at the last turn that would lead me to the entrance I'd used earlier in the week when the blare of an alarm sliced through the air. My heart stopped, and I hesitated for a moment before breaking into a full sprint. There should have been two minutes left before the marines even made it back to their barracks. How had someone already discovered the theft? The security camera? My careful calculations didn't matter now. I was out of time.

My leg muscles were on fire when I finally skidded around the last corner that would lead me to freedom, just in time to see the emergency gate come crashing down. The bars sizzled with the high-voltage electrical charge designed to prevent a dinosaur from entering the compound and I barely stopped before colliding with them. Ten feet away, just beyond my reach, sat the compound entrance. My eyes raked over the gate, but I knew there was no way through. The blue electricity that raced over the iron bars would stop my heart if I touched it. For a system designed to keep monsters out, it was horribly effective at keeping me in. I balled my hands into fists as angry tears pressed against the backs of my eyes. Swallowing a scream, I slammed my closed fist against the side of the tunnel wall. Stone bit into my knuckles, sending white-hot pain up my arm, but I didn't care. It didn't matter. Nothing mattered now. I'd failed before I'd even begun.

The sound of running footsteps came up the tunnel behind me, and I turned, my jaw clenched, my feet braced. If this was the end, I would meet it head on. A figure emerged from the shadows and the flashing emergency lights illuminated Shawn's familiar face. I felt a momentary rush of relief, followed immediately by gut-wrenching fear.

"What are you doing here?" I cried as Shawn dashed past me to the holoscreen embedded in the concrete of the tunnel wall.

He began typing something, his forehead scrunched in concentration. "I'd ask you the same question, but apparently I know you better than you know me."

"You don't understand." I could hear the desperation in my voice and I glanced nervously back down the tunnel, wishing there was somewhere for us to hide. "You need to leave. They're going to think you stole stuff."

He gave up on typing and ripped the entire cover of the holoscreen off the wall, letting it fall to the stone floor with a crash. He began pulling at wires. "Sorry, can't do that. Give me a second."

"You might not have a second," I warned. I could hear pounding feet and shouts getting closer. I flicked my eyes up to the security camera. The red light winked at me and my stomach clenched. Someone had fixed it. I turned back just as the gate suddenly flickered and then powered off. I blinked in shock. Without the snapping electrical charge that made it so deadly, it was nothing but widely spaced iron bars.

"Hurry up," Shawn said. "I could only deactivate it for thirty seconds." Before I could say anything, he'd ripped my backpack off and shoved it through the bars, pushed me after it. Turning myself sideways, I held my breath and squirmed through. As soon as I was clear, Shawn's pack flew through the bars and he threw himself into the same gap I'd used. He got about halfway through before he got stuck, his chest and back wedged tight between the unforgiving bars. He grunted and squirmed, his eyes wide with panic. Lunging forward, I grabbed his arm and, bracing both feet against the bars, I yanked for all I was worth. If the gate came back on now, we were both dead.

"Come on, come on," I pleaded through gritted teeth as I strained backwards. My joints creaked as I pulled with all my might. Suddenly, with a pop, Shawn came free of the gate and we both flew backwards, landing in a tangled heap on the rough stone floor. The gate reactivated. My heartbeat hammered in my ears as I untangled myself from Shawn and darted for the tunnel entrance. With a flick, I turned on the holoscreen. Shawn rushed up beside me and together we began frantically scanning the ground above.

"It looks clear," Shawn said.

"Looks can be deceiving," I said, biting my lip so hard I tasted blood. "Those things stalk compound entrances."

Shawn adjusted his pack. "They've seen lunch-on-legs pop out of the holes in the ground too often not to. We will have to risk it. I'll go out first and signal if it's safe."

"You aren't coming," I said, pulling him away from the ladder. I glanced back at the holoscreen. Still clear. "Stay here. Claim I tricked you into this or something."

"Stop!" The shout came from behind us, and I whirled round to see three of the compound's marines trapped behind the sizzling gate that had almost killed us. One of the marines was messing with the same holoscreen Shawn had. I looked back just in time to see Shawn's feet disappear through the compound hatch. Gritting my teeth in frustration, I followed.

CHAPTER 8

As soon as I was out, I clipped the large metal padlock from the storage closet on to the hatch lid, sealing it shut. The marines would just have to backtrack to a different entrance hatch before they could follow us; this one was closed for business. I'd known that I'd need a head start, but I hadn't planned on needing it this badly. I also hadn't planned on being responsible for a life other than my own. I stood up and jumped when I noticed that Shawn had a small black stun gun in his hand. How in the world had he got that? The guns packed a big enough electrical punch to stun a five-ton dinosaur, and I had thought it was impossible to steal one. Obviously, I'd been wrong.

"Which way?" he asked. He was whipping his head left and right, his eyes frantically scanning for potential threats. I yanked my compass out of my shirt. The dial spun crazily before finally settling on north.

"That way." I pointed towards a tightly packed

bunch of pine trees to our left and took off, Shawn close at my heels. Moments later we were among the thick trees. I sighed in relief and felt myself relax a fraction. The trees grew too close together for most of the larger dinosaurs to manoeuvre through. It was our only advantage over the beasts. Most of them hadn't been built to survive in Indiana's dense forests and were confined to the open areas where their massive bulk could move freely. The smaller ones that made their homes in the trees wouldn't bother us unless they were hunting in a pack. I hoped.

An ear-splitting screech brought me up short and I looked back at the compound entrance. A few marines had somehow broken the padlock and got out through the entrance hatch, but they were now in retreat. The pack of deinonychus I'd met the day before had returned, and I bit my lip as I saw one of the marines stumble three feet from the entrance. Shawn cried out as the man scrambled for the hatch on his hands and knees. He made it inside, but part of his right leg did not. I choked back the bile that rose in my throat as the dinosaur swallowed his prize and began clawing at the concrete surrounding the hatch.

"We need to move," Shawn said. I nodded as guilt

tugged at my guts. That man had lost part of his leg because of me. We ran.

Ten minutes later the compound sirens had faded behind us, and I stopped, breathing hard. I'd never been topside this long before, and the air felt heavy and moist, as though I were breathing water. It wasn't a pleasant sensation. The deinonychus attack had ensured that no one would be able to come after us for at least a few hours. We could rest, just not long. The fact that the marines had even bothered to risk their lives over a few ration packs and a suit of body armour was shocking. I would have thought they'd be glad to be rid of me. I turned to face Shawn. He had his hands on his knees, and his face was an alarming red. Sweat drenched his grey uniform.

"OK, Shawn Michael Reilly." I huffed. "Spill it. What are you doing here?"

"First of all," he said, holding up one finger, "don't call me that. I feel like you're about to assign me a work detail." I rolled my eyes and pulled out my canteen, taking a small sip. I would have to ration it until I found fresh water. When I tried to offer it to Shawn, he shook his head, pulling out a much bigger canteen than my own and taking a few deep pulls. I eyed his backpack curiously. He'd apparently got his hands on more than a stun gun.

"Yesterday," I accused, "you went on and on about how no one survives topside."

Shawn shrugged. "That's because no one does."

"Then why are you here?"

Shawn sighed and shoved his canteen back in his bag before looking at me. "To cut a long story short, I decided that I wasn't going to let you go alone. So this morning, I was planning to sit you down and tell you that I was coming too. I even brought all my gear along to show you that I was prepared." He frowned. "Then I got to your room, and you were already gone. I thought I was too late. I beat a path for the compound entrance, and that's when I heard the alarm and found you stuck behind a dinosaur stun gate. So here I am. You're welcome."

"You're welcome?" I asked, eyebrow raised. "Says the boy who got stuck in the gate."

"Oh, right." Shawn looked down, a little sheepish. "My grand rescue did lose a little something when that happened."

I shook my head stubbornly. "This is a horrible idea, Shawn. You can't come with me."

"I can," he countered. "And –" he paused dramatically, looking around himself – "it looks like I already am."

I just scowled at him, my arms crossed.

"Seriously, why would it be so horrible to have me along?" he asked.

I began pulling on my new camouflage body armour, ignoring him. "There is no way you have all the gear you need," I pointed out, motioning to my suit.

"Already taken care of." He pulled out a suit identical to my own.

I gazed at him in surprise. "How?"

"You aren't the only one who knows how to steal things around here." He began to pull his own suit on over his grey compound-issued pants. I noticed with envy that his suit fitted him like a glove where mine hung in loose, wrinkly folds, the high-tech fabric bunching awkwardly at my elbows and knees. I was just under five feet tall and small-boned, which meant that nothing the marines stocked would have fitted me well. I brushed aside the thought; I would have to fix that later.

"What about your aunt?" I cajoled. "Won't she be frantic if you just disappear? Go back now and you can claim you had nothing to do with me leaving or stealing the body armour or—"

"Stop," Shawn interrupted me. "We have two options. Option one is that we both go back to the compound. Where it's safe. I know my aunt could smooth this whole mess over." He saw the look on my face and sighed, resigned. "Option two is that you stop whining so we can get on with finding whatever is in the middle of Lake Michigan before something shows up to eat us."

My resolve to send him back faltered. "But your aunt?"

"She'll be fine. She has her new baby to worry about. She barely notices I exist these days." Shawn grinned, but something felt off about that. His aunt was the only family he had left, and I couldn't imagine her being OK with her nephew's illegal escape from the compound.

"You said yourself that no one survives up here," I tried one more time. "I believe the word you used was *insane*?" When he just looked at me, I sighed. "Option two."

Shawn grinned.

"But if you die, don't blame me," I snapped.

"Do dead people blame you for things often?"

I groaned. "I'm already regretting this decision."

He raised an arrogant eyebrow at me. "Do you even know how to use that suit you're wearing?"

"I know how to use it," I said. I did know how. You put it on, and it made it harder for dinosaurs to see you. I didn't think they had instructions beyond that.

"Do you know what this button does?" He flicked a button on my right shoulder, and the suit started to constrict around me like a balloon deflating. I gaped at it in surprise.

"How did you know how to do that?"

"Just do. A side effect of being brilliant. Should we get going again?"

I bit back my retort and nodded. He was right. The further we got from the compound, the better.

"Shawn?" I asked as I readjusted my pack on my back. "Why do you think the marines bothered to come after us?"

He shrugged. "I'm not sure. I was kind of surprised by that too."

"And they had guns on them. Did you notice?" I asked, thinking back. "I know stealing supplies is illegal, but it still seems extreme. Don't you think?" I swallowed hard, remembering the marine who had made it back to the compound hatch, but not in one piece. I hoped he'd survived.

"Maybe," Shawn said. "But you know the marines will do anything and everything to ensure the continuation of the human race. Maybe they thought we stole something more than a few supplies?"

"Maybe," I said, fingering the compass that sat around my neck. Something about the whole situation was bothering me, but I forced myself to focus on the lush forest around me instead. In this world, the marines were the least of our worries. I looked around at the dappled green light that filtered down through the thick canopy of leaves. It seemed so peaceful, but I knew that it hid deadly predators. We needed to be on high alert if we had any hope of surviving. Still, when Shawn was preoccupied with his pack, I ran my hand down the bark of the nearest tree trunk, soaking in its rough texture. I needed to reassure myself that this was really happening. I was a little worried that I was going to wake up and find myself back in my room in the Guardian Wing. Everything had happened so fast that I hadn't really processed what it would mean to come topside. And now that I was actually here, it seemed unbelievable. I looked up from my musings to find Shawn giving me a strange look, and I immediately stopped petting the tree. My face flushed red, and without another word, I glanced at my compass and headed north.

It turned out that we weren't very good at hiking. After spending our lives walking on smooth tunnel floors, we found ourselves on uneven earth for the first time. Rocks, tree branches and animal holes seemed to come out of nowhere. We both fell. A lot. To make matters worse, our thin compound shoes didn't do much to protect our feet, so that we might as well have been walking barefoot. Blisters were growing on top of blisters and I was pretty sure there was at least one hole in my right shoe. I chose not to look. There was nothing I could do about it. My only consolation was that Shawn looked just as bad as I did. Maybe worse.

I tried to stay alert to noises, but there were just too many sounds swirling around us to concentrate. Our feet crunched over the forest floor, and although at first I enjoyed the chirping birds and buzzing insects, before long it was nothing but deafening background noise. Dinosaurs were everywhere, but luckily since the trees we walked through grew practically on top of each other, they were all smaller species. I recognised a lot of them, noting in my head which ones were plant eaters and which weren't. Shawn kept his stun gun out, but the dinosaurs only stared at us curiously, scurried away or ignored us entirely. They'd probably never seen a human before, and since we were too big to eat, we were ignored. It was going to be a different story as soon as the trees started thinning out

The forest was also a refuge for a lot of the animals that had managed to survive the dinosaur takeover. I smiled at a family of chipmunks that watched us with interest. They were so much cuter than I'd ever imagined. When I'd read about them in class, I'd pictured smaller versions of the rodents that sometimes got into the compound supplies. But these were nothing like the scrawny rats and mice that lurked under supply crates and hissed when cornered. These were little balls of furry energy with their black button eyes and twitching whiskers. I wondered what other animals my science class had failed to do justice to. The thought worried me. To my surprise, the chipmunks didn't run at the sight of us. They'd forgotten that humans were predators. We probably looked like kittens compared with the giant scaly guys stomping around these days. I thought about the pictures I'd seen of deer. Those gentle souls hadn't stood a chance and had gone extinct shortly after humans went underground.

Three hours later, the sun was high overhead and we were still alive. I was kind of shocked. We'd lived our whole lives underground, convinced that the topside world was an instant death sentence, but we hadn't died yet. We were walking in silence, aware that noise could alert predators, when Shawn's voice made me jump.

"Remind me again why you thought topside was better than the compound?" he asked, slapping at one of the mosquitoes that had plagued us for the last hour or so.

"It's beautiful," I said defensively. "You just aren't used to it."

"You aren't either. Your face is bright red. I think it's sunburn." He pressed a finger experimentally against my nose, and I flinched. "I always thought that was just a myth."

"I never thought about sunburn," I admitted.

"How dare you not think of everything," Shawn said. And even though I knew he was joking, I suddenly and stupidly felt like crying. Shawn noticed and threw a companionable arm across my shoulders and squeezed.

"It's a little different than the compound, isn't it?"

"That's the understatement of the century," I agreed.

"Would it have made you feel better if I'd said I told you so?"

"No," I said, jabbing him in the ribs with my elbow.

He grinned. "Let's take a break and eat something before we pass out."

I nodded gratefully, and we plopped down next to a large tree.

"I didn't grab enough for two people," I apologised as I dug through my bag. "So we'll have to make do and keep our eyes peeled for anything edible."

"It doesn't look like you brought enough for one." Shawn eyeballed my meagre stash of stolen supplies. "Here." He offered me a muffin from his own bag. My stomach snarled greedily as I took it. I pulled off a piece and popped it in my mouth. It was gritty and bland, but it tasted divine. Shawn pulled out a muffin for himself and dug in. Apparently, he'd managed to get more food than I had. Suddenly he sprang to his feet and pulled his gun as he focussed on something behind me. I whirled round to see a pair of black eyes peering at us from the gloom of a pine bough.

"Can't be that big," he breathed. "It would never be able to come in this far." The eyes blinked, and then slowly a tiny dinosaur emerged into a slant of sunlight. It stood just under two feet tall and perched on its well-muscled back legs. It had a head like a triceratops, but its two front legs were short and carried in front of it like a T. rex. It cocked its head to the side and sat back on its haunches.

"What's wrong with it?" Shawn asked. "All the other dinosaurs this size avoided us."

"Maybe it's just friendly?" I shrugged as I crouched down to get a better look at the tiny creature. "I think it's a microceratus. I read about them. They are supposed to be really smart." I had a picture of one somewhere in my journal. I'd got the front claws wrong, though; given it too many toes. I made a mental note to fix it later.

"Could you explain to me why dinosaurs all have such complicated names? I mean seriously, who decided that every one of them needed a name with ten syllables?"

I snorted. "You're just bugged because you failed all those spelling tests when we were in third grade."

"It's hard to believe that people used to keep these

things as pets." Shawn had lowered his gun, but he kept a wary eye on the creature. "Ugly little suckers, aren't they?"

"I don't know. I think it's kinda cute in an awful, *I'm the reason you almost went extinct* kind of way."

Shawn snorted. "You would."

"Do you think it bites?" I cautiously extended a piece of muffin towards the creature.

"Probably." He settled back down against the tree. "If you feel sentimental about keeping all your fingers, I wouldn't do that."

"Oh, you worry too much," I muttered. However, deciding that it wasn't worth the risk, I tossed the piece of muffin so that it landed a few feet in front of the creature. I jumped as it darted forward to take the muffin and then scurried back to its hiding place under the trees. I pulled my journal out of my pack and made a note about the quickness and began reworking the claws with my pencil.

"Don't feed it any more," Shawn cautioned as our tiny green friend came creeping back out from under the pine, its nose twitching as it eyed my muffin hungrily. "It isn't Shamus hiding in the storage closet waiting for you to save him. That's a dangerous animal, Sky.

And I didn't pack enough supplies to feed the entire dinosaur population."

"Right." I flipped it the last bite of my muffin, which it caught dexterously between its two tiny front feet and carted away. "Just enough to give Herman a nice snack." After years of being hungry, I got a weird joy out of feeding things. I'd never told Shawn about the mouse I used to feed in the Guardian Wing. I'd named him Herman too. I named most things Herman. He'd been killed in a trap, and I'd cried for days.

"Herman?" He rolled his eyes in exaggerated exasperation. "You're impossible." He stood up and brushed himself off. A quick glance at my compass to orient myself and I led the way into the woods. Out of the corner of my eye, I saw that Herman was still following us, and smiled. I now had two friends along on this journey.

CHAPTER 9

We made our way to the edge of the pine trees and peered out at a vast meadow. Knee-high grass, shrubs and tiny purple flowers covered miles of flat ground that spread out in all directions. In the distance I could just make out a faint tree line, but to the left and right the meadow seemed to go on forever. It wasn't empty either. A small herd of what I thought were triceratops grazed about a half mile to our right, and tiny dots of green and red to our left had to be dinosaurs, but they were too far away to make out what kind. I looked up, and for the first time in my life, I saw more than just a small patch of sky. Fluffy white clouds piled on top of one another as they shuffled across a blue sky so vibrant it made my eyes hurt. I felt small as I took in all that space. I could have stared at it all day, but the snort of a triceratops snapped me back to the task at hand.

These open areas were the main thoroughfares for

the larger dinosaurs, and they were dangerous. Really dangerous. It was obvious that this particular meadow used to be a farm field of some sort, based on the rotting bits of wire fencing still visible here and there, but then again, most of Indiana had been farmland if the history books were correct. Once humans were out of the picture, though, nature had reclaimed what was rightfully hers.

I pulled out my dad's map and consulted it again. Unfortunately, it didn't have much detail on it, but that hadn't stopped me from checking it frequently as we hiked. Lake Michigan lay above us to the north, and my dad's hand-drawn path was fairly easy to follow. I wished it showed things like this meadow, so we could have avoided it. But now that we were here I was too impatient to waste hours going around it when we could cut across it in minutes. Shawn wanted to camp in the trees for the night, but even though I was more tired than I'd ever been in my life, I wanted to keep going. The marines chasing us topside had spooked me more than I was willing to admit. The more distance between North Compound and myself, the better.

"Remember," Shawn breathed in my ear, "they can hear and see about a billion times better than us."

"Duh," I snapped as a coil of nerves twisted in my stomach.

"Sorry. This just freaks me out. I've heard my whole life that these things can outrun us, outthink us and swallow us whole, and we're about to invite ourselves to dinner."

"What about Herman?" I glanced around for the little dinosaur. He'd followed us for the last few hours, no doubt wondering if we were going to provide him with any more muffins, but I didn't see him anywhere now.

"Typical Sky. Incredibly dangerous situation, and she's worried about her new pet. Perfect." Shawn muttered. I scanned the large meadow in front of us. It was a lot like scanning from a holoscreen, except this time we weren't safely underground.

"Don't stop running until we reach the trees on the far side," I said through gritted teeth, feeling ill. "Ready?"

"As I'll ever be," Shawn replied. I leapt out of the cover of the trees. Shawn was right behind me as we sprinted headlong across the meadow. My eyes were focussed on the distant trees, and I commanded my body to move faster. It responded. I felt alive, free.

My feeling of freedom faded as my muscles started to tire. I'd run on the compound's treadmills for years and never had a problem logging mile after mile. This was different, like sprinting through water or wet concrete. Each step felt weighted and heavy, and my feet slipped and slid over the uneven surface. Despite the discomfort, I pumped my arms and forced myself onwards for another minute, then two, then three. I felt a spark of worry. The trees didn't appear much closer. No sooner had this thought flashed through my mind than I heard one of the triceratops give a warning bugle and the ground shuddered beneath my feet. I darted my eyes to the left just as a gigantic scaled head emerged at the far end of the meadow, followed by a massive lumbering body. My breath caught in my throat as I took in the sheer size of the thing. It was enormous. Bigger than any dinosaur I'd encountered near the compound and the last dinosaur I'd wanted to meet. It was a tyrannosaurus rex.

I reacted on instinct, diving into Shawn and bringing us both to the ground with a sickening thump. All of the air gushed out of my lungs, but I managed to clap my hand over Shawn's mouth before he could make a sound.

Shawn was about to rip my hand off when the ground beneath us shook again, and his eyes went wide. Now he understood. Together we peeked our heads up through the grass. The T. rex swung its massive head back and forth, scanning the newly deserted meadow. No doubt wondering where his dinner had gone. I prayed that the camouflage body armour worked as well as the marines claimed it did.

The T. rex took a teeth-rattling step in our direction, its nose flaring. The rancid smell of decay and death floated across the field, and every muscle, nerve and instinct wanted me to run, to hide, to save myself. But I fought it. There was a small chance it wouldn't spot us, but there was no chance of outrunning it. Just then I heard a rustling sound behind me and my blood turned to ice. The sound got closer, and I felt Shawn reach for the stun gun.

"Don't move," I breathed. A compound-issued stun gun didn't have a hope of dropping a T. rex. The rustling grew louder and closer to where we crouched, and the T. rex swung its head around to focus on our position. I tensed to run, but before I could command my muscles to react, Herman burst out of the tall grasses to my left, chattering angrily and scampering past our heads. Shawn tensed to run as the T. rex pounded towards us, but I held on to his arm.

"Sky, it sees us!"

"Stay." I tightened my grip. The T. rex's gigantic legs ate up the distance faster than I would have thought possible. The new possibility of it crushing us crossed my mind right before it paused. Its head swung from side to side, scanning. I held my breath, not daring to make even that small sound. The moment seemed to hang in the air, frozen, time stretching endlessly. Suddenly, with an angry chirp, Herman sprang from the grass ahead of us and darted underneath the surprised T. rex's feet and back towards the trees. With a roar, the T. rex whirled, its massive tail swinging only inches above our heads.

It thundered across the field, making it to the trees seconds after Herman. The little creature stopped inside the safety of the pines, clucking and squeaking angrily. If dinosaurs could insult each other, Herman was calling the T. rex all sorts of horrible things. Enraged, the T. rex began grasping trees with its massive jaws and ripping them from the ground, their roots flinging dirt in an explosion of breaking limbs.

"Now," I breathed, grabbing Shawn's hand and

yanking him to his feet. We ran. I didn't look back to see if the T. rex had noticed us, but when the sound of trees being ripped from the ground stopped moments later, I knew we'd been spotted.

The trees were getting closer by the second, but so was the T. rex. Its hot breath blew my hair forward, and I gagged on the smell. Panic clawed at me. Our head start wouldn't be enough. We were ten feet away.

Five feet.

Two.

I dug deeper for one last burst of speed, and as we dived headlong into the dark safety of the trees, I heard the angry snap of the T. rex's jaws closing on empty air.

CHAPTER 10

I was aware of Shawn's body falling next to mine as we tumbled across the pine-covered forest floor, but my eyes were filled with nothing but the revolving image of trees and sky. When I finally came to a stop, I flopped down in the dirt, sucking air into my greedy lungs. After a few moments, I propped myself up on an elbow and looked back towards the clearing. The T. rex was furious. It ripped at the trees with its teeth, shredding the branches into small chips of mulch, which floated down around me.

"Can you believe how fast it made it back across that field?" Shawn huffed, sitting up beside me and running a trembling hand over his eyes. "I was about to tell you off for tripping me. I was so focussed on running that I never even saw that thing."

"You're welcome," I said, echoing his words from earlier.

"Yeah, thanks. I really appreciate not being dead right now."

"How about that smell? Something curled up and died in its mouth. Like, last month. I had no idea smells like that even existed." I watched as the T. rex pawed angrily at the ground, sending chunks of dirt the size of refrigerators spewing out behind it.

"Really?" Shawn flashed a lopsided grin at me. "I thought it smelled a lot like the boys' locker room back at the compound."

I giggled as the relief of being alive washed over me. Shawn gave me a funny look.

"What?" I asked.

"Nothing," he said, shaking his head. "It's just that you seem different up here. You never really giggled in the compound."

I shrugged, feeling awkward. "I'm glad Herman got away," I said, changing the subject as I began picking sticks and leaves out of my hair.

"Yeah, I was real worried about the dumb lizard that almost got us killed." He rolled his eyes, and I elbowed him in the ribs.

My compass still hung around my neck, and a quick glance revealed that it had survived my tumble.

The T. rex moved away from us and began hunting around the edge of the trees, probably hoping for another chance at Herman. Shawn was preoccupied with reorganising the contents of his pack, so I walked back towards the meadow to get a better view. The thing really was massive.

A strong hand clasped me by the shoulder, making me jump. I was about to tell Shawn to knock it off, that I was fine, but when I turned around Shawn was ten feet away from me, his eyes wide with alarm. I looked up into the green eyes of a stranger.

"Let go of her!" Shawn yelled, his voice cracking. He pulled out his stun gun and trained it shakily on the strange boy holding my arm. It was a pointless gesture. A dinosaur stun gun would knock us both out if he shot it. Shawn was clearly terrified, but I was too shocked to be scared. What was another person doing topside? The boy beside me chuckled.

"That's a cute toy, but it isn't going to do you much good out here."

"It's no toy. Let her go, or I'll shoot," Shawn said, his voice squeaking again.

The boy snorted. "Doubtful." I saw Shawn's shoulders slump slightly in defeat as his bluff failed.

When was he going to learn that I could take care of myself? Twisting, I smashed my elbow into the boy's stomach. He cried out in pain, and I ripped my arm up and out of his grasp. Not taking my eyes off his astonished face, I leapt backwards. Instantly Shawn was behind me, and we stood glaring at the stranger.

"Impressive," the boy gasped, bending over to catch the breath I had knocked out of him. I studied him. He was younger than I'd first thought, probably around our age, although his dark, close-cropped hair and bronzed skin made it hard to tell.

"Come any closer and I'll shoot," Shawn warned.

The green-eyed boy smirked, and snatched the gun from Shawn's hands faster than I'd have thought possible. Shawn barely had time to grunt in surprise.

"They told you this could drop a dinosaur, huh?" He gave the gun a yank and a twist, disassembled it in three moves. He looked inside and laughed. "I think they gave you a bum gun," he said. "I'd heard they couldn't penetrate dinosaur hide, but yours can't penetrate anything." He handed back the iron fragments. I gaped at what was supposed to be the deadliest technology in the compound. The gun was nothing but a shell. No wires, no bullets, no place for an electrical charge, completely useless.

"But…" Shawn sputtered. "This was supposed to, the marines said…"

"I wonder if all of the stun guns are fake," I said, turning to Shawn. "It would explain why the marines don't allow anyone else to use them."

"You're a quick one, aren't you?" The boy grinned. "And I'd heard you moles take a while to come around."

"Moles?" I asked, looking from Shawn's shocked face back to the boy's.

"That's what we call you compounders, because you all live underground," the boy explained, as though this were common knowledge. "Like blind moles in your tunnels."

I blinked at him stupidly. "Who's *we*? Don't you live in a compound?"

He snorted. "Uh, no. Never have. Never will. I prefer fresh air and this little thing I like to call freedom."

"That's impossible," Shawn said. "No one can survive topside. The Noah said…"

"My mum said that compound moles were brainwashed, but I didn't think you were that stupid. Don't you go to some kind of fancy school?"

"You really don't live in a compound?" I repeated.

124

My mind whirled with all of the possibilities.

The boy sighed in exasperation. "I take back what I said about you being quick. I think I passed judgement too soon. No, there's no compound around here. I would no more live underground than kiss Big Ugly over there." He grinned and nodded towards the meadow, where the T. rex was still visible in the distance. Shawn bristled beside me.

"Who are you, anyway?" Shawn asked as he tucked the fragments of his useless gun into his pack.

"I'm Todd." He held out his hand to Shawn, but Shawn just glared and made no move to shake it. I'd never seen someone our age shake hands before. That form of greeting was usually reserved for compound officials and old men. I was apparently wrong about a lot of things. Todd shrugged and offered his hand to me. I shook it hesitantly. He was tall, with a stretched-out look like he'd grown a foot overnight. Despite his gangly appearance, he moved in a fluid, graceful way that I envied. His bright green eyes were set over a long nose that looked like it'd been broken on more than one occasion.

I heard a familiar chatter and watched in amazement as Herman trotted out of the trees and right up to Todd.

The little creature sat back on its haunches, buzzing and chirping in its birdlike way. Todd chuckled and pulled a small strip of meat from a leather pouch on his belt, flipping it to the creature. Herman caught it midair, making happy little clucks.

"You know Herman?" I asked.

"Herman?" he snorted. "This is Verde, and *she* knows me very well. I raised her from an egg."

"That thing almost got us killed," Shawn fumed. He took a threatening step towards the creature, and I seized his arm to stop him. Todd yanked a large bow off his back and had an arrow on the string and pointed at Shawn almost instantaneously.

"Take another step. I dare you," Todd growled. "Verde saved your life, although now I'm thinking that wasn't one of her brighter moves."

"Saved our lives?" I asked as I warily eyeballed the massive bow in Todd's hand. How had I not noticed that thing? It was huge. It appeared to be made of a single carved bone, a dinosaur rib, maybe? Although it seemed more flexible than normal bone. The arrowhead was the size of my palm. I wondered if it could pierce dinosaur hide.

"I was on lookout and saw that stupid stunt you

two pulled. Don't you know that you never, and I mean never, run through an open field? Lucky for you, I was feeling particularly charitable and sent Verde out to distract Big Ugly over there." I glanced back towards the T. rex and shuddered.

"Thank you, Verde," I murmured. Verde peeked around Todd's legs warily, her small, beaklike nose sniffing in my direction.

Todd lowered his bow and glared at Shawn. "Unless you want some ventilation holes poked in your sorry hide, I wouldn't hurt her…" He stopped, cocking a questioning eyebrow at Shawn.

"Shawn Reilly," I filled in for him.

"Don't tell him anything about us," Shawn said, frowning.

Todd slid the bow back on to his back. "Actually, I would be delighted to hear what two compound moles are doing bumbling around my forest."

"It isn't your forest," Shawn said.

"If you're not from a compound, then where are you from?" I asked, a protective hand over my compass.

"Why should I tell you? How do I know you aren't one of that Noah guy's lackeys?"

I laughed. I couldn't help myself. The idea was too

absurd. "Because the Noah doesn't hire twelve-year-olds to be his… what did you call us? His lackeys?"

Todd stiffened, and I stopped laughing, not wanting to offend.

"That's not what I've heard," Todd said. "My mum said that guy is so power-hungry he'll recruit just about anyone if it means keeping control."

"You don't know what you're talking about," Shawn bristled. "The Noah saved us. The compound protects us; without it, the human race would be extinct."

"I'd like to present exhibit A," Todd mocked, gesturing to himself, "that proves that statement is dead wrong."

"Well, this has been fun," Shawn said, "but we need to get going." He started to turn away, but I jerked him back.

"Wait," I said, irritated. I turned my attention back to the dark-haired boy in front of me. "Have you ever met anyone else from a compound? We are looking for someone. His name is Jack Mundy?" When Todd didn't say anything, I went on. "He's around six feet tall, brown hair, a beard? Kind of skinny?"

"No, sorry," Todd said, and I could tell he didn't want to give us any more information than he already had.

"Sky," Shawn said. "I doubt your dad came this way."

Todd's eyes softened a little. "Your dad?"

"Yeah," I said. "He's been missing for five years."

Todd hesitated, biting his lip. "Well," he finally said, "Jett might have heard of him. He's the leader of the Oaks."

My heart gave a hopeful squeeze. "Could you tell me where to find him? Please?" I stopped, processing what he'd just said. "Wait. What's the Oaks?"

Todd studied us. "Are you sure you aren't government spies?"

I groaned in exasperation. "I promise."

Todd stood for a moment, torn, and I held my breath.

"I'm really not allowed to show you where I live," he finally said, and I deflated a little in disappointment. "But after that stunt you just pulled, I don't think you two would survive much longer without some help." I grinned at Shawn, but he didn't grin back.

"But," Todd said, pointing a long finger in our faces, "if you betray us, don't think I'll hesitate to put those ventilation holes in you I mentioned earlier." He patted his bow.

I gulped, nodding. "Thank you."

"Don't thank me yet," Todd said. "Jett might not let you up."

"Up?" I whispered to Shawn as Todd turned and headed away from the meadow, obviously expecting us to follow. I was about to when Shawn grabbed my backpack.

"What?" I hissed as Todd stopped and turned back, waiting.

"How do we know we can trust this guy? For all we know, he's taking us back to his mud hut to eat us. He's not from a compound, which means he's been living with no laws his entire life."

"He saved our lives."

"So *he* says. I don't like it, Sky. He has no respect for our Noah."

I groaned in frustration. "Listen. I'm willing to risk it if it means finding out about my dad. If things look dicey, we run for it. Deal?" Shawn's lips pulled into a tight line. I rolled my eyes. "I promise I won't let him eat you in his mud hut or whatever."

"I'm holding you to that."

"Aren't you even a little bit curious about how people have managed to survive if it wasn't in a compound?"

"No."

I gave him a look, and he huffed in defeat.

"OK, fine. Maybe a little."

"Make up your mind," Todd called, glancing nervously at the sky. "It's almost dark, and you've already cheated death once today."

"We're coming!" I called. "How far away is it?"

"Not far," he said, smirking. "Let me show you how the *real* people live."

CHAPTER 11

I stared up at the trees, amazed. Fifty feet high, the treetops were laden with small wooden houses, suspended by poles and beams that balanced and adhered them to the branches. Long ropes hung down, and men and women were using them as pulleys to ferry wood and people up to the tree houses.

"You live up there?" I breathed. "In the sky?"

"Up among the stars, and much too high for any passing 'saur to reach us." Todd grinned proudly. Shawn had the same amazed look on his face.

"How did you build those?" Shawn asked. "How long have you been here? How many of you are there? What do you do about pterosaurs?"

"Easy, man," Todd chuckled. "One question at a time." I couldn't blame Shawn. I had a million questions buzzing inside my head too.

"As long as you've been living underground, we've been living in the trees. Not everyone was lucky enough to fall into government-funded safe houses," Todd explained. "Don't tell me you didn't learn about us in that fancy school? And I have no idea what a ptero-whatsit is. If you are talking about the flying dinosaurs, most of them have flown south this time of year, but they've learned to avoid the village. We're all pretty good shots." He tapped his bow to show us what he meant before striding over to a tall, bearded man and clapping him on the shoulder companionably. "Jett," he said. "This is Sky and Stew."

"My *name* is Shawn," came a growl from behind me.

"Right. Sorry, Seth." Todd turned back to the man with a smug look. "Jett here is the leader of the Oaks. His word is law." The man extended his hand, eyeing us warily, and we shook it. For the first time I realised how odd we looked in our skintight camouflage. Todd and Jett were more simply dressed, in loose brown trousers and simple green tunics. The fabric had a slight shimmer to it when they moved that made them blend into the green foliage around them. I was about to open my mouth to ask about my dad when I saw the look on Jett's face and stopped myself.

"Todd," Jett said sharply, nodding to us, "a moment, please." Todd's cocky demeanour melted a little at

Jett's tone as he followed the man. Jett motioned to two other men standing near him; both wore massive bone bows like Todd's strapped to their backs. They walked over to stand by us, and although they didn't pull out their weapons, it was obvious we were being guarded.

"I don't like this," Shawn whispered.

"Relax," I murmured, not taking my eyes off Todd and Jett.

"I don't trust him."

"Who? Todd or Jett?"

"Both. We should just leave. We were doing fine on our own."

"I don't think we could leave if we wanted to," I muttered, trying to swallow my own nerves.

"For your information," he said, "getting eaten in a tree house isn't any better than in a mud hut."

"Shhh," I cautioned. "He's coming back."

Todd strode up to us, his arrogant smile no longer in sight. "Sorry about that."

"Are you in trouble?" I asked.

"No. Not yet, anyway," he replied, his face clouding over momentarily. "Jett said you can stay here tonight. But before I take you up, he insists that you submit to a search. We need to make sure you aren't carrying a tracking device." Shawn jerked in surprise, and I blinked at Todd in horror. A tracking device? They were used in the compound as a way to locate important citizens in case of emergency. And the marines had them built into their uniforms. They were all around me in the compound, so why, when I set out on the most important trip of my life, hadn't I thought to check the stuff I'd stolen for them? I mentally kicked myself. I slipped off my backpack as two men approached, serious looks on their faces. One of them began pawing through my pack, while another began patting Shawn down, running his hands over his legs and arms, down his chest and over his back. When the man finished with Shawn, he searched me.

"Well, I think that's it," Todd said as the two men walked back over to Jett. They hadn't said one word to us.

"Did you ask him about my dad?" I asked, peering around Todd's shoulder to get a better look at Jett.

"I didn't." Todd shrugged. "He was too busy telling me off for bringing you to the Oaks in the first place."

"Sorry." I grimaced. I hadn't wanted to get this strange tan boy in trouble.

"It's OK," Todd said, brushing off my apology. "He tells me off about once a week for something or other. He did say that he was going to stop by to talk to you both tomorrow. You can ask him then."

"Does it have to wait till tomorrow?" I asked, biting my lip as I glanced at Jett again.

Todd looked surprised. "What's your rush?"

I fidgeted, shifting from foot to foot as I tried to decide how much to say about why we'd come topside. "It's just that I kind of have this thing I'm trying to do," I finally said evasively. "And I'm already late doing it."

"I thought you wanted to ask about your dad?" Todd looked over at Shawn. "Is she always this confusing?"

"You have no idea," Shawn grumbled, slapping at another mosquito on his neck. *Poor Shawn*, I thought. He looked so miserable and bedraggled standing next to Todd.

"You can try," Todd said, shrugging, "but if Jett says tomorrow, he means tomorrow."

Before I could think better of it or lose my nerve, I ducked around Todd and jogged over to Jett and the sombre-looking men that had searched us.

Jett watched me approach with icy blue eyes set

under a furrowed brow. "Yes?" he asked. I swallowed hard and squared my shoulders.

"I'm looking for my dad. His name's Jack Mundy. He would have come by here around five years ago? He's tall and skinny with brown hair and a beard." I was about to go on when Jett held up a wide calloused hand to stop me.

"We have never had anyone from a compound come this way besides you and your friend over there." Jett jerked his head to where Shawn and Todd were watching us, Shawn with a wary expression, Todd looking slightly impressed.

"Never?"

"Never," Jett repeated. I sagged with disappointment, but immediately chided myself for my reaction. I hadn't expected to find him on my first day topside, if I found him at all.

"Are you sure?" "Maybe you've seen footprints in the woods that you couldn't explain?"

Jett shook his head and his stern demeanour softened a little. "I'm sorry, young compounder, but I know all that happens in this village. Your father never came this way. If he was compound born and raised, his odds of survival weren't very good. Why did you say he left the compound?"

I forced myself to look him in the eye. "I didn't."

Jett studied me for another long moment, and then he turned a wary eye to the surrounding trees. "We will have to discuss this at a later time. Night is almost upon us." Surprised, I glanced around and was startled when I noticed how dark it had become. The shadows under the trees were lengthening as the night seemed to weave itself into the very fabric of the trees. I'd never seen anything like it before. It was so much subtler than the instantaneous darkness of the compound. When I turned back, Jett had already grabbed the rope in front of him and was preparing to climb.

"But I have more questions for you," I cried, thinking of the map in my pocket. I mentally kicked myself for wasting my time asking about my dad when what I should have been asking about was how to get to Lake Michigan. *Focus*, I told myself sternly. Dad had asked me to do something important, and that something wasn't to find him. If I managed to successfully deliver the plug, then I could comb through the never-ending wilderness looking under every rock and shrub for my dad. But until then, I needed to put him out of my mind.

"We can talk tomorrow," Jett said dismissively. "I'll

stop by Todd's house in the evening."

"I won't be here in the evening," I said firmly. "Shawn and I need to keep moving."

Jett paused in his preparations with the rope and raised an eyebrow in surprise. "Then I will stop by Todd's house tonight. I believe you are planning to spend the night with young Todd?"

"We are." I nodded. "Thank you for allowing us to stay."

"You are welcome," Jett said, looking over my shoulder at Todd. He shook his head in disapproval. "Todd tends to leap and then look, and not the other way around. He shouldn't have brought you here. Now that he has, we can only hope that you are who you say you are."

"We aren't spies," I said indignantly, "if that's what you mean."

"Until later tonight, then," Jett said, clearly done with the conversation. I shot Todd and Shawn a triumphant grin. When I turned back to Jett to thank him, he was gone. Craning my head back, I saw him already halfway up one of the long ropes, climbing hand over hand as he headed towards a large tree house sixty feet overhead. I hurried back over to the boys.

"He's coming to your house tonight," I told Todd.

Todd shook his head. "I'm impressed."

"I'm not. Sky is the most stubborn person I know," Shawn said drily. "Why do you think we're topside right now instead of sleeping safely in our bug-free beds?" He slapped at another mosquito, smearing a streak of blood and bug guts down his sunburned arm.

"We better head up. It's getting late, and I'm betting you and Shep are hungry." Todd winked at me. I tried not to smile at the murderous look that crossed Shawn's face as Todd led us towards one of the long ropes. I eyed it warily and then looked up at the tree house silhouetted against the darkening sky.

"Nervous?" Todd smirked. "Don't worry; we haven't dropped anyone on their head in over a week." The colour drained from my face, and Todd chuckled. "Kidding, it's been at least a month."

"Not funny," Shawn frowned.

Todd just shrugged as he flipped open the lid of a large wooden crate buried in the ground at the base of the tree and pulled out a bundle of straps. "It's your only option unless you are planning on staying on the ground tonight. And if that's the case, then I might as well have let Big Ugly get you back in the meadow."

"These trees are dense enough to prevent large predators," Shawn objected.

"The big ones aren't always the ones you need to worry about," Todd said. I noticed that we were the only ones still on the ground. Everyone else was climbing or being pulled up to the safety of their homes.

"I'll send you both up in the harness, just to be safe," Todd continued, tossing us each a bundle of straps. "Untangle those and get yourselves buckled in." I jerked mine over my head and began tightening the ropes around my legs. I was so engrossed in figuring out which strap went where that I almost didn't notice that Shawn hadn't started moving.

I sighed. "What's the hold-up?"

"How are you getting up?" Shawn asked Todd, jerking his chin at the tree. "Where's your harness?"

Todd cocked his head to the side, a wide grin on his face. "Don't need one. I've been climbing these ropes since I could walk."

"Then I don't need one either," Shawn said, chucking his harness back in the crate. "I'll climb too."

"Shawn," I groaned in exasperation, "don't be an idiot. You've never climbed anything before. What if you're scared of heights?"

"I'm not," he said, folding his arms across his chest.

"Suit yourself," Todd said. "But let's get a move on." Seeing that I was successfully strapped into my harness, he clipped the back of it to a dangling rope. My stomach churned.

"It's really not that bad," Todd assured me.

I looked up and gulped. I didn't think I was scared of heights, but then again, I'd never had the opportunity to test that theory. Suddenly, Todd stiffened at my side. The dim forest around us had gone eerily silent. The hairs on the back of my neck stood on end.

Todd swore, yanking on a small cord as a rumble came from the shadows to our left. "Grab on," he bellowed at Shawn. A pack of green scales and teeth erupted from the trees. I screamed just as my harness went tight. Todd leapt towards me, curling his hands in the harness straps at my shoulders just as Shawn seized the straps across my back. We were jerked skywards as below us a pack of man-sized green dinosaurs snapped at the air where our feet had been only moments before.

"What are those?" I choked.

"Nightmares," Todd said breathlessly, following

my gaze. "The buggers are crazy smart and come out at night. They travel in packs. I didn't realise how late it had got." His description made me think they were probably troodon, but I hadn't realised they had feathers. These creatures were sleek, with feathers fading into scales along their joints and heads, their oversized eyes set in the front of their heads like humans staring up at us, as though they were trying to figure out the pulley dragging us to safety so they could disable it. I'd read about the troodon's massive brain, but it was eerie to see that kind of humanlike intelligence at work.

"Shawn? Are you OK?" I craned my head, trying to look over my shoulder.

"Been better," he grunted. He tried to readjust his grip, and the motion sent us swinging.

"I bet you're wishing for that harness about now, aren't you, compound boy?" Todd grinned.

"Not even a little bit," Shawn said through gritted teeth. Todd barked a laugh. I peered down at the green predators with their arrow-shaped heads and mouths full of teeth, and shivered.

"Just hold on," Todd said. "We should be up in the house soon." I realised then that he was right. The creatures were growing increasingly small, and I looked around myself for the first time. I could see out over the tops of the trees and glimpsed the horizon for the first time in my life. The sun was huge and blood-red in the sky, and I gasped as the whole world spread out before me.

"It's beautiful," I breathed. "Shawn, are you seeing this?"

"All I can see is the back of your head," he grumbled.

"Are you sure you guys are OK hanging on like that?" I asked.

Todd smiled. "I could do this all day, don't worry about me. It's your buddy I'm worried about." With a sharp jerk, our ascent stopped, sending us swinging back and forth alarmingly.

"Dang it!" Todd glared up at the tree house still thirty feet above us.

I wasn't enjoying the view any more. "What happened?"

"Stupid lifter must have busted again; too much weight. Thought I'd fixed the thing."

Shawn groaned. "This just keeps getting better and better."

"What do we do?" I asked.

"We climb, or we hang here all night," Todd said

with a strained smile. "And as much fun as this is, I don't fancy sleeping this way with our hungry friends below. Do you?" I shook my head. The harness was already digging painfully into my shoulders and back.

"I'll go first. Shawn, follow me, and then Sky," Todd instructed.

"Now you remember my name," Shawn grumbled.

"You compound moles don't have much of a sense of humour, do you?" Todd said.

"I'm actually hilarious," Shawn grunted. "Just not when I'm hanging thirty feet above angry dinosaurs."

"Fair enough," Todd said. He eyed me sceptically. "One piece of advice: don't look down. Or up, for that matter."

"She'll be fine," Shawn said.

"I wasn't worried about her." Todd winked at me, and I forced a smile on to my face. He reached for the rope attached to my harness and began pulling himself up, hand over hand. I watched him go, impressed. In less than two minutes, he had disappeared through a small square hatch in the bottom of the tree house.

"Well, this is just great," Shawn grumbled as he muscled his way up to the rope, cracking me in the back of the head with his flailing knee in the process.

"Just climb, will you?" I asked. "And don't fall. I don't want to watch you break your neck."

"That makes two of us," he said, craning his head to look down. "If it makes you feel any better, I don't think those green guys would even let me hit the ground before ripping me apart."

"How would that make me feel better?" I muttered. He started climbing, and I watched until he made it to the tree house, not wanting to swing the rope any more than it already was. I took a deep breath to fortify myself and reached for the rope above my head. It was my turn.

CHAPTER 12

The rope felt rough in my hands and the muscles in my arms were shaking within seconds. Cold sweat that I couldn't wipe away trickled down my face, and I questioned the sanity of people who lived this high up. As I climbed, my harness kept getting in the way, tangling in the slack of the rope. There was no way I would make it up to the tree house this way. I hesitated, hanging in midair, and made a snap decision. Unclipping the harness, I let the rope swing free. Someone muttered darkly above me, probably Shawn. I began climbing again, unencumbered. If I wasn't so focussed on not falling to my death, I knew I would be terrified. Instead, I felt nothing but a cold, determined focus as I pulled myself up inch by painful inch. Finally, I felt two sets of hands grab my shoulders and haul me upwards. I collapsed on to the hard wooden floor of the tree house and lay with my eyes shut, panting.

"You OK?" Shawn asked. Opening one eye, I saw

him glaring down at me. I blinked and nodded, still breathing too hard to reply. "I'm not even going to ask why you thought unhooking that harness was a good idea." He extended his hand to me and heaved me to my feet. "It wasn't. In case you wanted my opinion."

"I don't. And it wasn't nearly as dumb as not wearing one to start with." I shrugged out of the harness and scanned the inside of the small house. Todd was talking quietly to a short grey-haired woman. When she turned to look at us, I could see where Todd had got his startling green eyes. She strode over, holding out her hand to me.

"I'm Emily Birch. Mother to this devil," she said, giving Todd an indulgent smile. "I'm told your name is Sky, and I've already met Shawn. Poor lad's been having fits while you took your sweet time climbing." Emily Birch leaned in and took my arm in her hand, encircling my bicep with her fingers. "Here's the problem, child. You have noodles where your arms are supposed to be. You need to toughen up. You're a pretty one, but pretty won't keep you from being someone's lunch."

"Lovely welcome, Mum," Todd said drily. "But they learned that the hard way today with a Big Ugly in the meadow." Emily arched her eyebrow at her son and looked back at us sharply.

"Did you now? Well, you must have some luck."

"They had Verde. I sent the little rascal out to create a distraction. She earned her dinner tonight."

"You feed that thing?" Shawn asked.

"Of course we do," Todd said. "I'm surprised she isn't here yet." His face darkened momentarily with worry. "I hope she didn't get caught by those Nightmares."

"She's much too smart for that, dear. I'm sure she is just lying low until the Nightmares move on. I'm sure she'll turn up by breakfast. Speaking of food, dinner is almost ready, and I can't remember the last time we had guests." Emily smiled, turning back to the pot simmering on the small fireplace positioned in the corner of the room.

"She can't remember because we've never actually had any," Todd whispered conspiratorially. "You just made her day. She's been hoarding extra plates for years *just in case.*"

I smiled. I thought that I might like Todd. He had a spark to him, as though he was so full of life that it slipped out of his pores. I wondered if I'd be like that too, if I'd been raised in the sunlight and fresh air.

I looked around the tree house, marvelling at the differences between this home and the one I had left just that morning. The walls and floor were made of a warm worn wood, and a cool breeze drifted in through the large windows. A few strategic holes had been made in the walls and roof of the house to allow the tree's branches to grow and wind their way through unencumbered. Emily had taken advantage of these, hanging an odd assortment of pots and pans off one and stacking clothing on another. The main frame of the house was made out of something knobby and white, and on closer inspection I realised they were massive dinosaur bones. Todd saw me looking and grinned.

"They're light," he explained. "We realised a long time ago that we could construct bigger houses if we used bones as the main supports."

"They don't look light," Shawn said sceptically, standing on his toes to peer at what had to be a femur that ran along the length of the ceiling.

"Didn't you know that a lot of dinosaur bones are hollow?" Todd asked, surprised. "They have more in common with birds than reptiles."

"I'd heard that," I admitted, "but I never really

believed it." I looked around the tree house in amazement. Despite the bones, it was cosy and inviting in a way that I had never felt in the sterile grey of the compound. A threadbare couch and two heavily patched wing-back chairs stood around the fireplace. A small, round table perched in the corner. I wandered over to one of the windows and looked out at the neighbouring tree houses, their lights twinkling in the fading light.

Todd had begun to set the table. I moved to his side to help, taking the stack of plates from his hands. Each plate and piece of silverware was mismatched and chipped, and some even had delicate faded patterns of flowers around the edge. I held up a pale pink one and studied it. It was so different from the compound plates of identical size and shape. The glasses Todd handed me were equally unique, each one a different size, shape or colour, but when they were all arranged on the worn table, it looked wonderful. Emily carried over a large cast-iron pot and motioned for us to be seated.

"So what happened to the lifter?" Todd asked as he pulled off the lid and began ladling something thick and brown into our bowls.

"You know that thing is hit-or-miss." Emily shrugged dismissively. "If you hadn't put triple the weight on it, you probably would have been fine. You'll just have to fix it tomorrow morning."

"Can't wait," Todd grumbled around a mouthful of stew.

"How many people live here?" I motioned to the surrounding tree houses, thirsty for information about this strange village.

"About thirty of us." Emily smiled. "I think it might be thirty-one since Maggie had her baby last week." I looked down at the delicious-smelling brown stew in front of me and took a tentative bite. It was richer and chewier than anything I'd had in the compound.

"This is amazing," I murmured in appreciation. "What is it?"

"Roasted Duck Face," said Todd. "Jett brought one down two days ago."

"Duck Face?" I asked.

"Yeah. Really funky-looking dinosaur with this long nose that kind of looks like a duck."

I almost choked in surprise, but forced myself to swallow my mouthful.

Shawn spat his stew back into his bowl. "This is

dinosaur? We're eating dinosaur?"

"They don't seem to have a problem eating us," Todd chuckled. "So why not?"

"What do you eat in that compound if you don't eat dinosaur?" Emily asked curiously.

"Root vegetables, mostly." Shawn shrugged. "Things that can be grown or processed using grow lights. No live animals."

"No wonder you're both so scrawny." Todd grinned. I bit back a smile at the dumbstruck expression on Shawn's face. I didn't think anyone had called him scrawny in his life. People had called him short, but those people had regretted that decision.

Shawn reorganised his expression and swallowed whatever smart-alecky comment he was about to say. "So how does the government not know about you? I can't believe the Noah would let you live topside like this if he knew."

Emily and Todd stiffened, shooting each other a look before Todd responded. "You're right. That's why he doesn't know, and we plan on keeping it that way. Jett was nervous about that earlier, but I think the fact that you're just a couple of kids won him over. It's why you had to be searched. It's important that we stay off the government's grid."

I nodded. It made sense, but I noticed that Shawn looked troubled. I didn't blame him. The fact that these people even existed made me feel unbalanced. I glanced at the door of the tree house for the fifth time in less than ten minutes and hoped that Jett really would stop by tonight. I hadn't been lying when I said that Shawn and I needed to keep moving. Maybe he would know what was in the middle of Lake Michigan, or at least be able to tell me the best way to get there.

"Todd," Emily said, interrupting my thoughts, "I've just remembered that tomorrow is gardening day. You are going to need to look at that lifter tonight. I don't feel like climbing down that rope tomorrow with my shovel and pruning shears."

Todd groaned, but Shawn sat up straighter.

"Can I help?" he asked. Todd looked at him like he was nuts, but shrugged his assent and they left through a small door at the rear of the house. Emily stood to clear the dishes, and I scrambled to join her.

"You have a garden?" I asked. I wanted to know more about these people who'd cheated extinction.

"Of course," she said. "The Oaks has a rather large plot of ground just south of here." When she saw my look of confusion, she smiled warmly. "We cleared about three acres of trees in the middle of the forest. We used the timber to build the houses here in the Oaks."

"But don't you worry about the dinosaurs?"

"The garden is surrounded by fairly thick trees," she explained. "So we don't have to worry about any big-footed dinosaur stepping on our tomatoes. Now, the little ones," she said, shaking her head in disapproval, "those will destroy a crop of green beans faster than you can say scat. We have a fence, but they still get in every now and then."

"I'd like to see it," I said as I watched Emily scrub the dishes in a large pail of soapy water that she then dumped out of a slot in the side of the house.

"No running water?" I realised, amazed.

"Too high," Emily explained as she handed me another dish to dry. My eyes flicked to the door again, but when it opened moments later, it was only Shawn and Todd. Shawn was covered in what looked like thick black grease, and he was grinning broadly.

"The lifter is fixed," Todd told his mum, flopping on to the couch.

Emily raised a sceptical eyebrow. "That was fast."

"Shawn did it," Todd said. "I've never seen anything like it."

"You have a really neat system rigged up," Shawn said. "It would be even more efficient if you used a bigger wheel mechanism: more torque that way."

Todd laughed at Emily's confused look. "That's exactly what I looked like when he started talking like that." He turned to Shawn, a disbelieving grin still plastered on his face. "I can't believe they taught you how to use a lifter in that fancy school of yours."

"They didn't." I smiled, feeling a surge of pride for my friend. "Shawn's always been really good at that kind of stuff."

"Not always," Shawn corrected. "There were about three years there where I could take anything apart, but I couldn't put it back together again."

I laughed. "I had kind of forgotten about that. Remember when you got a month of extra work detail for taking apart the microphone in the assembly hall when we were eight?"

"Assembly hall?" Emily asked.

"Work detail? Microphone? What in the world are you two talking about?" Todd shook his head. "It's like you're from a different planet."

"I think we might just be speaking different languages," Shawn said. "What you called a lifter, I call a simple luff tackle pulley and winch. Although I really think that a twofold purchase pulley with a larger wheelbase would work a lot better for you."

"Right," Todd drawled, sounding unconvinced.

"Hold it right there," Emily said sharply as Shawn went to sit down on the couch next to Todd. Shawn jumped guiltily and stepped away from the couch. Emily chuckled. "Relax, dear. No one is going to bite you. I just didn't want you sitting on my couch with those grease smears everywhere." Shawn looked down at himself, seeming to notice the smears of black for the first time. Without ceremony, he shucked off his body armour, leaving him in the grey pants and shirt from the compound.

"Well, that just won't do," Emily said, peering at Shawn's shirt. Large patches of the grease from his body armour had soaked through, leaving oily-looking splotches on his shirt and pants. "Todd," she said as she absentmindedly examined the fabric of Shawn's sleeve, "please go grab a pair of trousers and a tunic for Shawn. What is this made of?" she asked, wrinkling her nose.

"Recycled nonbiodegradables," Shawn said.

"Strange," she muttered. Todd handed Shawn a pair of brown trousers and a green tunic very similar to the one he was wearing.

Shawn took the clothes, but then looked around the completely open room and frowned. "Um, where should I change?"

Emily chuckled, and walked over to pull a long piece of fabric with rings on the top so it slid across the length of the tiny house. Shawn gratefully slipped behind the makeshift curtain. When he emerged moments later, I felt a pang of jealousy. Although the trousers were too long and the shirt was a little too tight across the shoulders, he was wearing colour. And not the muted colours of his body armour, either. This tunic was bright, vibrant, more alive somehow. I'd never worn colour like that. Sliding my own body armour off, I shoved it in my pack. I avoided looking at my grey-on-grey clothes that had been washed and worn more times than I could count. Before I could pad over to sink down in one of the chairs, a brisk knock on the tree-house door made me jump.

"Now who could that be at this hour?" Emily asked

as she wiped her hands on a towel and walked towards the door.

"Oh, hey, Mum," Todd said, grimacing. "Jett's coming over tonight to talk to these two."

"Thank you for the ample warning, dear boy," Emily said, narrowing her eyes at her son as she opened the door. "Hello, Jett," she said warmly, as though she'd been expecting him. "Do come in and have a seat. I'll get you a cup of tea."

"No need, Emily." Jett ducked his head under the low doorframe and walked in. "Sorry to impose on you like this."

"No trouble at all." Emily waved a hand dismissively. "Take a seat. You must be exhausted. Did you and the boys bring down anything today?"

Jett shook his head. "No, but we saw some decent tracks that we will be following tomorrow."

Jett perched in one of the wing-back chairs, motioning for me to take a seat. I plopped down next to Shawn on the couch as Emily settled down into the other chair, pulling a basket on to her lap. The basket contained three large balls of coloured thread, and she proceeded to use two smooth sticks to begin weaving them together.

"Now then," Jett said, sitting forward, his elbows braced on his knees as he looked at us with those penetrating blue eyes, "why aren't you two tucked safely underground in that compound of yours?"

I frowned. I'd been planning on doing the questioning, not the other way around.

"I've been asking myself that same question," Shawn said, scratching at one of the numerous mosquito bites that peppered his arms.

"Here, dear," Emily said, standing to retrieve a small brown bottle. She handed it to Shawn. "Rub this on those bites. You really should avoid getting bitten. Those bugs carry diseases."

"I didn't exactly volunteer as their dinner," Shawn muttered, but he groaned in relief as he rubbed the thick green lotion on to the bites. "You're my hero," he said to Emily. "Got anything for Sky's blistered nose?"

"It's blistering?" I asked, reaching up to touch my nose. My fingers encountered raw skin, and I winced.

"I most certainly do," Emily said. "Shame on me for not getting something for you earlier. I'll blame it on the excitement of having guests." She leaned out of one of the windows and pawed through an overflowing window box. I heard a soft crack, and then she handed me a pointy bit of oozing leaf.

"Thank you?" I said as I looked at the leaf. What did I do with it? Eat it? I sniffed at it experimentally.

Todd laughed. "It's part of an aloe vera plant. You rub the broken end on your burn. And I've got to say, you have one of the most impressive sunburns I've ever seen."

"Your skin does almost match your hair." Shawn smirked, in a much better mood now that his bug bites had been tended to.

"I've only ever met one other person with red hair," Emily said. "A dinosaur hunter who used to trade with us on a regular basis. I remember him mentioning that redheads burned easily."

"Dinosaur hunter?" I asked. That couldn't be a real occupation. Could it?

Jett cleared his throat, and we turned to look at him. "If we could get this discussion back on track now that bug bites and sunburns have been dealt with?" he asked. I nodded sheepishly, and tried not to be too self-conscious about the thick goo now coating my nose.

"Please explain your presence in our woods. From Todd's description, you aren't very knowledgeable about survival among dinosaurs. What made you two leave the safety of the compound? From what I've heard, it's against compound law." I frowned. I hadn't really thought through how much I should or shouldn't tell these people.

"It's not exactly against the law," Shawn said before I had a chance to formulate a reply. "Most people just aren't stupid enough to go topside."

I glared at him.

"Don't give me that look, Sky Mundy," Shawn warned. "I'm here too. That makes me just as stupid as you."

"Stupid was running across that meadow today," Todd muttered as he walked over and settled himself with his back against the wall, his long legs stretched out in front of him. He pulled a small knife out of the holster on his arm, fished a rock out of his pocket and began sharpening the knife.

I ignored him and turned to Jett. "I left the compound because my dad told me to."

"If your dad is missing, how did he tell you to leave the compound?" Todd asked.

"If you'd stop talking, she's trying to tell you," Jett growled.

"Sorry," Todd muttered.

"Maybe it's easier if I just start at the beginning," I said, squirming under Jett's icy gaze. I looked away to watch the crackling fire instead as I began. "My mum died when I was born, so it was always just me and my dad. He was a technology specialist at North Compound. He fixed port screens, that kind of thing."

"Are we supposed to know what a port screen is?" Todd asked.

"It's like a handheld computer," I explained.

"What's a computer?" Todd asked. I sighed; this was going to be more difficult than I'd imagined.

"Just let her talk," Emily said. "She can explain what a portski is afterwards."

"Port screen. Not portski." Shawn chuckled, but I shot him a look, and he stopped.

"So," I went on. "One night, a few days after I turned seven, everything changed. I woke up in the middle of the night to our apartment being searched, and my dad was gone. They claimed he'd stolen valuable compound property, and they called him a traitor." I cleared my throat. "There was an assembly where they explained how what he'd done could jeopardise the survival of everyone in the compound. Needless to say, I wasn't very well liked after that."

"But you were seven!" Emily said indignantly.

"Age doesn't really matter in North Compound," Shawn said. "Everyone, regardless of their age, is held accountable so everyone has a chance to survive. Most of the time, it's a really good arrangement. It just wasn't so good for Sky."

"Age isn't important here either," Jett said. "But we'd never blame a seven-year-old for her father's crimes."

"My dad wasn't a criminal." I swallowed hard at the sudden tight feeling in my throat. "I think." I wished I knew for certain.

"How did he send you a message?" Jett prompted.

"He left me a note, asking me to do something for him," I said evasively.

"He asked her to go to the middle of Lake Michigan," Shawn blurted out, and I glared at him in exasperation.

"But there's nothing in the middle of Lake Michigan," Todd said, turning to look at his mother and Jett for confirmation.

"There has to be," I said. Whether I liked it or not, Shawn had laid our cards out on the table. I unscrewed the back of my compass, took out the map and handed it to Jett. I was just going to have to take a chance and trust these people. "My dad was one of the top scientists in the North Compound. If he marked something on this map, it's because it's there. Are you sure you've never heard of anything?"

Jett unfolded my map and studied it before shaking his head and handing it back to me. "We make occasional hunting trips to the lake, and I can testify that there is nothing there."

"Maybe there's another village like this one there that you haven't heard about?" I tried, fully aware that I was starting to sound a little pathetic.

"How would you propose to build a village in the middle of a lake?" Jett asked, eyebrows raised in amusement. My cheeks burned in embarrassment, and Todd snorted. I glared at him. It wasn't that funny.

"Well," I said, fighting to keep my temper in check as I took my map from Jett and tucked it back in my compass, "maybe it's not a village. But if my dad said there was something in the middle of the lake, then there is something in the middle of the lake."

"I did mention Sky was incredibly stubborn, right?" Shawn asked, a crooked grin on his face.

"I prefer the word *determined*," I snapped.

"The only things in Lake Michigan are fish and swimming dinosaurs," Jett said.

"Plesiosaurs," I said absentmindedly.

"Is that like a portski?" Todd asked.

Now it was my turn to laugh. "No. Jett said swimming dinosaurs, but there really are no such things. There *are* plesiosaurs and mosasaurs, though." When Todd continued to look at me blankly, I added, "They are giant marine reptiles that were brought out of extinction at the same time as the dinosaurs."

"What's the difference?" Todd asked.

"No clue," I admitted. "That's just what we learned in school." I hadn't done nearly the research on them that I'd done on regular dinosaurs. For one thing, I'd never thought I'd be close enough to water to see an actual plesiosaur.

"Sky is an amateur dinosaur expert," Shawn explained. "She's got an entire journal filled with sketches and notes on the things." If I could have kicked Shawn without anyone noticing, I would have. I wasn't ready to show them everything. Not yet.

"Really?" Todd said. "How did you manage to research dinosaurs underground?"

"We had a few books on them," I explained. "Mostly about the dinosaurs from millions of years ago, but we had one or two that were published during the years right after dinosaurs were brought out of extinction."

"Can I see the journal?" Jett asked.

Not sure what else to do, I pulled my journal out and offered it to him. He opened it up gingerly, and I got the feeling that books were just as rare topside as they had been in the compound. Todd got up to look over Jett's shoulder, and I squirmed self-consciously as they flipped through page after page. It felt odd to show people my journal after years of keeping it a secret.

"I know it isn't completely accurate," I said, folding my hands firmly in my lap to keep them from snatching the journal back. "I think a lot of the dinosaurs have evolved and changed since those books were written."

When Jett was done, he handed the journal to Todd, who ran his finger along my notes, sounding out the words to himself.

Jett turned his attention back to me. "I didn't know that people in the compound were interested in dinosaurs. I thought you all lived underground and pretended they didn't exist."

"That's pretty accurate," Shawn said. "The Noah promised that he is going to fix the dinosaur problem, so we can all move topside again."

Jett snorted. "That's what he called it? The dinosaur problem?" I could tell from Shawn's face that Jett had just offended him. I dug my elbow into his ribs before he could say something stupid. When he turned to look at me, I shook my head. Now was not the time or place for him to start talking about how great the Noah was. Jett and the rest of the Oaks clearly weren't fans of our leader, and I didn't want them to go back on their offer to let us spend the night.

"This isn't bad, but some of your facts aren't quite right," Todd said, and I looked over at him, grateful for the change in topic. He was holding up the picture I'd drawn of the troodon, the dinosaurs he'd called Nightmares. "These only come out at night," he said. "See how big their eyes are? It's so they can see in the dark." He flipped to the next page. "This one you call a *Tarchia gigantea*?" he said. "The forehead shape is a little off. And by the way, what kind of name is *Tarchia gigantea*? We just call them Boneheads."

"I'd love for you to tell me what else I got wrong. I've never actually seen most of those. I was just trying to learn everything I could." I frowned. "Although it turns out I should have been researching sunburns and bug bites."

"And shoes," Shawn groaned, stretching his legs out in front of him so we could see the impressive display of blisters that had bloomed across his feet. "Man, do I wish you'd figured out better shoes."

"Why did you do this to the back half?" Todd interrupted, holding up the journal to display the hole.

"My dad did that." I motioned to my compass. "He hid this inside it."

"What is it?" Todd asked, leaning over to get a closer look.

"It's a compass," Jett said, before I had a chance to respond. "It tells you which way north is."

"Why wouldn't you just use the sun?" Todd asked.

Shawn looked up from inspecting his feet. "You can tell direction that way?"

Todd rolled his eyes. "Which just proves Jett's point that although this is nice," he said, gesturing to my journal, "it isn't going to help you survive up here."

"Gee, that sounds familiar," Shawn said. "Who told you topside survival was impossible again?" He put his hand on his chin, pretending to think. "I know somebody must have mentioned it. I think it was someone incredibly good-looking and smart."

"It's not impossible," Emily corrected. "It's just difficult."

"I think you should go back to your compound," Jett said abruptly, standing up from the couch. "When you do, make no mention of the Oaks. It is very important that the Noah not know we exist."

"Going back isn't an option," I explained. "But even if I could go back, I wouldn't."

"Then stay here," Todd jumped in. "There are plenty of people who would take you in if you didn't want to go back to that underground mole hole." He glanced at Jett and his face flushed red. "I mean," he stuttered, "if Jett says that's OK."

"I don't believe you are the Noah's spies," Jett said after a painful pause, and I squirmed again. There was something about the way he looked at us, like he could read our minds, that made me nervous. "If you would like to stay here in the Oaks, you are welcome. You will have to work hard. This life is not an easy one."

"Thank you for the offer," Shawn said. "But I think Todd has a point; we shouldn't be out here on our own. I say we just go back. I'll talk to my aunt about getting us a pardon."

"You can go back," I said stubbornly. "I'm going to

finish what I started." I looked over at Emily's kind face and Todd's hopeful one before turning back to Jett. "But after this is all over, I would love to live here. Thank you for the offer. And don't worry, I know how to work hard." I saw Shawn's jaw drop beside me, but I ignored him.

Jett nodded stiffly, thanked Emily one more time for allowing him to intrude on her night, and left.

I turned to Emily, Jett's thank you reminding me that I hadn't been nearly as grateful as I should have been. "Thank you again for letting us spend the night. We will be out of your hair first thing in the morning."

"At least let me take you to the trading post before you go," Todd said. "You're unarmed and so unprepared it's pathetic." I bristled, but I realised that Todd was right. Apparently the gear we'd stolen was a step away from useless, and since our stun gun actually was useless, we needed weapons. Todd seemed to think our camouflage body armour was our best bet to trade for what we needed, and I reluctantly agreed.

Over the next few hours, we discussed life in the Oaks. I was amazed by their ingenuity. They had engineered everything in their village from scraps and remnants of the world before dinosaurs. Todd and

Emily were equally amazed by our stories of lunch tickets, meal allotments and work details.

I must have drifted off at some point, because the next thing I knew, Shawn was gently shaking me awake. I looked around blurrily to see that the fire had gone out. Todd and Emily were bustling around the small room. I watched in sleepy amazement as they moved slats of wood to the side and lowered two beds from the walls, one large and one small. Emily pulled the woven curtain to make a divider and the small tree house transformed.

"We don't have much room for guest beds," Emily said apologetically. "Shawn, you'll share my bed with Todd, and I'll make up the couch for Sky."

"Do I get to vote on that?" Todd asked.

"No," Emily said, shooting him a look that made me smile.

"The couch would be wonderful," I murmured. Shawn scowled but followed Todd behind the curtain. Emily shook her head as the boys disappeared. She handed me a soft woven blanket and a pillow. I curled up on the couch, the exertions of the day catching up with me. Todd and Shawn bickered quietly behind the curtain, something about snoring and smothering each other with pillows, but I was too tired to care. I managed to keep my eyes open just long enough to draw a quick sketch of the tree houses and to fix my facts about the 'Nightmares' that had almost eaten us, before my eyes shut, and I drifted into dreams about people who lived in trees.

CHAPTER 13

I jerked myself from a nightmare, and my eyes popped open in the dark. I felt a moment of confusion as I took in the walls of the tree house before remembering the events of the previous day. Wow, was I stiff. Muscles I didn't even know I had hurt with an almost impressive intensity I hadn't known was possible. The room felt stuffy, and I eased myself off the couch and tiptoed past a sleeping Emily. It took everything I had to stifle a laugh when I noticed that Shawn was sleeping on the floor next to the bed, having obviously decided against sharing with Todd. Todd sprawled on his stomach, his hair rumpled. Both boys were snoring softly. Careful not to make a sound, I opened the door I'd seen earlier and slipped out into the night.

On the other side of the door was a small wooden deck with a rope bridge leading to the next tree house. I peered tentatively over the edge of the deck railing, but the dark forest floor was too far below to make out and my stomach flopped uncomfortably at the sight. Sliding my back down the wall of the house, I tilted my head up to take in the breathtaking expanse of stars. I'd never been outside at night before. I felt like I'd travelled to a new planet instead of to the topside of my own.

The chill of the night bit through my thin shirt, and I curled my legs up against my chest. The crisp air almost had a flavour to it compared with the recirculated air of the compound. Todd could probably tell me what tree or flower I was smelling, but to me it just smelled like topside − fresh, earthy and alive. The soft click of a door being opened behind me made me jump guiltily. Shawn emerged, looking around frantically before rushing to the rail and peering down into the gloom. I put my hand over my mouth to cover a giggle. What did he think? That I'd decided to jump? He was turning towards the rope bridge when he spotted me. His whole posture relaxed, and he ambled over to sit down beside me and gaze up at the stars.

"Couldn't sleep?" he asked. I nodded. He craned his head back, and I joined him, drinking in the night. "There are a lot more stars than I thought there would be."

"We've missed so much," I murmured.

"Maybe not; maybe we just waited to start our adventure until we were ready."

"*Our* adventure?" I raised a sceptical eyebrow.

"You didn't think I was going to let you get eaten without me, did you?" he chuckled. I rolled my eyes, glad the dark hid my grin. Sometimes Shawn Reilly was utterly impossible in the best possible way. Ever since he'd come into my life five years ago, I couldn't picture it without him. Maybe that was why I'd given in when he'd followed me, because some selfish part of me wasn't brave enough to do this without him. I'd never tell him that, of course. Instead, I dug a friendly elbow into his side.

"I thought you were all about us going back to the compound?"

"Oh, don't get me wrong. I am."

"Then why did you come with me?"

Shawn shrugged. "I realised that I would rather die helping my best friend on her wild adventure than end up an old man in the compound. So it was really a no-brainer."

"I'm terrified that I'm going to be responsible for getting you killed." My voice cracked a little at the word *killed*.

Shawn was quiet for a while, and the night noises whirled around us. Finally he said, "We all die eventually."

"I hope you didn't make a mistake." I would never say it out loud, but I was starting to worry that I'd led us on a deadly wild-goose chase. The fact that Jett didn't know of anything in the middle of Lake Michigan worried me more than I was willing to admit. Everything had happened so fast. From finding my dad's note to escaping the compound, and Shawn tagging along. It all felt horribly overwhelming at times.

I cleared my throat. "Todd and Jett seem to think we're crazy."

Shawn snorted, not taking his eyes off the impressive expanse of stars twinkling overhead. "Sky, if knowing you has taught me anything, it's that being crazy makes life a little more interesting."

"It was plenty interesting today," I muttered.

"A little too interesting," Shawn agreed. We sat in silence for a minute, and then Shawn turned to look at me. "Can you tell me something?" he asked.

"What's that?" I asked.

"Be honest now," he cautioned. "You were just being nice when you said you'd come live here. Right?"

"I told you I was never going back to the compound," I said quietly.

Shawn stiffened in surprise beside me. "You can't really want to live in a tree without running water? Did you notice the other villagers when we met Jett? I didn't see anyone older than forty. I have a feeling no one around here dies of old age."

"I don't care," I said stubbornly.

"I know you aren't going back to North Compound, but why wouldn't you go back to a different one?" When I didn't say anything, he sighed. "You'll change your mind."

I scowled. "I won't."

"Whatever. We'll cross that bridge if we survive that long." Shawn rubbed his hands vigorously up and down his arms in an attempt to warm them. "Want to go inside? I think you're turning blue."

"Not yet. I've been inside too long."

"OK," he conceded. We sat quietly for a while, looking up. I'd always appreciated that I didn't have to fill the silences around him. Finally, we both got to our feet and crept back into the house.

"The floor?" I whispered, pointing at the still-snoring Todd.

"I don't care. It's better than sharing a bed."

I shook my head and crawled back on to the couch.

The next morning dawned bright through the window and I woke up to sunlight for the first time in my life. I reflected that the last twenty-four hours had been filled with a lot of firsts, not all of them as nice as sunshine and stars.

Emily was already up and bustling around the fireplace.

"Can I help?" I whispered. She nodded and pointed to a small basin sitting on the dresser.

"Get washed, and you can go down to Myrtle's for some eggs. She owes me." I decided not to ask what she wanted eggs for and did as I was told. I splashed the cool water on my face and ran my fingers through my tangled curls. After rummaging around in my bag, I located my hairbrush and managed to tame the mess somewhat, then reported to Emily for instructions.

"There are bridges that connect each of our homes." She handed me a large wooden bowl. "Myrtle is three houses down and two houses over. Tell her Emily is wanting those eggs she's been promising, at least a half a dozen, as we have company."

I nodded and tiptoed outside past the sleeping boys. The village was just coming to life, and I looked out across the treetops to see people opening their windows and a few already descending the ropes to the ground below. I considered the flimsy rope bridge I'd seen the night before but, vowing not to look down, I started across the first one. It pitched and wobbled, but by the time I reached Myrtle's house, I was feeling pretty confident. I knocked on the wooden door and waited. A tall, boxy woman with wild black hair answered and peered down at me suspiciously.

"And who might you be?" she asked.

"Sky Mundy, ma'am. Emily Birch sent me to collect the eggs you owe her. A half dozen, please."

"I owe her, huh? Miss Bossy Pants wants a half dozen now, does she?" The woman grunted. This wasn't going to be as easy as I'd expected. "Well, I haven't gone out to the coop to collect them yet, but if you want them –" she gestured towards a small hut perched above her house with a rope ladder dangling down to her deck – "go get 'em."

"OK." I gulped, wondering how exactly I was supposed to do that.

"Here." She thrust a pair of thick leather gloves at me. "If you want to keep your fingers, you'll need these." She wiggled her hand at me, and with a jolt I realised two of her fingers were missing at the knuckle. I took the gloves and made my way over to the ladder, eyeballing it warily. I was about to begin climbing when I heard the creak of the rope bridge and turned to see Todd jogging towards me. The entire bridge swayed wildly, but it didn't seem to faze him.

"Hey. What are you doing here?" I asked.

"Hey yourself. I thought I'd help. Old Myrtle can be a handful."

"I heard that, Todd Birch!" Myrtle's voice boomed out of her window, and I flinched. Todd just grinned. "Get those eggs collected or I'll show you a handful," Myrtle called. Todd plucked the wooden bowl from my arms and clambered up the ladder. I scrambled up after him.

"How many did my mum want?" Todd asked.

"Um, I'm supposed to collect a half dozen." I gestured towards the small shack. "But I've never done it before."

"No problem," he said, taking the gloves from my hands. He took a bucket off a hook on the wall and ducked under the low doorway. I followed him into the gloom and almost gagged at the smell. Looking over his shoulder, I saw three large birdlike lizards sitting on nests. If I remembered correctly, their name was rhamphorhynchus. I recalled thinking that these were especially creepy-looking when we studied the different kinds of pterosaurs in school. But creepy didn't even begin to cover it. Their beaklike jaws jutted out, showing off an impressive set of needle-like teeth as they rustled their massive webbed wings. My biology book also hadn't bothered to mention that they smelled like the compound's sewer. As if on cue, the one in the middle broke wind. Charming. Their huge eyes watched us warily.

"This is what you get an egg from?" I whispered.

"Why are you whispering? The old girls know why we're here." Todd bent down to pick a small dead fish out of the bucket at his feet. In one practised move, he tossed it against the far wall of the hut. The creatures lunged to the left, their beaks snapping. Todd leapt forward and scooped out a handful of fist-sized white balls from under two of the creatures. He carefully placed them in my bowl.

"Want to give it a go?"

"Not really," I admitted. "That Myrtle woman was missing a few fingers."

"Ha!" Todd laughed. "She used to scare me with that one when I was a kid. She was born without those fingers. Don't get me wrong, these girls would take one off if you offered it, but you'd have to be really slow to lose one."

"I don't know…" I hedged.

"Spoken like a kid who's never had to provide for herself." His tone had just the slightest edge of condescension. I stiffened and yanked the gloves off his hands, jamming them on to my own.

"So I just throw the fish?" I asked through gritted teeth.

"Throw, grab, retreat, repeat. I was doing this at five years old," Todd bragged. I took a fish from the bucket, trying not to cringe at its slimy texture, and threw. It bounced off the wall and the creatures dived for it as I lunged. My hand closed around two warm spheres, and I threw myself backwards, colliding with Todd as the disgruntled rhamphorhynchus thrashed their whiplike tails and resettled on their nests. I was so relieved that I almost didn't notice the warm liquid running through my fingers. One of the eggs had smashed, and my gloved hand was now covered in what looked like a gigantic glob of snot. I looked up at Todd in horror, and he burst out laughing.

"Smooth one, Ace. Lucky for you, we only needed one more egg. Don't leave any yolk or shell, or Myrtle will pitch a fit." Back outside, I scrapped the sticky mess off my hand, letting it fall to the ground far below.

"This is disgusting." I wrinkled my nose as Todd provided a few leaves to clean off the last of the gunk. "What does your mum want these for?"

"You aren't serious, are you?" he asked. "You really don't know what eggs are for?"

I sighed. "To be on the safe side, just assume I don't know how anything works up here."

"You eat them."

"Oh." My stomach rolled sickeningly at the thought. "Do they fall for that trick every time?" I asked.

"They are about as bright as a log," he said as he took the bowl from my hands and climbed down. "We're lucky that they are one of the dumber species of dinosaur. There aren't many of those, so we take advantage when we can."

I debated telling him that those weren't technically dinosaurs, but I decided against it as I followed, substantially less expertly, and reclaimed the bowl.

"Thank you. I'm not sure I could have done that without your help," I admitted grudgingly.

"Which proves Jett's point that you and your little boyfriend aren't built for life aboveground."

I scowled. "OK, first of all, Shawn is my friend, not my boyfriend. That's just dumb. And secondly, Shawn is short, not little. If you value keeping your face arranged the way it is, I would suggest you remember that. And third, if we wanted your opinion, we would have asked for it." I turned on my heel to stomp away, but two feet later I had to stop and proceed more cautiously across the bridge, completely ruining the effect. Todd chuckled, and suddenly he was swinging across the gap on a long rope, letting out a war whoop as he went. He landed on the tree house platform twenty feet away, turned to wink at me and then charged off across the next bridge. "Show-off," I muttered through gritted teeth. Careful to hold the fragile eggs steady, I followed him.

He waited for me a few bridges later, a wide grin on his face as he munched on an apple. I watched him bite into it curiously. I'd heard of apples, even tasted one in the third grade, but I'd never seen someone eat a whole one before. He saw me staring and stopped mid-bite.

"Hungry?" he asked, offering me the half-eaten fruit.

"A little," I admitted. "Do you get to eat these all the time?"

"When they're in season." He shrugged. "There's an old orchard not far from here. Ever since my dad died, I do most of the hunting and gathering for my mum and me. So we eat a lot of apples."

"You're lucky," I said.

He grimaced. "I guess. We get by. I'd rather be hunting, though. I'm a really good shot. I wasn't joking when I said I could punch a few holes in Shawn."

"Would you really have done that?"

"Probably not. I was mad, though. Verde and I grew up together. That little squirt was just a hatchling when my dad brought her home from one of his trading missions. An old trapper he knew had found her nest, was going to mercy kill her before she starved, but my dad stepped in."

"Verde is an unusual name," I said.

"It's Italian for *green*. My mum is one hundred

per cent Italian; that's rare. My dad had no clue what he was. My mum called him a mutt."

"So does that make you a half mutt?"

"I guess. I never really thought about it."

"How long ago did your dad die?" I asked.

"Two years," he said. "Trading mission gone wrong. All Jett and the search party found was a smear of blood and his bow. It's my bow now."

"I'm sorry," I said.

He shrugged. "Why? You aren't the one who ate him. Besides, we always knew that what he did was dangerous. Travelling back and forth from village to village. Mum always gave him this big, sloppy kiss when he was leaving on a trip. Like she'd never see him again. It used to gross me out, ya know? But I don't think it would any more."

"I know what you mean."

Todd nodded, and headed across the last bridge. We made it back into the tree house with all the eggs intact, and I opened the door cautiously, not wanting to wake up Shawn, but he was already up and dressed. The green tunic he wore made his blond hair stand out in startling contrast.

"Just in time." Emily smiled as she scooped the bowl

of eggs out of my arms. "I was worried you'd got lost."

"I was just giving her an egg-gathering lesson," Todd said, smirking. "She was a natural." I stuck my tongue out at him, biting back a grin as I wandered over to stand next to Emily by the fireplace. The bulge of muscle on her arms and shoulders was apparent even through the tunic she was wearing. She was used to a life of hard work. I watched sceptically as she banged each egg roughly on the edge of her pan to crack it. They just looked too much like snot to be edible.

Once the blankets on the couch were folded, I looked around for my body armour. Emily saw and motioned with her hand towards the dresser.

"Since you're going to trade that thing, don't bother with putting it back on, dear. I got you something more decent to wear from one of our neighbours with a daughter your size. Just step behind the curtain there and throw them on." Behind the curtain, I found a pair of tight brown leggings and a forest-green tunic, more fitted than the boys' but similar. I felt the tunic's unfamiliar softness. After years of coarse fabrics, this was a luxury I could get used to. I shrugged into the clothes and neatly folded my scratchy grey leggings and shirt and put them in my pack. When I came back around the curtain, Emily was serving the boys their eggs. Todd dug in immediately, but Shawn looked down at the fluffy yellow mixture apprehensively.

I sat down beside him, eyeing my own plate with suspicion, but I picked up my fork and took a bite despite my qualms about where this particular delicacy had come from. The flavour was unlike anything I had ever tasted. I smiled reassuringly at Shawn. "Go with it," I murmured. He did. When we were finished, I helped Emily clear the table. Shawn had eaten every bit. So had I.

"I'm glad you liked the eggs," she smiled. "Todd told me these were your first."

"They were wonderful. Thank you for letting us stay the night, and feeding us…" I trailed off, feeling very indebted to these strangers. "We appreciate your kindness."

"My pleasure." Emily waved us off. "No trouble at all. It's nice to see new faces."

At that moment, Verde came scampering up to the table and sat back on her haunches. Todd flipped her a chunk of egg, and she chuckled happily. He picked up the body armour I'd set on the table, and wrinkled his nose as he held it up to the light. "We'll need to trade these for a bow and knife for each of you. Minimum. Knowing how to use them would be even better. I could give you basic training if you wanted. In a month I could have you shooting straight."

"Nope." I shook my head. "Not going to happen. I need to get to Lake Michigan, and I need to get there fast."

"She's in a big hurry to get eaten," Shawn said conspiratorially, winking at Emily. Emily didn't smile.

"Getting eaten isn't funny around here," she said quietly, taking the boys' empty plates. Shawn's ears burned red. I felt sorry for him. There was no way he could have known that Todd's dad had been eaten only two years ago.

Todd bounded to his feet. "Let's go."

"Why don't you take them to see Roderick first," Emily said. "I think he'd like a look at their map, and he might be able to tell them the best route to Lake Michigan."

"Why didn't I think of that?" Todd said. "Mum, it's easy to see where I get my brains from." He gave her a quick peck on the cheek and turned to us. "Roderick first, then the trading post."

CHAPTER 14

"So who's Roderick?" I asked a few minutes later as we made our way into glaring sunlight. I blinked, my eyes watering a bit. Had spending the first twelve years of my life underground damaged them somehow? Todd didn't seem bothered by the sun at all.

"You'll love him," Todd said. "He's a little nuts, but he's a collector."

"What's a collector?" Shawn asked.

"Sorry," Todd said, charging across a rope bridge, not even bothering to hold on as it pitched and jumped. My breath hissed out between my teeth at the sight of the forest floor feet below us. "I keep forgetting you two don't know much."

"It's fine," Shawn grunted, clutching at the rope bridge with both hands. "We keep forgetting too."

"A collector is someone who specialises in something from the old world. You'll see."

We moved from one bridge to another, snaking our way through the trees. When I wasn't preoccupied with trying not to fall to my death, I studied the surrounding tree houses with interest. Just like Todd and Emily's house, they were all constructed of a dinosaur-bone frame with wood walls, but that was where the similarities ended. Some sprawled across the entire width of a tree, obviously containing several rooms, while others utilised the trees' height, sporting two or even three levels. Circular, square, rectangular and octagonal shaped windows dotted the houses, obviously scavenged from the wreckage of abandoned buildings. Shawn bumped into me from behind when I paused too long to study one particularly beautiful window I thought must be made of stained glass. And under every window was a window box overflowing with flowers, herbs and bright red tomatoes. Each tree contained only one house, and trees without houses had small wooden decks built on them that acted as hubs for the various rope bridges that crisscrossed through the branches.

We stopped on one of these decks and I looked out at the village. The day was in full swing now, and people called to one another across the gap between trees, and rope bridges bustled with activity. Brightly coloured clothes hung out to dry on long lines tied from one tree to the next. I watched in amazement as a little boy, no bigger than two or three, tottered out of a tree house unaccompanied. I grabbed Todd's arm in terror as he climbed up on to the railing and, with a giggle, threw himself off the deck. I shrieked, and Todd laughed.

"It's fine," he said. "Look." A moment later, a flustered woman came out on to the deck, looked down and then grabbed on to a rope and hauled the giggling toddler back over the railing. It was only then that I noticed the boy was wearing a harness, very similar to the one I'd worn the day before.

"I think I just had a heart attack," I said, sagging in relief as the mother disappeared into the house, toddler in hand.

"I used to get in so much trouble for deck diving," Todd said, smiling wistfully at the memory.

"Deck diving?" Shawn said. "That's a thing?"

"All kids are required to wear safety harnesses until the age of five," Todd said. "It's the law here at the Oaks. The harnesses are attached to a rope tied in the house. That way no one accidentally falls." When we still looked unconvinced, he shrugged. "It's a real rush. If you two were going to stick around, I'd show you. A few of us still do it every now and then for fun."

"I'll pass," Shawn said, looking a little green.

"I'll let you know once my heart starts beating again," I said. Todd laughed. Five bridges later, we were standing in front of a two-storey tree house built into the branches of one of the biggest trees I'd ever seen.

"These houses really are amazing," Shawn said, poking experimentally at one of the deck railings.

"Thanks," Todd said. "We rebuild them every ten years."

"Why?" I asked, thinking of the compound, in use now for over a hundred and fifty years.

"Wood rots," Todd explained. "We tear houses down before they fall out of the tree." He smiled when I shuddered, picturing one of the houses crashing to the ground. "It's not that big a deal. The houses seem to get better each time we do it. My great-grandpa was one of the Oak's founders, and he said the first houses were barely more than a few boards tossed together.

"Now I'm even more impressed," Shawn said grudgingly.

Todd grinned cockily. "You haven't seen anything yet." He knocked on the door of the house. I heard the excited snort of an animal inside, and then something collided with the door.

"Back! Back!" came a nasal voice from inside, followed by the sound of a brief scuffle. Moments later the door opened and a tall, thin man stood in the doorway, holding the collar of what I initially thought was some kind of strange pig. But it couldn't be a pig, I reasoned. For one thing, pigs were extinct; for another, this creature was a rubbery grey colour with a longer snout than a pig was supposed to have. Before I could say anything, it pulled free from the man's grasp and charged over to snuffle at my boots excitedly.

"Tilly, no!" the man said, lunging forward to grab the collar again. "I apologise," he said as he dragged the animal back into his house. "She loves people." He grunted as he pulled back on the collar as Tilly attempted to greet Shawn. "Maybe a little too much," he added. "Please, please, come in."

We walked into a house very similar to the one Todd and his mum shared, except the walls were covered in maps. I turned in a slow circle, taking in the faded pieces of paper tacked to every square inch of the available space. Maps were rare in the compound and, like books, they were not something the general public was allowed to own or display.

"What can I do for you?" the man asked.

"Roderick, this is Sky and Shawn. They are just passing through on their way to Lake Michigan," Todd said. He didn't mention that we were from a compound, a fact I appreciated. "They were hoping you could take a look at their map."

Roderick's eyes brightened with excitement. "I'd love to look at their map; just let me put Tilly outside." He brought the snuffling animal to the door and, with a little pushing and shoving, sent her out on to the deck. "Go play!" he instructed, shooing her away from the door. "Sorry about that," he said, turning back to us.

"Is it rude if I ask what Tilly is?" Shawn whispered to me, and Roderick whipped his head around.

"Of course not!" he said. Shawn jumped.

"Roderick has killer hearing." Todd grinned.

"He does," Roderick agreed. He turned to Shawn. "Tilly is one of the smaller dinosaur breeds. I believe her species eventually evolved into elephants. Or was it pigs?" He stopped a moment, thinking. "No," he said, "definitely elephants. The irony is that elephants and pigs are now extinct, and she isn't any more. Funny how that happened, isn't it?"

"Funny," Shawn mumbled. "Not the word I would have used."

"She seems nice," I said, not wanting to be impolite.

"Oh," he smiled, "she's my baby. She's quite smart, but she hogs the bed like you wouldn't believe." I saw Shawn's jaw drop, and I stifled a laugh.

"Show him the map," Todd said.

"Right," I said, and I handed Roderick the folded map. He opened it eagerly, and while he studied it, I wandered around his house, looking at the faded images of Hawaii, South America, China and Japan. Were any humans left in these places I'd heard of but would never get to see? Sighing, I turned my attention back to Roderick's maps, specifically the ones of the surrounding areas. Someone, presumably Roderick, had written down things like *Long-necked dinosaur nesting ground, large blueberry patch, Nightmare hunting ground* and *freshwater well.*

"Roderick keeps track of things for us," Todd explained, peering over my shoulder at the map I was studying. "It helps us remember what places to avoid."

"How did you get all these?" I asked Roderick.

"Hmmm?" Roderick looked up to blink at me as though he'd forgotten I was there. "Oh, my father fell into what used to be the basement of a travel agency while he was hunting. He brought back everything he could carry. I've had them ever since." He pointed at my map. "This is a very good map. It's older than mine but in better condition." He pulled out a pen and, before I could protest, he was writing on my dad's map.

"Right here, here and here," he said, drawing wiggling lines across the map, "are freshwater streams. And here," he said, sketching in another long line, "is an old highway. The actual road is gone now, of course, but the larger dinosaurs use the old road networks to travel. It's best to avoid them altogether, if you ask me." He dabbed his pen in a bottle of ink and reached up to draw a large circle. "This is where the city of Chicago used to be. You are going to want to avoid that too."

"Why?" I asked.

"Lots of road relics, concrete and building ruins," he said. "Very few places to take cover, and the larger dinosaurs roam that area a lot." He drew a line to the right of the circle. "I would go this way. It was much less developed, with more tree cover. Although some of the larger dinosaurs still hunt in this area if the trees get thin."

"Thank you," I said when Roderick handed the map back to me.

"Happy to help." Roderick smiled. A loud bang came from outside, and we all jumped. "That would be Tilly." He glanced out of the window to see the sun. "She thinks it's lunchtime." He stood up and went to the door to let the overexcited Tilly back into the house. No sooner had he turned the doorknob than Tilly was back inside and racing for a dish sitting on the floor of the tree house. Finding it empty, she turned and charged Shawn. He threw his hands up protectively, but Tilly got a few good snorts in his ear before Roderick managed to pull her off. We took that as our cue to leave.

CHAPTER 15

"This is so gross," Shawn said as he attempted to wipe dinosaur slobber off his liberally coated neck.

"She liked you." Todd smiled.

"I got the feeling that she likes everyone," Shawn said. "Do all of you Oaks people have dinosaurs as pets?"

"No," Todd said as he headed back across the rope bridges and Shawn and I followed. "A few people do, though."

"Which one of these is the trading post?" I asked, looking around at the surrounding tree houses. The sun was creeping higher and higher overhead, and I was anxious to be on our way.

"We can't get to it by bridge," Todd said over his shoulder. "We need to go to ground level."

"How do we do that?" I asked.

"My house," he said simply. Five minutes later,

Todd opened up the panel in the floor of his house, and I peered down to the distant forest floor and gulped.

"Harness?" Todd asked, offering one to Shawn and me.

"Not you?" Shawn asked.

"Not me," Todd said. With the practised ease of someone who had done this a thousand times, he wrapped the rope around his foot and, holding on with only one hand, disappeared from sight. I rushed to the edge to watch him slide down and sighed in relief when he reached the ground safely.

"It doesn't look that hard," Shawn said. I groaned, already knowing what was going to happen next. He grabbed the rope and began his own descent.

Emily shook her head at Shawn's stunt and turned to me. "Would you like to show off how tough you are too, or do you want to use the harness?" I was about to say harness, but then stopped. Todd was right; life topside was not for the weak.

"I think it's time I got tough," I said.

"Good choice." Emily smiled. "Please remind that rascal of a son of mine that I'll be at the garden plot until noon." I nodded and, taking a deep breath, took the rope in both hands, and began to climb down.

"Welcome back to terra firma," Todd joked when I reached the ground. I brushed my sweaty hands off on my trousers and glanced nervously around the forest, our near miss from the night before still fresh in my mind.

"Is it safe to be standing here like this?"

"Sort of." Todd shrugged and readjusted the bone bow across his shoulders. "We have a morning patrol that makes sure the area is secure before anyone comes down." I relaxed a little. "Don't do that," he cautioned.

I jumped. "Do what?"

"Relax like that. Never relax."

"But the trees are thick here," I said. "And you said the Nightmares only come out at night. Shawn and I were in the trees all day yesterday, and the only dinosaurs we saw were tiny."

"Then you were really lucky," Todd said. "Some of the bigger dinosaur breeds will venture into thick trees if they get hungry enough. Plus, the forest is where a lot of the adolescent dinosaurs hide out until they get big enough to protect themselves. You have to stay alert. It was my dad's number-one rule."

"His dad?" Shawn whispered.

"Got eaten two years ago," I replied quietly. Shawn

winced, realising why his comment at breakfast had gone so badly.

"Now I feel like a jerk," he whispered.

"Keep up, you two," Todd called over his shoulder.

Five minutes later, we were standing underneath a massive oak tree. Todd walked up to a small dangling rope and gave it three hard tugs. Nothing happened. He frowned and yanked again. This time a small rope ladder was lowered.

"Remember," Todd cautioned as we climbed, "let me do the talking."

"Why isn't the trading post connected to the rest of the village?" I asked.

"Two reasons," Todd said. "One, old Adler is paranoid. He is convinced everyone is out to steal from him. So he's close enough to benefit from the Oaks' protection, but far enough away that no one can get to his store without his knowledge."

"What's reason two?" Shawn asked.

"Oh," Todd said, "he hates people."

"This just keeps getting better and better," Shawn muttered.

We finally reached the top of the ladder and Todd held out a hand to help me up on to the wide wooden deck. The trading post was a small, dark structure crammed floor to ceiling with mismatched plates, old pots and pans, small scraps of fabric, and the woven material I'd seen over Emily's windows. Every available surface was covered in an assortment of jumbled, dusty items, and I recognised a few tools from my history textbook. It smelled of spices, burned wood and something I couldn't quite place.

Todd ignored all of it and strode to the back of the hut, where a tall, skinny man with a thin face that reminded me of a rat stood behind the counter. He nodded briskly to Todd and looked Shawn and me over with suspicious black eyes.

"What can I do for you?" Adler asked. He had an oily voice that matched the long, matted hair clinging to his partially bald scalp.

Todd grinned wolfishly at the man. "We need some supplies for my friends here: two good bows and arrows to go with them, arm sheaths, and knives to go in them. Oh, and boots."

"That's a tall order," said Adler. "What are you planning to trade for all that?"

Todd snatched the suits from Shawn's hands and flipped them on to the table. Adler's eyes grew large, and he ran his long, thin fingers over the iridescent fabric hungrily.

"I believe we can make a trade. I'll give you the bows and knives, but no boots." Todd just crossed his arms and raised an eyebrow.

"What if I throw in this?" Shawn asked, taking a box out of his pocket and setting it on the counter.

"What is it?" Adler asked, poking at it gingerly, as though it might explode. My heart sank. I knew what that was. Shawn had been carrying it in his pocket for as long as I could remember.

"It's a music box," I said. "And it's not part of the deal." I went to pick it up, but Adler swiped it off the counter.

"Will it get us the boots?" Shawn asked.

"Shawn, what are you doing?" I hissed.

"Does it work?" Adler asked.

In reply, Shawn reached over and turned the key at the back, and the faintest of lullabies filled the small hut. I still remembered the day Shawn had finally fixed it. He'd been sitting in my room in the Guardian Wing, and he'd jumped up and down, doing a little jig in celebration.

"Boots and another knife and sheath for each of

them," Todd said quickly. "That's more than a fair offer. You and I both know that thing will trade well." Adler looked back at Todd and, after a moment's hesitation, nodded and stuck out his hand. Todd shook it, sealing the deal. Adler began piling the merchandise on to the counter. The knives in their arm sheaths looked particularly lethal. Once all the items were accounted for, we handed over the suits and left.

"You didn't need to do that," I muttered to Shawn once we were back in the sunlight.

"She's right," Todd said. "Adler would have come around to my deal eventually. Didn't I tell you not to talk?"

Shawn clenched his teeth, and I knew he was regretting his rash decision. "I wanted to make sure we got everything."

"Whatever, just put the boots on," Todd instructed, handing me a tall leather pair. "Those slippers you two are wearing are useless." The boots were old, the leather soft and supple under my fingers as I pulled them on to my aching feet. It looked like they'd been resoled about a million times, but they fitted surprisingly well. When we got back on the trail, I didn't feel every stick and rock like I had in my compound shoes. It was fabulous.

Todd took a few minutes to help us fasten the knife sheaths on to our arms. What I had thought was a pile of leather straps turned out to be a quiver to hold the massive arrows that went with our bows. Arrows we didn't know how to use. I frowned but then pushed the thought away. There wasn't time for the lessons Todd had mentioned, even if they were tempting.

"So now that we've got our supplies, what's the plan?" Shawn asked.

"We're wasting daylight," I said, glancing up. "We should really get going."

Todd looked disappointed. "What's your rush? It's not like Lake Michigan is going anywhere."

"He has a point," Shawn said, pulling back the string of his new bow experimentally. "I'd like to practise with this thing." He let the string go and yelped when it snapped back into place. Todd laughed as Shawn hopped around, flapping his stinging hand.

"Not as easy as it looks, is it?" Todd said.

"We'll be OK," I said. "We'll learn as we go."

Todd shook his head. "Doubtful." I frowned. It probably *was* stupid to turn my back on the chance to train, but the burning sense of urgency in my stomach wouldn't let me take him up on the offer. I was already a year behind from where my dad thought I'd be. I wanted to get to the lake. And I wanted to get there yesterday.

"Well, at least come back to the Oaks for lunch," Todd said. "My mum has something for you."

"I don't know." I hesitated, not wanting to be rude. "We really should get going. And we already owe you guys too much as it is." Suddenly Todd stiffened, and a moment later I heard the thudding roar of an engine.

On instinct, I grabbed Todd and Shawn, pulling them into the underbrush and out of sight.

"What are they?" Todd asked, gazing wide-eyed as three large black shapes buzzed past us overhead.

"Helicopters," Shawn supplied, his voice awed as he stared up at the whirring propellers. "I didn't think any of those existed any more." I watched them fly past, the golden ark emblazoned across their sides, and for the first time, the Noah's symbol sent a shiver of fear up my spine. The feeling surprised me. The symbol had never made me feel anything but grudging admiration before.

"What's a helicopter?" Todd asked.

"It's a flying machine," Shawn said. "It carries passengers. Not as many as the Noah's plane, but they are supposed to have more mobility than a plane."

"The Noah?" Todd said, and I saw terror cross his face. Before I could stop him, he was up and running towards the Oaks.

"I have a bad feeling about this," I said, getting up to run after him. "Really bad."

"Why?" Shawn asked, scrambling up to follow me. "The Noah probably just spotted the Oaks, and he wants to help."

"And what if he doesn't want to help?" I called back over my shoulder as I raced through the woods after Todd.

"Why else would helicopters be here?" Shawn called, struggling to keep up as we ducked under low-hanging tree branches.

"I don't know," I admitted. The crack of a gun reverberated throughout the forest, and I pushed to catch up with Todd.

Todd was fast, but by some miracle I was faster. Moments before he would have burst into the open, I made a flying leap and brought him to the ground in a tumble of legs and arms. We skidded to a stop behind a low pile of bushes, and I smashed my hand over his mouth.

"What are you doing?" Shawn whispered, catching

up. I shook my head and he helped me pin down the flailing Todd. I peered up through the bushes and froze as I saw what was happening less than fifty yards away. My stomach clenched painfully as panic raced through my system. With an effort, I pushed it back, ducking my head under the cover of the bushes. I needed to think. I could panic later. Todd struggled beneath me, biting down on my hand, hard, and I had to stifle a scream. I pressed my lips against his ear and whispered as quickly and as quietly as I could manage.

"Stay down. The Noah's marines are here." Todd struggled again, biting down harder on my hand, and tears slid down my cheeks. "Stop it," I hissed through gritted teeth. "If we make a noise now, we'll get caught. Then we won't be any good to anybody." I looked in his eyes, hoping to see reason return. Slowly he released the skin of my hand; my palm burned. I waited another few seconds and then took my hand away.

"What's going on?" Shawn whispered. He sat behind me, Todd's legs and one arm pinned firmly underneath him.

"It looks bad," I admitted. I glanced at Todd again.

"If we let you up, do you promise not to go charging in there? They have guns." Todd's face went white, but he nodded.

"Marines always have guns when they go topside, Sky," Shawn whispered. "What's the big deal?"

"They don't point them at innocent people," I snapped back. Shawn looked confused, but he got off Todd's legs and together we peered out over the top of the bush.

Standing in the clearing were ten marines in black body armour with the gold ark crest across their chests. Thick visors covered their eyes. Five of them had lethal-looking guns levelled at a cluster of villagers huddled under one of the trees. They made the stun gun Shawn had stolen look like a toy. I frowned. The gun Shawn had stolen had turned out to *be* a toy. There was a pile of broken and splintered arrows littering the ground at their feet. Todd's village hadn't been prepared for body armour. As I watched, more arrows rained down on the remaining marines, who were attempting, unsuccessfully, to climb the ropes leading up to the tree houses. Suddenly someone grabbed on to my arm, and I whipped around to see Shawn, a look of pure disbelief on his face.

"This doesn't make any sense," Shawn said. "What are they doing?"

"Surrender!" yelled a voice I recognised. I went numb as General Ron Kennedy stepped away from the pack, wearing the same thick metal body armour as the rest of the marines. And that's when I knew for certain that we'd been followed. These weren't random rogue marines. These were *our* marines, the marines of North Compound that I had grown up with and worked under for all of my life. We had been followed, and now Todd's village was going to pay the price for our crimes. Shawn went rigid beside me, and I knew he'd just realised the same thing.

General Kennedy walked over to the group of villagers, most of whom were women wearing dirt-smeared clothing and holding shovels and spades. He grabbed Emily roughly by the arm and dragged her into view of the tree houses above. Putting his gun to her temple, he glared up at the trees. "Surrender or she dies," he yelled. "I'll kill your women one by one. And when I have no one left to kill, I'll set fire to the trees." He tightened his grip on Emily, and Todd lifted his bow to shoot.

"He's wearing body armour," I whispered in Todd's

ear. "All you'll do is give away our position. Or, worse, your shot will ricochet and hit your mum."

Todd lowered the bow, but the look on his face broke my heart. *My fault*, I thought numbly. *This is all my fault.* I tried to push aside the sense of hopelessness that was threatening to overwhelm me. I needed to think of a way to save these people who had been kind and welcoming to us. Seconds later, ten bows fell to the ground with muffled thumps. Two of them broke on contact, but the others were gathered by the marines. I looked up as the remaining villagers came climbing down the trees, but the fear and hatred I saw etched in their faces had me looking away guiltily.

No longer being pelted by arrows, the marines climbed the ropes and entered the tree houses. They ran from house to house, guns drawn. A gunshot came from one of the houses and I jumped. Todd's face tightened. A few of the captured villagers screamed, and I saw Emily scanning the surrounding woods with wide, frightened eyes. It didn't take much to know who she was looking for. The marines had their backs to us, so when she looked our way, I pulled aside the leafy branch we were concealed behind and made eye contact. Her face, already drained of colour, got even whiter. She shook her head ever so slightly, and I nodded.

Just then one of the villagers broke from the group and ran for the woods. The marines shouted, and someone screamed as a gunshot rang out. The man crumpled and didn't move. I tightened my grip on Todd's shoulder. Kennedy tucked his gun back into his belt and turned to the villagers. I swallowed hard, worried I was going to be sick.

"Let that be a lesson on how our Noah deals with rebels and traitors," Kennedy sneered, nodding to the marines standing guard. "Get them into the choppers. If anyone gives you any trouble, shoot them."

I watched in helpless horror as, one by one, Todd's fellow villagers were loaded into the bellies of helicopters.

"This one seems to be the leader," one of the marines said, shoving Jett forward roughly.

"Good," Kennedy said, and with his gun pointed at Emily's temple, he looked straight at Jett. "I hope I don't have to tell you that telling the truth is in this lady's best interest." Jett nodded, his eyes hard. "We are looking for two kids. A boy and a girl. They are escaped convicts from North Compound. Have you seen them?"

Jett's eyes flicked to Emily's panicked ones. "No," he said evenly. "I haven't."

Kennedy nodded, and the marine standing behind Jett raised his gun and slammed the butt of it into the side of Jett's head. Emily cried out, and I slapped my hand over my mouth to hold in my own cry. Todd jerked beside me, and I tightened my grip, my fingers digging into his arm.

"I'm going to ask again," Kennedy said, this time holding the gun to Jett's head, his eyes on Emily. "Have you seen a boy and a girl? The boy is short, and not very bright. The girl has red hair."

"No," Emily said, her voice shaky but firm. Kennedy stared at her, evaluating and I held my breath. Then with a jerk, he pulled the gun away from Jett's head and gave him a disgusted kick.

"Load them into the chopper with the rest," he said. Kennedy motioned for two other marines to follow him into the woods. They hurried over to obey orders, and I realised with a jolt that they were heading straight for us. We ducked our heads, and I bit my lip so hard I tasted blood.

"Well?" Kennedy barked.

"She was supposed to be here, sir," responded the

taller of the two marines. "Our tracking methods have a very high degree of accuracy."

"Your methods didn't work." I could hear the venom and hate dripping from his every word. "Somebody screwed up, Jeffrey. And when I find out who that somebody is, heads will roll." When I glanced towards Shawn, his face looked just as sick as I felt. Even though Jett had searched us, something we carried with us had led them straight to the Oaks. The urge to rip off my pack and begin going through my things was overwhelming. I felt tainted. Like I carried around something disgusting and dirty. But I didn't dare move a muscle. Not now. Not with Kennedy standing mere feet away from where we crouched.

"Sir," said one of the marines, "if I may ask, why are we putting so much effort into finding two children? They were probably eaten within minutes of venturing topside."

"Those children stole valuable government property. The Noah commanded we recover that property," Kennedy said, his voice dangerous. "Is that not enough for you, soldier?"

"Yes, sir," the marine said, ducking his head. "Sorry, sir."

"Go tell the pilots we leave in two," Kennedy said. The marines hurried back to the helicopter, and Kennedy stood for a moment staring out into the woods, a frown on his face, before finally turning to join them. Seconds later the choppers took off in a whirr of thrumming propellers and roaring engines. I blinked back angry, helpless tears as I watched Todd's entire village disappear over the trees.

CHAPTER 16

Todd stumbled to his feet as soon as the choppers were out of sight, and ran to the fallen man. When Todd rolled him over, I realised it was Roderick, the man who'd helped me with my map. His blue eyes wore a frozen expression of shock, and I turned away, my stomach churning. Todd scrambled to his feet and pulled his bow off his back and pointed it straight at us. "What tracking method was he talking about?" he yelled. Hot, angry tears were falling from his eyes, but I didn't think he even realised it.

"Easy," I said, taking a few hasty steps back. I felt myself bump into Shawn. I looked over and saw him eyeing Todd's bow warily.

"You led them here. Why? Why would you do that?" Todd asked, his features twisted in pain and rage. Todd had trusted us, vouched for us, and we'd betrayed him in one of the worst ways imaginable. He would never trust someone so completely and easily again, and it wouldn't matter that our betrayal had been by accident.

"I don't know what tracking device he's talking about," I said, feeling helpless. I looked at Shawn. "Do you?"

He shook his head, a look of pure confusion on his bone-white face.

"Jett's guys must have missed something," I said, dropping my pack to the ground with a loud thump. "There must be a tracker hidden somewhere that I don't know about." I immediately began pulling out each of my belongings, going over them carefully, inch by inch, centimetre by centimetre, looking for the telltale bulge of a tracker. After another nervous glance at Todd, Shawn dropped his own pack and began looking over his belongings as well. Todd watched us for a second, and then he took a threatening step towards us, bringing his drawn arrow within inches of my face.

"Where are they taking them?" Todd cried. "Tell me or I'll shoot. I swear I will. This is all your fault."

"It's not," Shawn said, looking up from the canteen he was inspecting and over at me with a grimace. "OK. It kind of is."

"We didn't lead them here on purpose. I promise," I said, pulling out the few ration packs I'd managed to steal. I couldn't imagine anyone putting a tracker in one of those, but I looked anyway. "We would never do that to you. You heard General Kennedy. They are trying to find us. He called us convicts."

"What's a convict?" Todd sniffed.

"A criminal," I explained. "Which we technically are, since we stole supplies before we left. But I've never heard of the marines going after someone."

"No one was ever dumb enough to go topside besides your dad," Shawn muttered, then, seeming to realise that he'd spoken out loud, he glanced at me. "No offense." He turned to look at Todd. "Why did your mum and Jett cover for us? I don't get it." I didn't understand it either. No one in the compound would have lied for us.

"Because we're good people," Todd spat. "Unlike you."

"Todd," I said, finally done with my inspection, "I know you probably hate us right now, but I really didn't think anyone would come after us. I never would have put your village in danger like that." I sighed as I cinched my bag shut again. "And I know you aren't going to believe me, but I still can't find a tracker."

Shawn looked up at me, his forehead wrinkling in

the familiar way it always did when he was trying to figure out a problem. "Maybe it was on the body armour we just traded?"

"Maybe." I frowned. "But we wore that stuff all day yesterday; we'd have felt a tracker. Wouldn't we?"

Shawn shrugged, his face clouded and anxious as he busily checked the lining of his bag. "They make them tiny now. Plus –" he shook his head, eyes baffled – "trackers need to be manually turned on. How could they have done that?"

"Well, they did," I snapped, and then immediately felt ashamed. This wasn't Shawn's fault. This was mine. If I was angry with anyone, it was myself.

"Even if they had a tracker, they shouldn't have come after us," Shawn said, considering. Then he looked at the compass hanging around my neck. "It has to be your dad's info plug that they want. It's the only thing that makes sense."

I nodded grimly; he'd confirmed my suspicions. They wouldn't have bothered sending helicopters and armed men after us for stealing a couple of body armour suits and some ration packs. They would only do that for something big, and it had to be the plug.

"What plug?" Todd asked.

"But they didn't know about that. I never—" I stopped, thinking back to my escape, and my heart sank in realisation. My compass had fallen out of my shirt when I'd leaned over to look at the marine's ports. I'd opened to it see if the plug would fit in any of the port screens. There had been a security camera. Guilt, hard and heavy, settled in my stomach. I turned to Shawn. "Oh, no."

"Whatever is on that plug must be worth killing for," Shawn said. "The Noah wouldn't risk sending marines topside if it wasn't."

"Stop talking," Todd said as silent tears streamed down his face. I jumped. I'd almost forgotten that Todd was standing there, his huge bow still pointed at our heads, listening to us discuss tracking devices. I swallowed hard at the anger I saw boiling just beneath Todd's skin.

He held out a trembling hand. "Hand over that plug thing you keep talking about." I looked at his outstretched palm in disbelief.

"What?" I asked.

"You heard me," he said. "If they want that stupid plug, then I'm going to give it to them and get my mum back."

"But…" I stuttered. "That won't work."

"Why not?" he snapped. "You are going to tell me where they are being taken, and then I'm going to hand that plug over to them." His voice was too loud in the silent forest. I looked helplessly at a speechless Shawn before turning my attention back to Todd, all too aware of the sharp arrowhead inches from my face.

My hands went up. "They could be taking them to any one of the four compounds." I took a cautious step back. Could I outrun one of Todd's arrows? Doubtful.

"Why would they do that?" Todd asked.

"Because humans aren't supposed to live topside. It's against the law," Shawn said.

"Your laws," Todd snarled.

"Even if I gave you the plug," I said cautiously, "the marines still wouldn't release your mum and the rest of the villagers. They may have come here looking for it, but they took those people away even though they knew they didn't have it."

Todd looked at us for another moment, and then he lowered the bow.

"Keep your stupid plug, then." He sniffed. "You can tell Roderick over there how important it is to you." With that, he stormed past us towards the abandoned tree houses. I glanced over at Roderick's still body and felt sick. When I let go of my compass, I saw that I'd been clutching it so tightly that it had left an angry red imprint on my palm. Was Todd right? Should I just give him the plug? I rolled this idea around for a moment before shaking my head stubbornly. Kennedy and his marines wouldn't hand over the villagers for the plug. Not now. I could only hope that Roderick hadn't died in vain. That whatever was on this plug was worth the sacrifice. My dad had certainly thought so, or he wouldn't have risked my life and his.

When I finally looked up, Todd was halfway up one of the long ropes. I went to follow him, and Shawn grabbed my arm to stop me, shaking his head.

"Give him a minute to cool down," he advised. "We aren't his favourite people right now. In fact" – he looked up nervously – "part of me thinks we should run while we have the chance."

I crossed my arms and glared at him in disbelief.

Shawn sighed. "How did I know you wouldn't be on board with that plan?" As one, we craned our heads back to follow Todd's progress. He was fast, faster than I'd thought possible. Soon he was through the hatch in the floor.

"We need to fix this," I said as we watched Todd running from house to house, the rope bridges swinging wildly. My heart tugged painfully.

"How do we do that?" Shawn asked.

"I don't know." I frowned and tapped the compass. "Whatever is on here, we need to get it to Lake Michigan."

I looked up as Todd began lowering cloth bundles down on ropes. The first three were light and appeared to be nothing but rope and thick fabric, and I wondered what Todd wanted them for. The last bundle was heavy, and when it landed in my arms, I felt a warm weight that made my heart sink. It was a body. A small one. I laid it down gingerly, too scared to open it. Todd soon followed, a large pack strapped to his back and his bow over his shoulder. He was holding three shovels.

"Anyone up there?" I asked.

"No. Come on," Todd said. "We need to bury Roderick before scavengers find him." He bent down and gingerly picked up the heavy bundle.

"I'm so sorry, Todd," I said. "This is all my fault."

"No," Todd said, laying the bundle down beside Roderick. "It's my fault. I should never have brought you to the Oaks." I flinched as he began digging a hole.

He was right; he shouldn't have helped us. Roderick would have still been alive if Todd had let that T. rex eat us in the meadow. Shawn and I picked up the shovels and helped dig. Soon we had an acceptable hole, and Shawn helped Todd carry Roderick over. Todd walked over to the other bundle and threw back the wrappings to reveal Tilly. She could have been sleeping if it hadn't been for the neat bullet hole in her head. A sob caught in my throat, and I turned away as Todd laid her down next to Roderick.

Shawn stood staring bleakly into the hole. "I never thought I'd be sad to see a dead dinosaur." He turned his face away, and I saw a tear glistening on his cheek before he wiped it away. "But this is awful." He picked up his shovel to begin covering them with dirt, but Todd held out a hand to stop him. He reached down and removed a leather necklace from around Roderick's neck and put it around his own. On it hung a simple silver circle. I looked closely and recognised the old pre-Dinosauria-Pandemic currency: it was a quarter. It had a hole punched through it to allow the leather to pass through.

Todd saw me looking and tucked it in his shirt. "It's a symbol of our village," he explained. "You don't get one until you turn eighteen, but as I'm the only free villager left, I didn't think anyone would mind."

"I'm sorry, man," Shawn said. "Not everyone in the compound is like Kennedy. He's as mean and nasty as they come. I'm sure the Noah didn't authorise him to shoot people." He glanced back down at the hole and swallowed hard, and I knew he was thinking that the Noah probably *had* authorised the marines to shoot dinosaurs. Todd just grunted, and we finished burying Roderick and Tilly in silence.

The job done, Todd walked back over to the pile of packs we'd left by the base of the tree. I noticed that there was something about the way Todd moved, a wary edginess that Shawn and I lacked. His eyes flicked this way and that as he took in the surrounding woods. Every now and then, his head would snap in the direction of a noise, and I'd see his hand jerk involuntarily towards the bow that never left his back. Shawn and I had left ours sitting in a pile next to the packs. Not good. I hurried over to sling mine on, not that carrying it was going to do me much good. I had no clue how to use the thing.

"What is all this?" I asked, pointing to the remaining bundles Todd had lowered from the tree houses.

Todd picked one up and tossed it to me. "They're tree pods."

"Thanks," I said.

"What's a tree pod?" Shawn whispered to me.

"No clue," I muttered, "but say thank you."

"Thank you," Shawn said obediently. Todd ignored us as he secured his own tree pod to his pack.

"If you don't sleep in a tree, you're as good as dead. This lets you do that without breaking your neck. My mum wanted you two to have them. Of course, she didn't plan on you getting our entire village kidnapped, but you won't last one night without them."

I looked around, my heart jumping into my throat. "Wait, where's Verde?"

"Verde is staying here. She's too small to come with us, and I don't want anything to happen to her." He glanced back at the freshly dug grave and frowned. "It's lucky she was out. I've left enough food for her to last a few weeks, so hopefully she won't try to follow us." He readjusted his pack and glared at us. "Are you ready to go?"

"You're coming with us?" I asked, and as I said it, I realised it was what I was hoping he'd do. Our chances of making it to Lake Michigan alive were much better with him along, and he was my only hope of learning how to use the bow strapped to my back.

"I'm not going with you," Todd said as though this should have been obvious. "You're coming with me. You have to help me find my mum and get my village back. I have no clue where that stupid compound of yours is, and it's your fault they got taken."

"I want to help you," I said. "I do. But I can't. Not yet. I have to finish what I started. I think the reason those marines came after us in the first place was because of this," I said, holding up my compass. "I need to get it to Lake Michigan, and I need to get there fast before anyone else gets hurt."

"And what?" Todd said. "You are just going to leave my mum and everyone I love in the hands of your crazy dictator? No way. You got them taken, and you are going to help me get them back."

"I promise I'll help you get them back," I said. "I'll march you right into North Compound myself if that's what you want. But I can't go anywhere near a compound until I see this thing through. I have to."

Todd frowned. "There isn't anything in Lake Michigan. If you make it there alive, which you probably won't, all you will have accomplished is wasting time."

"So come with us," I said. "We make it there faster, and we make it there alive. As soon as I've delivered this plug to, well, whatever is in the middle of Lake Michigan, Shawn and I will help you get your village back."

"We will?" Shawn muttered quietly, and I stomped down hard on his foot. He grunted in pain, but he got the message.

"We will," I said. "I promise."

Todd stared at us, then he looked back up at the deserted tree houses, their rope ladders swinging gently in the breeze. "If I help you," he said after a moment, "we can make it to Lake Michigan in less than three days."

"Really?" I said, feeling hopeful for the first time since the helicopters had shown up.

Todd nodded. "If it was any further, I'd say forget it, you're on your own. But I can spare a few days, especially if it means you help me. I know about as much about survival underground as you know about survival aboveground."

"So… you know nothing," Shawn said. Todd laughed despite himself. Shawn had a knack for making people laugh when they felt like crying.

"Really? You'll come with us?" I asked.

Todd nodded. "I've never actually gone to the lake, but I did do some trading trips with my dad to Ivan's, and I know his place is only a day or so from the lake."

I froze.

"Did you just say Ivan?" I asked. Not daring to hope. "You know an Ivan?"

Todd looked at me strangely. "You know Ivan? Crazy trapper Ivan? Dinosaur hunter Ivan?"

"Um –" I glanced at Shawn – "maybe?" I unscrewed my compass and pulled out my dad's note and handed it to Todd. It was time to put all my cards on the table.

"How many things do you have in that direction-finding thingy of yours?" he asked.

"More than you'd expect," I said with a strained smile. "Just look at it." He read it quickly and then handed it back to me.

"So that plug thing you guys were talking about is in there?" Todd asked, eyeing my compass speculatively. I nodded, fighting the urge to grab it protectively. Todd saw my look and shook his head ruefully. "Don't worry. I'm not going to take it."

I nodded.

"Your dad wasn't real specific in that note, was he?" Todd said.

"You can say that again," Shawn grumbled.

I glared at him. "You should be happy. If it is the same Ivan, then we might not have to go all the way to Lake Michigan."

"Now that," Shawn said, pointing at me, "is the best news I've heard all day."

I frowned as something occurred to me, and I turned to Todd. "Can we go back to Adler's trading post before we head out?"

Todd looked startled. "Why? You have all the gear you need."

"That's not it." I shook my head. "I don't trust this stuff any more." I gestured to my backpack. "I want to trade it all in. I couldn't find a tracker, but there has to be one, or those marines wouldn't have found us. The last thing we need is for them to track us to Ivan."

"We can try," Todd said, "but Adler's not going to want anything potentially carrying a tracker."

I frowned. "I didn't think about that."

As it turned out, Adler wasn't a problem. The rope ladder leading up to his house swung back and forth lazily in the wind, and the small hut was abandoned.

"The marines must have got him," Shawn said, running his fingers over some of the dusty pots and pans hanging from the wall. He picked up a small box of bits of metal and began pawing through it.

"Or Adler heard the gun shots and took off without even trying to help," Todd said in disgust. His face darkened, and he glared at me. "Although I shouldn't be too judgemental. All we did was hide in the bushes."

"There was nothing we could have done," Shawn said, setting down the box of metal. "If we'd shown ourselves, we'd be in those helicopters too." Todd just grunted in response and disappeared down a dusty row of what looked like cooking utensils. Shawn's eyes roamed over the cluttered shelves of the store. He was looking for his music box.

I took my bag off my back and plunked it on the counter. It didn't take long to empty out my worn grey clothing and the few items I'd stolen from the compound. Todd thumped two large canvas bags like his own down without a word, and turned around to poke through the shelves again. Shawn joined me at the counter and quickly emptied out his own bag. His pile of supplies dwarfed mine, and I stared in wonder at the items he'd managed to get his hands on. I picked up the med kit and the small bag of tools, wishing we could take them with us. But in the end, I put them back on the pile. One of these items had a tracker in it, and nothing was worth getting caught for.

Ten minutes later, we had filled our new canvas packs with supplies from Adler's stash and were heading back down the rope ladder. The only thing I'd kept was my journal, tucking it safely in the bottom of the unfamiliar pack. Shawn had kept his old patched-up port. I hadn't known that he'd brought it along, but after a little arguing, he'd convinced me that there was no way a tracker was in the port he'd personally assembled piece by piece. I'd finally agreed. I knew part of the reason was because we hadn't found his music box. He'd tried to hide his devastation when it hadn't turned up, but failed. Everything familiar had been left in the tree house above us. It was bittersweet and freeing all at once.

Todd jumped the last few feet to the ground, landing gracefully. He'd barely spoken to us through the entire exchange of supplies. He stood now, taking in the forest around us, his face wary, his bow strung. At least it wasn't pointing at us any more, I thought as I hopped off the ladder to land clumsily beside him.

Shawn dropped next, but missed the landing and fell on to his butt. I bit back a smile as I helped him up. "So we're heading to this Ivan's house?" he asked glumly as he dusted himself off.

"We are," I said, nodding, but then I stopped and looked at Todd as something occurred to me. "Can you even find Ivan? My dad said that he didn't know where Ivan was located."

"I can find him," Todd said. "I think. He relocates every few years, but I know Mitchell just saw him a few months ago to trade for some teeth and bones, and he said Ivan was back at the house I visited with my dad once."

Shawn didn't look convinced. "Only once?"

"Once is enough," Todd said, shouldering his pack. "Let's get going. I want to get as far as I can before night falls." He took a few steps into the woods, then stopped and turned back to us. "Remember what I said about being alert," he warned. "If the smaller meat-eating dinosaurs are hungry enough, they might try to take one of us out, especially if they are hunting in a pack. We need to stay close together, and we need to have our bows ready."

"But we don't know how to use our bows," Shawn pointed out.

"Worst-case scenario," Todd said, "use it as a club." He turned and headed into the woods at a jog.

"Was that supposed to be reassuring?" Shawn asked me.

"I don't think so," I said, heading in after Todd.

CHAPTER 17

I wondered if I would ever get used to this topside world. As I ran after Todd, every breath scraping up my throat in a wheezing gasp, I decided the answer was probably not. Growing up in the filtered, monochromatic quiet of the compound made all the colours and smells and sounds up here overwhelming. There were so many things I wanted to look at but couldn't because I needed to watch where I was going. I managed to catch a glimpse of a bird here or a chattering squirrel there, but I always paid for it with a rather painful face-plant and an irritated look from Todd. And while I appreciated the beauty of the fallen leaves, moss and tiny patches of multicoloured flowers we ran over, I also found them annoyingly uneven. I caught myself longing for the smooth compound tunnels and almost laughed out loud at myself. I'd spent a lifetime wishing for exactly what I was doing right now, running in the fresh air and the dappled green light that shone down from the trees. I just hadn't imagined it being so uncomfortable.

My feet were killing me. My new boots were wonderful, but the blisters from the day before were still raw, and the bottoms of my feet felt bruised. Todd kept us at a brisk trot for what felt like hours. His face was a thundercloud, and it was clear that talking was out of the question. Except for the occasional glare or snide remark when Shawn or I tripped, he didn't say much. I tried to mimic his constant state of wary watchfulness, but it was impossible. He saw things ages before I did, heard things I couldn't and smelled things I didn't even notice. Watching him, I realised that Shawn and I had been way too relaxed the day before. I'd thought we were safe in the thick trees, but Todd made it obvious we were not.

I was so busy thinking about how stupid we'd been that I almost ran smack into Todd's back when he pulled up short.

"Look there," he whispered, pointing through the trees to our left. I looked and spotted a small pack of dinosaurs, no taller than my waist. They were pawing underneath a fallen log, and as we watched one of them let out a high-pitched shriek as it came up with a fat bullfrog clutched in its jaws. Immediately the dinosaur next to it ripped the frog out of its jaws and swallowed it whole. The first dinosaur squealed in rage and went after the thief.

"What's so special about them?" Shawn huffed, his hands on his knees. "We've seen little dinosaurs like that all day."

"What did you call that Big Ugly back in the meadow? A T. rex? Well those, my friends, are baby T. rex," Todd whispered.

"Really?" I asked, looking again. These dinosaurs were a muddy brown instead of the flashy greens and reds of an adult T. rex. And while the adults had a smattering of thin, whisker-like feathers on their heads and backs, these had thicker feathers covering large portions of their body. Camouflage, I realised. The young dinosaurs blended in with the forest floor. The giants that roamed the open areas must send their young into the trees for protection. The youngsters crouched on all four feet, using their front legs to balance out their well-muscled back half. Their forelegs must stop growing soon, I thought, picturing the adult T. rex's useless front legs.

"I forgot this area was a T. rex breeding ground,"

Todd whispered. "Roderick only marked your map for the trip to Lake Michigan. If he'd known we were going this way, he could have warned us." He trailed off, and I knew he was remembering that Roderick was dead. I pulled my map out and Todd silently pointed to a spot to the right of my dad's original path. We were still heading north towards Lake Michigan, but we were now heading there at an angle instead of the direct route my dad had drawn. The miniature T. rex pulled their heads up to stare at us, their eyes bright and intelligent. Todd motioned for us to follow, and we were off and running again, leaving them to fight over the discovery of another frog.

Shawn and I kept up with Todd for another hour as he led us through the woods. He seemed to know instinctively exactly where the thickest trees were and led us out of our way to avoid any dinosaurs we came across – all while running at an almost unbelievable pace. I gritted my teeth, determined not to be weak, but I was worried if we kept our pace up much longer, I was going to pass out. "Todd," I finally called, "if you're trying to kill us as payback for getting your village taken, you might just get your wish."

Todd stopped and looked back at us, taking in our

sweat-drenched shirts and Shawn's bright red face. Todd wasn't breathing hard at all.

He frowned. "What's the problem?"

"We can't run much longer," I said, as Shawn dropped to the ground and started digging out his canteen. When he finally found it, he stared at it a moment, as though he'd forgotten that he'd given up his smooth metal compound one for the dingy glass one from Adler's. Then he shrugged and took a long drink.

"I think I hacked up a lung about a mile ago," he wheezed. "Don't worry. There is a fifty-fifty chance I'll survive without it."

"The air up here is too thick," I complained.

"Too thick?" Todd said. "What are you talking about?"

"It's the humidity," Shawn said, taking another long drink. "The compound didn't have any. We had filtered and recirculated air with a higher oxygen content to make up for the increased carbon dioxide levels of the tunnels."

"Whatever," Todd said. "We can walk awhile, but I want to get as far as possible before dark." He turned and started walking swiftly through the woods, his bow drawn. I offered Shawn my hand and helped him up.

"Why does he have to be so fast?" he groaned.

"Because he wants to survive," Todd called back.

"What is with the freakishly good hearing?" Shawn muttered to me.

"Different question, same answer," Todd replied, and I had to grin. I hurried to catch up with Todd. Shawn was right; I practically had to jog to keep up with his ground-eating strides.

"I know I've already said it," I told him, "but I am so sorry about what happened." Guilt was gnawing at me. I needed him to tell me we were OK before it ate me alive – even if it wasn't even close to being OK.

"I know you didn't mean for it to happen," he said, puffing out his cheeks and looking at me. "But I would forgive a lot quicker if Shawn didn't keep defending the people who took my mum."

"Yeah, about that." I sighed. "You have to understand that in the compound, the Noah's word is law. He's the world's protector, the reason we've survived this long. Every rule, every law, every everything in the compound is to ensure the survival of the human race. Shawn never could have imagined them capturing a village like yours. He couldn't even imagine a village like yours existed two days ago."

"And you have to understand that out here the Noah is somebody to be feared," Todd shot back. "He's a dictator who brainwashed the human race into thinking that they had to give up their independence to survive. According to Jett, the Noah will stop at nothing to keep power. Nothing. Even if it means eradicating the last pockets of freedom and acting like they never existed. And after what I just witnessed, my version of your precious Noah looks a lot more accurate." I stopped walking and stared after him, struck dumb as I tried to reconcile his version of the Noah with my own.

"What was that about?" Shawn huffed, catching up with me.

"Nothing." I frowned as I started walking again. "Just friendly small talk."

"It didn't look like Todd was feeling too friendly. Not that I can blame him."

I nodded, my mind churning as I thought about everything Todd had said. The Noah he described was not the Noah I'd learned about in school or heard from during mandatory assemblies.

I leaned over and picked up a fallen leaf so I could

shred it between my fingers as we walked. It gave off a tangy, lemony smell and made my fingers feel sticky. "He seems to think we're idiots for believing the Noah all these years."

"I've met a lot of idiots," Shawn said, "and I promise you, Sky Mundy, that you aren't one. What happened at the village was bad; I'm not denying that. But the Noah always has a reason. Remember history class? There have been three Noahs that have taken power over the years, right? And every Noah has always made laws and decisions with one goal in mind: to save the human race. I think you can forgive a lot when the alternative is extinction."

"I'm not so sure," I muttered. Something inside of me was shifting, and it made me uncomfortable. When I'd taken on my dad's mission, I hadn't really thought through whom I was working against. Stealing supplies and leaving the compound had been minor acts of rebellion. I'd spent years working to ensure the survival of the human race, following the Noah's every decree, obeying the rules. Now, it appeared, I was working against the very man I'd looked up to. The Noah obviously didn't want me to deliver whatever was on this port, and he'd sent his marines to stop me.

I glanced up from my shredded leaf to see that Todd was now twenty feet in front of us.

"Hurry up," Todd called. "And get out your bows. They aren't going to do you much good strapped to your backs."

Shawn and I hurried over, fumbling to unstrap our bows. After watching us struggle, Todd sighed and stopped to help us. He spent a minute or so adjusting our grips and tightening the bowstrings before nodding in satisfaction.

"OK," he said. "Let's go."

"What are we shooting at?" I asked, confused.

"Nothing," Todd said.

Shawn looked confused. "But shouldn't we have an arrow out?"

Todd shook his head. "I don't feel like getting shot today, and that's just what you'll do the first time you trip." Shawn looked down at his grass-stained knees sheepishly. "Until you get comfortable with the bow," Todd said, smirking, "and walking, you don't get any arrows."

"Is this how your dad taught you?" I asked.

"Yeah." Todd smiled. "I had to carry my bow around for a whole month."

"Did you feel like an idiot?" Shawn asked, gesturing to his bow. "Because I sure do."

Todd laughed, and the tension that had been hanging over us ever since we left the Oaks eased.

"What was it like to grow up topside?" I asked, wanting to keep Todd talking. I liked the easygoing, joking Todd we'd met in the woods the day before. This sombre, moody Todd put me off balance. He had every right to hate us, but I hoped he wouldn't.

"Topside," Todd said thoughtfully as he started walking again. "You two always call it that, but I've never known anything different."

"We were like that in the compound," Shawn said. "Until I was five, I always thought that the topside was just an interesting bedtime story."

Todd shook his head. "I can't imagine that."

"Did the Oaks have a school?" I prompted. "You know how to read."

"Not very well," Todd said. "We don't have a fancy school like you compound moles. A few people still have books, and Jett required that everyone know how to read by the time they were ten. He didn't want the skill to die out. Mostly we learn how to do useful stuff, like hunt, fish, build and garden. When you turn sixteen, you're apprenticed to someone in the village. I was going to ask to be Roderick's apprentice." He frowned. "He was going to teach me all about maps, so I could be a trader like my dad."

"But who did you trade with?" Shawn asked. "Certainly not the compounds."

Todd snorted. "Definitely not. There are three other villages within a week's travel of the Oaks. My dad used to make the trip to trade goods with them. And we trade with Ivan. He used to come to the Oaks about once a month. Now if you want something from Ivan, you have to go to him. I haven't seen him in years."

"You said he was a dinosaur hunter?" I asked. "That can't be a real thing. Can it?"

"You just wait and see." Todd smiled. "If his house is the same as I remember, you're in for a real treat."

"Has anyone ever tried to improve your pulley system?" Shawn asked, and I smiled as we fell into easy conversation. We shared stories about our lives and grilled each other about the oddities of each other's upbringing, and I almost forgot that we were walking through dinosaur territory. Almost. The bows in our hands served as a helpful reminder.

"We'll stop here to eat," Todd finally said, indicating

a small cave built in the side of a large rock formation. "My dad and I used this as a breaking point when I was a kid," he explained as he shrugged his pack off and let it fall heavily to the ground. "I was too little to make it very far in one day."

Shawn followed suit, rolling his shoulders gratefully. "I could have gone another couple of hours, but if you need to rest, that's no problem."

Todd let out a laugh. "Yeah, right. Sit down before you fall down."

I glanced at Todd. "Is it OK if I go over there?" I pointed to a clump of thick bushes about thirty yards away.

"Yeah," Todd said, looking confused. "But why?"

I felt my face grow hot. "Um…"

Todd's own face flushed. "Oh, yeah. That's fine."

I headed for the bushes to relieve myself. The boys had been able to take care of this necessity as we travelled, but I was much too self-conscious for that. Being a girl could really be a pain.

I was just heading back towards the boys when something made me stop. My skin prickled into goose bumps. Some ancient survival instinct made my heart rate quicken. I wasn't alone. Every muscle tensed, waiting to explode. Green scales flashed to my left, and I was running in an instant.

"Run!" I screamed as branches cracked behind me. The dinosaur was too big to manoeuvre easily, and on instinct alone, I began zigzagging through the trees. My first impulse was to run back to the boys, in the hope that Todd could drop the creature with his bow, but as the trees flashed by me, I realised that I no longer knew which way that was.

A feral roar sounded behind me, so close that my heart almost stopped in sheer panic. I commanded my muscles to move faster, and I began frantically scanning my surroundings for something, anything, that might save me. There was nothing. On a hunch, I dived suddenly to my right and doubled back, forcing the creature to spin. I gained a few yards, but it wasn't enough. Terror roiled through me. *Think*, I commanded myself. *Think or you're dead.* I felt one of my new knives bouncing on my arm and ripped it out. It was a long shot, but it was something. Whirling, I took aim and flung the knife. As it winged towards my attacker, I realised what a futile effort it was. The tiny blade looked laughable as it bounced off the creature's shoulder. It roared angrily, not even slowing down as

I turned to run again. Great, I'd just made it mad. And I'd lost ground. Brilliant.

The creature was gaining on me. Teeth snapped together only inches from the back of my head, and I knew that this was how I would die. There was movement off to my right, and I realised that the dinosaur might be part of a pack. I prayed that it would be quick, that the creature would break my neck and not rip me to shreds while I was still alive. Suddenly a sharp twang ripped through the air past my right ear and the dinosaur let out a bloodcurdling screech. The sound made me stumble, and my exhausted muscles faltered. I was falling. Time seemed to slow as I twisted and ripped my last knife from its holster in one movement. I thrust it out and felt it connect with hard scales right before everything went black.

CHAPTER 18

I knew I was dead, but I was surprisingly unbothered by this fact. It hadn't been as bad as I'd feared. All of my joints felt loose and detached, as though I were a puppet someone had put down and forgotten. Something was shaking my shoulder. I squeezed my eyes shut, willing it to go away. Voices drifted through my blackness.

"Sky! Oh man, don't be dead."

"She's just knocked out. She isn't even bleeding."

"What do you know?! If you'd been faster, this wouldn't have happened."

"Easy for you to say. I noticed your shot hit a tree. Very helpful."

"Why isn't she moving? Do you think that allosaurus broke her neck?"

"I don't think it's broken, but she sure is scratched up. She tried to take it down with a couple of four-inchers. Talk about guts."

"What was that thing doing this deep in the forest anyway? I didn't think dinosaurs that big could come this deep."

"No clue. This one is pretty young, though; these guys get to be huge as adults. Did she just squeeze her eyes shut?"

"I think so. Sky? Sky, can you hear me?"

"Give her a minute. That thing practically knocked her into next Tuesday."

"Are you sure it's dead?"

"Cut its throat myself. It wouldn't have tumbled on top of her if I hadn't got it in the eye. Remember that. The ones with the hard hide can't be stopped except for a shot through the eye."

"She's moving. Thank God, she didn't break her neck."

"Told you."

"Just be quiet, will you?"

I was finding it difficult to stay in my comfortable blackness. Prying my eyes open, I looked up into two blurry faces. Shawn looked ashen, and Todd was smirking. It was the first smile I'd seen since we'd left Emily that morning. Had it only been that morning? It felt like a lifetime.

"Welcome back to the land of the living," Todd said.

"I'm not dead?" I asked groggily as Shawn helped me to my feet. Sticks and leaves fell off my dirt-smeared clothing, and I looked down at myself in confusion. "Why am I not dead?"

"You almost were," Shawn said. "If Todd had waited two more seconds, you would have been done for. As it was, the thing practically tackled you as it went down."

"If I hadn't waited to make sure my shot was good, I might have missed, or accidentally hit her," Todd explained, annoyed. "Hence the delay of the shot."

Ten feet behind Todd lay the still body of the dinosaur. A dark red slit ran across its neck, but its yellow eyes still seemed to be looking at me. I felt myself begin to tremble.

"Don't worry," Todd said cheerfully as he strode over to the creature and picked up my knives. "This guy wanted you for lunch –" he wedged a knife between two scales in the creature's back haunch and began to saw – "so we'll return the favour and have him." Blood spurted from the hindquarters and on to Todd's hands, and my stomach rolled. I stumbled away to puke.

"We can't hang around here," Todd said a moment later, sealing his bloody prize inside two different drawstring sacks before putting it into his pack. "We need to get moving."

"Moving?" Shawn asked. "What happened to lunch?" As if on cue, his stomach snarled.

"That guy's still on today's menu." Todd jerked his head at the still-bleeding carcass behind him. I averted my eyes as my stomach rolled sickeningly again. "But we can't eat here. Hurry up and get your packs on. I'll explain once we have some distance between us and all that blood."

"You shouldn't have mentioned food if you weren't going to follow through," Shawn grouched, readjusting his pack.

"You'll get fed," Todd snapped. "Just hurry." I glanced at him, surprised by his tone, and realised he was on high alert, his head turning this way and that, taking in the woods around us as though he expected another attack.

I took a drink of water from my canteen, swished and spat. It improved the taste in my mouth, but not by much. Before I could put it back in my pack, Todd had snatched it from my hands to pour over his own blood-soaked ones.

"That seems like a waste of water," Shawn protested.

"Trust me," Todd said, his face grim. "It's not." He glanced around nervously. "Grab your stuff, Sky." Still feeling too dizzy and disoriented to argue, I limped over to my pack and eased its weight on to my throbbing shoulders. I staggered a bit, light-headed from the fall, and Shawn steadied me, frowning.

"Sky needs to rest," he insisted.

"No," Todd said. "Sky needs to survive. And that means she has to move." He glanced at me. "Sorry." Without another word, he took off at a fast jog, and we followed. We ran, crossing and recrossing two streams along the way. Todd made us run right down the middle of the last stream, our boots getting soaked in the icy water. Thirty minutes later, Todd finally stopped and set down his packs. I sank down next to them, putting my head between my knees and blinking the black spots in my vision away.

"Now we have lunch," Todd said.

"Thank goodness," Shawn said, plopping down next to me.

Ten minutes later, I watched the meat drip fat into the fire Todd had built. I'd never sat by an open fire before. I decided I liked it. Every movement sent a wave of pain through my muscles, and I was pretty sure every inch of my body was bruised. Shawn was pretty sure I had a concussion.

When I was handed a large piece of steaming dinosaur perched on a flat leaf, I almost didn't accept it. The thought of eating the creature that had almost devoured me made my newly empty stomach queasy. But it did smell good – a smoky, thick smell I was beginning to associate with the strange foods of the topside world. I watched as Todd dug in with gusto. Shawn shot me an apologetic look before biting into his own steaming piece. My belly felt hollow, and with a resigned sigh, I nibbled at the corner. It was amazing. Ignoring Todd's smug grin of approval, I tore off a larger hunk and chewed, my eyes squeezed shut as it practically melted on my tongue.

"So why couldn't we have done this at that cave?" Shawn asked. "Why'd we run away from a dead dinosaur?"

"Scavengers," Todd explained through a mouthful of meat. "I made a silent kill so it may take them a while to find it, but when they do, we'll be glad we're well away. If dinosaurs have the option, they always go for the easy meal. Why do you think they find us so appealing?"

"Scavengers?" Shawn asked.

Todd nodded. "Odds are that man-eater you called an allosaurus will be found within the hour and be nothing but bones by sundown. And when they finish with him, they would have gone after us."

"Isn't it dangerous to have a fire like this?" I asked. "Wouldn't *that* attract dinosaurs?"

"Nope." Todd shook his head. "We don't know why, but we think it has something to do with their instinct to flee from fire." I nodded and took another bite. Wiping my greasy hands off on my pants, I took my journal out of my pack and flipped to a new page. At the top, I wrote TODD'S TOPSIDE TIPS. Underneath I jotted down what he'd just said about fire, and a few of the other bits of information he'd thrown our way throughout the day.

"What are you doing?" Todd asked. I jumped and glanced up to find him looking over my shoulder at the list.

"I just don't want to forget," I said sheepishly, shutting the journal and sliding it back in my bag.

"No one's ever written down what I said before," Todd said, sitting back. "Todd's topside tips." He nodded. "It has a certain ring to it." Seizing another piece of meat, he dug in, letting the grease drip off his chin into the dirt.

"I wouldn't flatter yourself," Shawn said. "She has a head injury."

"Watch it," I laughed, and threw what was left of my piece of meat at Shawn's head. He caught it, inspected it and then popped it in his mouth. I shook my head. He'd come a long way for a guy who'd gagged the night before when he'd been told he was eating dinosaur.

The last of the meat eaten, Todd licked his fingers clean and stood to kick dirt over the remaining flames. Reshouldering his pack, he grabbed his bow and motioned for us to do the same.

I got gingerly to my aching feet. "What are we doing?"

"I'm going to give you both a quick lesson," Todd said. "I was wrong not to train you at least a little bit. Next time it might be me being chased, and I don't want you two attempting to club it to death." He turned and went over to a nearby tree. Pulling the knife from the sheath on his arm, he carved a rough target into the bark. I followed him.

"This should be interesting," Shawn muttered, but he picked up his bow and walked over.

"OK," Todd said, sounding resigned. "I don't want to spend too much time on this, so we are just going to stick to the basics. Both of you stand where I am and try to hit that target," he said, motioning towards the tree, twenty feet away. Shawn and I both got into position.

"Wow, that's horrible," Todd groaned, walking over before either of us had had a chance to shoot. "Sky, pull your arrow back again, then freeze." I did what he asked, my arm muscles shaking at the effort of pulling back the bowstring. I was using three fingers like he'd shown me when he first made us carry our bows around that morning, but he still looked exasperated. "You need to stand parallel to your target," he said, turning me roughly so my shoulder pointed at the target instead of my hips. "And don't have this arm stick straight." He adjusted the arm that was holding the arc of the bow. "If you do that, your string is going to snap you right in the arm, and it hurts like you wouldn't believe. And you'll also miss. Now give it a try."

I released the bowstring and my arrow shot wide, missing the tree by a good five feet. My face flushed in embarrassment.

"Not as bad as it could have been," Todd said. "You

drew the bowstring back to your eye to aim, right?"

"Yes," I said. "Was that wrong too?"

Todd shrugged. "I'm an under-the-chin shooter myself, but eye's fine. Just always do it the same way. Consistency is important." He turned to Shawn, and only had to make a few minor adjustments to his stance and arm positioning. I felt a bit better when Shawn's arrow went even wider than mine.

"It's a start." Todd glanced up at the sun. "I don't want to lose too much time, but I think we can spare about ten minutes for some practice." So Shawn and I shot arrow after arrow at the tree. By the end of the ten minutes, I had got one of my arrows to hit the target, and Shawn hadn't got any. I would have been smug, but the one that had actually hit had only hit because I'd decided to aim at a tree three feet to the left of the one with a target. Not that I was going to admit that any time soon.

"We need to start moving," Todd finally said. "Get your arrows and let's go."

This time the bow felt slightly more familiar in my hands as I carried it through the woods. All three of our bows were made of the carved rib of a dinosaur and were surprisingly light considering their size.

260

I couldn't get over the idea of hollow dinosaur bones. I'd known that a lot of the dinosaurs the old-world scientists had resurrected had shocked everyone by turning out to have feathers, but the dinosaurs were still way more birdlike than I'd expected.

The next few hours of hiking through the forest were blessedly uneventful. The only things we spotted were a few smaller dinosaurs that peered at us nervously before moving away. Every time we came to a clearing in the trees, we went around it. I caught glimpses of massive scaled bodies lumbering through the meadows, but Todd never let us get close enough to really see much. Watching Todd manoeuvre through the woods with such ease gave me hope that someday I might be that comfortable aboveground too. No sooner had I thought this than a distant screech made me jump about a foot. When Todd didn't even flinch, I tried to cover up the jump by pretending to trip, and then felt even more embarrassed when Todd rolled his eyes at me. I sighed, remembering that in order to get comfortable with the topside world, I needed to survive. And at the rate I was going, my odds didn't look good.

CHAPTER 19

"**Y**ou need to shoot dinner, or we're going to be eating dinosaur jerky tonight," Todd said as the light around us started to turn into the orangey-red tones that I now associated with sunset. I shuddered as I thought about the brown strips of hard meat Todd had made each of us pack when we swapped supplies at Alder's.

"Why can't you shoot it?" Shawn asked as his stomach rumbled audibly.

"Because I don't need the practice," Todd said. He had a point, so Shawn and I both started looking for something we could shoot. But I felt a little ill at the idea of killing any of the squirrels or foxes we'd seen scampering about the underbrush. They were all so beautiful and vibrant that I couldn't picture eating one. The problem was that as the tree cover thinned out, so did the animals. The woods had an almost eerie silence to them. Apparently the animals knew something we didn't and had made their homes elsewhere.

The terrain changed as we entered an area that had been more populated. It had been easy to forget that the ground we walked over used to be home to hundreds and thousands of people when we were surrounded by thick trees. Now the ghosts of the past were not so easily ignored. I stopped to inspect a crumbling brick wall. It had been decorative once, but time and passing dinosaurs had collapsed huge sections of it. A metal plaque had fallen off the front and now lay half buried in the dirt. Curious, I bent and pulled it out. *White Oak Estates* was etched elegantly into its surface. A piece of the sign crumbled in my hand, leaving orange flecks of rust all over the arm of my tunic. I dropped it and stood, brushing myself off.

"I'm pretty sure this area used to be called the suburbs," Todd said, and then frowned. "Or was it the urbsubs?" He shook his head. "I can't remember. But the point is that lots of people used to live close together."

Shawn walked up to stand beside Todd, looking around himself with interest. "How can you tell?"

"Look at the trees." Todd pointed. "See how the big ones all seem to grow in rows? They planted them to border the streets." I walked up beside him and saw that he was right: straight lines of trees mapped out the memory of roads, creating a green tunnel of leaves and branches for us to pass through. As we walked, I noticed that every thirty feet or so there was a perfectly square or rectangular space where small weeds and bushes grew out of the crumbling remains of concrete. *That's where the houses used to be*, I realised. I sucked in a breath as I looked out at the seemingly endless miles of trees and patches of ruined foundations. It was one thing to read about the billions of people who had died; it was another thing entirely to see the after effects in person.

I followed Todd and Shawn down what used to be the suburb's streets. Every now and then we'd come across a house that wasn't completely destroyed. These were creepier than the ruined foundations, and I shivered as their empty, windowless eyes watched us pass. I couldn't imagine what this place had looked like right after the takeover. It must have been a nightmare of dead bodies and ruined buildings. Nature had reclaimed most of it now, turning the remaining buildings into crumbling memorials for a civilization foolish enough to bring its own downfall out of extinction.

After another thirty minutes of walking, we stopped to refill our water supply in a stream that ran past an abandoned barn. The hulking relic had faded red paint and one of its walls had caved in, giving it a lopsided and forlorn appearance. I shut my eyes and tried to imagine what it had looked like a hundred and fifty years ago. Back when its paint had been a bright red, its roof whole and its surrounding field filled with cows and sheep. I opened my eyes when I realised that I didn't really remember what a cow looked like. Were they the ones with the long mane and tail, or was that the horse? Or maybe I was thinking of a goat? I'd spent all my time researching the dinosaurs and hadn't spent much time on the extinct animals that used to populate the earth.

Just then, a loud chirping squawk emanated from the barn. Todd whirled, drawing his bow in one fluid motion. Shawn and I pulled our own bowstrings back, much less gracefully. I noticed with a twinge of smugness that I'd been a hair faster than Shawn on the draw. The squawk came again as a herd of armoured dinosaurs came snuffling out of the crumbling remains. Their black eyes roved over the clearing and over us; their blue-green scales winked and glimmered in the fading light.

"Don't shoot," Todd breathed. "No sudden movements."

"Why?" I asked, my arm quivering with the strain of the drawn bow.

"See those armoured plates covering every square inch of them? Our arrows don't have a prayer of penetrating them," Todd growled through gritted teeth. He lowered his bow, and I did the same. Shawn still had his drawn. "You'll just tick them off, and they'll trample us," Todd explained.

"What if they attack?" Shawn whispered.

Todd glanced at Shawn's tense form and cocked an amused eyebrow. "Run."

Shawn scowled.

Todd rolled his eyes. "They're plant eaters, not meat eaters. They won't mess with us if we don't mess with them. Just don't spook them." Shawn finally lowered his bow.

A few were babies, small by dinosaur standards, just a little shorter than me, as they trotted along in a tight bundle behind their mother. She was more concerned about us than the rest of the herd, and she raised her head, sniffing the air. I wondered if she could smell our fear; after all that hiking, I knew we certainly smelled bad. She hesitated as the rest of the herd ambled off into the trees, watching us with her intelligent eyes. Like the rest of the pack, she had a large armoured ball on the end of her tail, and every inch of her was covered in sharp edges and angles. After a few tense moments, she seemed satisfied that we weren't a threat and gave a derisive snort.

I watched her walk away towards the rapidly setting sun. Would I always be enamoured with the outside world? Or would my wide-eyed wonder eventually wear off? The mama dinosaur looked so at home here as the pinks and oranges glinted off the armoured plates running down her back. She belonged here – maybe as much, if not more, than we did. Nature had erased the world that humans had built, and this was her world now. I wondered if that thought made me a traitor to the human race. I hoped not.

"Sky?" Todd said, and I realised that he'd been talking to me for a while. I shook my head to clear it.

"Sorry, what?"

"I asked if you wanted me to get dinner, or if you were going to shoot it yourself?"

"Dinner?" I asked stupidly. "I thought we couldn't shoot those things?" He sighed in exasperation and pointed up at a tree branch thirty feet above our heads. I looked up and spotted what I originally thought was a bird, glaring down at us. But as I peered up at it, I realised that it was no bird.

"What is it?" I asked Todd.

"A Four-Wing Glider," Todd said. "They hunt at night by gliding down and grabbing lizards and other small dinosaurs."

"Four wings?" Shawn asked.

"And four massive claws," Todd said. "They can't actually fly. They use those claws to climb up the trees and then glide down on to prey."

I studied the strange creature. "It must be a microraptor."

"Oh good, a flying lizard," Shawn said drily, "just what I was hoping to have for dinner."

"Whatever," Todd said. "They taste really good. So will one of you shoot it?"

I carefully raised my bow, took aim and froze. The microraptor cocked its head at us and ruffled its green-and-black feathers. I dropped my bow.

"I can't do it," I said quietly. "I don't want to kill it."

"Lucky for us, I don't have that problem," Shawn said, and he raised his bow, took aim and missed by about two feet. The raptor raised its four massive wings, but before it could escape, Todd had whipped his bow up and shot. His arrow buried itself with a *thunk* in its feathered side.

The birdlike reptile squawked and pinwheeled down to the ground, where it flapped awkwardly until Todd wrung its neck in one deft movement. The sight of the limp body made me feel nauseous.

"We'll set up camp here," Todd said, dropping his pack next to the base of a gigantic tree at the edge of the clearing.

"Aren't we a bit exposed?" I asked, glancing around at the shadowed forest nervously.

"We are," Todd admitted. "But the closer we get to the lake, the more exposed we are going to be. We should be fine if we get up a tree before full dark hits." He glanced over at Shawn. "Do you want to start the fire or dress the glider?"

"Dress the glider?" Shawn asked, looking uncomfortable. "Like in clothes?"

Todd gave him an odd look, and then sighed. "Let me guess. You have no clue how to do either of those things?" Shawn looked like he was debating hitting Todd, so I quickly stepped between the two.

"No, he doesn't," I said. "Neither of us knows how. But I bet you have no idea how to fix a grow light or make a flashlight completely from scraps."

Todd rolled his eyes again and flapped an impatient hand at Shawn. "Just get some dry sticks, and I'll show you how to start a fire. I'm too hungry to let you screw up dinner."

"Fine," Shawn said grudgingly. Soon we had a roaring fire, and I sat beside it and updated my journal while Todd prepped the raptor for roasting. It turned out that that was what he had meant by dressing it. His practised fingers ripped handfuls of feathers out, revealing the pimply pink skin underneath. I went to run my hand through my hair, but my fingers got stuck in the tangled, sweaty mass. The smell of dirt and sweat wafting off my clothing hit me, and I cringed. I was disgusting.

"I'm going to walk down the creek a little way," I said, jumping to my feet and brushing at the smudges of dirt that stained my pants and tunic. "I want to clean up a bit."

"Take your bow," Todd cautioned without looking up. Shawn stopped collecting firewood to give me a questioning look. "We don't want a repeat of the last time you wandered off on your own."

"Be nice to Todd," I mouthed at Shawn. He stuck his tongue out at me and went to gather more sticks for the fire. I wasn't going far. I'd learned my lesson earlier and had no desire to repeat the near-death experience. Grabbing my bow, quiver of arrows and the rough brown soap I'd got from Adler's, I turned and followed the stream into the woods. A few yards in, I pulled off my boots and set them down beside a tree before I stepped into the water. It felt amazing on my raw and blistered feet. I walked down the shallow creek bed, relishing the cool stones beneath my toes.

Coming around a corner of the stream, I found a small pond, its surface so smooth that the sunset reflected perfectly off it. Glancing back, I could just make out Todd and Shawn through the trees. Reassured, I rolled up my sleeves and splashed some of the water over my arms and face. It ran down my palms in dirty rivulets, and suddenly, it wasn't enough. I was filthy, the sweat and dirt a second scaly skin that I wanted to rip off.

Not giving myself the opportunity to change my mind, I set my bow on the bank of the stream and lowered myself down into the pond's cool depths. The water came up only to my chest and, fully clothed, I submerged myself, scrubbing at my arms and face with the gritty soap. It felt wonderful.

A far-off rumble startled me, and I yelped, yanking my knife out of its sheath. I cursed the stupidity of leaving my bow onshore. Over the tops of the trees, I could see three large heads on top of thickly muscled necks making their leisurely way towards me. My insides relaxed fractionally: they weren't carnivores. Deciding not to risk the run to shore, I sank down into the water, hoping that it would hide me. The dinosaurs emerged moments later, their enormous shoulders turning the branches and foliage into green confetti. I slid backwards in the water as they lowered their massive heads to the pond's surface and drank. Their eyes were a soft brown, and they blinked at me, probably wondering what kind of strange fish I might be.

They were beautiful. These were probably brachiosaur, based on the long curved neck, but my research hadn't done them justice. Their skin was slick and had an iridescent quality that flickered and changed as they moved, making them blend with the shadows of the forest. The largest one blew out hard through its nose, sending water showering down around my head. They made low guttural sounds that echoed across the water, and I realised they were talking to one another.

A tree branch snapped behind me, and I turned to see Shawn and Todd standing on the shore behind me, their bows in hand. I shot them a look that I hoped said, *don't move, stupid.* We sat like that, frozen, as the gentle giants continued to drink. I realised for the first time just how cold the water actually was and started to shiver. When they finally raised their giant heads and moved off in the direction they'd come from, I exhaled in relief.

"You just gave me a heart attack! Are you nuts?" Shawn hissed.

"No," I snapped back. "I was filthy."

"Heart attack," Todd said. "That's the second time you two have said that. Is that really a thing? What exactly is attacking your heart?"

"I'll explain in a second," I said through chattering teeth. "I want to get out of here first."

"You're going to get sick," Todd said. "There's a reason why people don't bathe in ponds in September."

The sky was getting dark, and my bright idea to take a bath now seemed incredibly stupid. I sloshed up out of the water and stood in front of the boys, shivering.

"Wait here," Todd said, sounding irritated, and he crashed back through the trees. He returned a moment later with a blanket and thrust it at me. "Go behind those trees and get out of those. We can dry them on the fire."

Doing as I was told, I wrapped the huge blanket around myself before following the boys back to our camp. I sank down, letting the warmth of the crackling campfire work its way into my bones. Todd turned the spit that was roasting the raptor, and I felt a pang of guilt that it had had to die. Like the brachiosaur, it had been beautiful in its own way. Shawn was still scowling at me. Finally, I gave up pretending I didn't notice and turned to face him.

"Don't give me that look, Shawn Reilly. I haven't felt clean since I left the compound."

"You'll be nice and clean when you catch pneumonia," Shawn griped. "If you die from this stupid stunt, I'm going to be furious."

I grinned. "Thanks for caring." Shawn pulled a face at me and bit off a piece of the raptor leg Todd offered him.

"Your clothes should by dry soon," Todd said.

"You'll want them for climbing."

"Climbing?"

"Tree pods?" Todd prompted impatiently. "The only way to sleep out here without getting eaten. Remember?"

"How soon do we need to get into them?" I asked. As if on cue, the scream of an animal came from the woods to our left. I stiffened, but the cry was miles away.

"Soon," Todd answered, ripping into his second piece of meat, the grease running down his chin. I had just enough time to sketch a picture of the brachiosaur from the pond before we were kicking dirt over our fire. I hurried behind some bushes and scrambled back into my fire-warmed clothes. They were still stained, but they smelled like the campfire instead of sweat, which was a definite improvement.

Todd showed us how to unroll the dark brown canvases we'd been carrying. The edges were threaded with a sturdy rope. We were to tie the rope to tree branches once we were high enough, and somehow sleep in the contraptions. I welcomed the distraction of untangling knots and coils of rope. My nerves were on edge as the darkness of the forest pressed in around us, and the growls and snarls from the woods grew more frequent.

Finally satisfied that we were ready, Todd began expertly climbing up the gigantic maple tree we'd had our campfire under, the remains of the raptor safely tucked away in his pack. I followed, carefully placing my hands and feet exactly where Todd placed his. Soon we were fifty feet up. Todd motioned for us to keep quiet and silently demonstrated how the loops and hooks of the tree pod worked to attach it to the tree.

Soon he had a sort of closed hammock. He expertly wriggled into his, sending the pod swaying gently back and forth, suspended above nothingness. He did not re-emerge. Clearly this was our cue to hang our own. I cautiously crept to the opposite side of the tree and began to clumsily hang my own pod. Each branch I tied it to got a thorough yank to make sure it would hold my weight. The thought of falling fifty feet in my sleep was not an appealing one. When I was finished, I squirmed ungracefully into my pod. The fabric closed tight above my head as my weight pulled its edges together. I squeezed my eyes shut as it swayed back and forth over empty air. The space was close and the musty smell of old fabric was overwhelming. But as my breathing relaxed, I realised that the pod was warming up, my breath creating a pocket of heat. Using my pack as a pillow, I rolled on to my side, sending the whole pod swinging again. This would take some getting used to.

I listened to Shawn hanging his pod somewhere to my left and slightly below my own. I had to smile as he muttered and fussed at the stubborn fabric. Taking pity on him, I climbed out and crept through the dark tree to help.

"I don't need help," he said as I took a stubborn knot of canvas out of his hands. "I can figure it out."

I pulled gently at the snarl. "I know you could."

Shawn frowned, and I could tell by his posture that he was upset, even though he was nothing more than a dark outline now against the ever-darkening sky.

"What is it?" I asked.

"Nothing."

"Shawn, spill it."

He didn't say anything for a minute, and I didn't pressure him. We were almost done hanging his tree pod when he broke the silence, his voice barely audible above the night noises of the forest. "I just hate it up here."

"In the tree?"

"No, topside," Shawn said. "I feel useless. Everything I thought I knew is turned all upside down and inside out. I had this grand idea that I would come along on your big dumb adventure to keep you safe and to talk some sense into you. But so far all I've witnessed is you almost getting eaten by multiple dinosaurs while I bumble around like an idiot. I hate it. I'm starting to wonder if you were right, if it would have been better for me to just stay underground."

I took his chin in my hand, forcing him to look up. "You aren't useless," I said. "At least no more useless than I've been. And I was wrong before."

"Sky Mundy wrong? Never." He smirked, and I smiled back, relieved. I wasn't sure how to handle a serious Shawn.

"You might want to document this, because it's never going to happen again. But I *was* wrong. I'm glad you came with me. I couldn't have made it this far without you."

"Could too," he grumbled. "But I appreciate you lying to make me feel better. I just wish… I don't know. I wish I knew what Todd knew."

"You know what Shawn knows," I said. "And we

can learn what Todd knows."

"If you say so."

"I do. I also say we need to go to bed. All that fault admitting has worn me out."

"Really? I would have thought it was all that horrible hiking we did today, or the near-death experiences, or the humidity, or…"

I laughed and held up a hand to cut him off. "I get it. Topside is a bit more than we bargained for. We'll get used to it, though. I promise." He still looked unconvinced, and I had a feeling there was something else bothering him. I didn't push him, though. I knew my best friend well enough to know that he would tell me when he was ready. Shawn crawled into his newly hung pod, and I heard him mutter something incoherent as it swung through the air. I smiled.

"Good night, Shawn."

"Night," came the muffled reply.

I crept back into my own pod and pulled off my boots. If it hadn't been for Shawn selling his mum's music box, I might still be walking around in those useless compound slippers. I made a mental note to point that out to him in the morning. I'd never properly thanked him for sacrificing it. If the situation was reversed, would I have been able to hand over my dad's compass for a pair of boots? Shawn Reilly might be a better person than me, I decided. Not that I'd ever tell him that. I'd never hear the end of it. Smiling, I settled down in my pod again, letting the sounds of the night swirl around me as I fell asleep.

CHAPTER 20

I awoke to a shaking world as my pod swung back and forth alarmingly. I shrieked as I tumbled inside it, my bow, pack and boots clattering around me. It took a while, but I finally managed to crawl to the end of the pod and hurl myself out and on to the shaking branch. The tree that had felt solid enough last night was trembling so hard my teeth clanged together. To my left, Todd was emerging from his own pod.

He blinked at me uncomprehendingly before glancing down. A look of pure terror crossed his face, and he dived headlong back into his pod. I followed his gaze and froze. Stomping around underneath the tree, its three-foot-long crocodile-like snout raised to sniff the air, was the scariest dinosaur I'd ever seen. Bigger even than the T. rex that Shawn and I had encountered on our first day out of the compound. The dinosaur turned its massive head to snuffle and snort at the remains of our campfire before rearing back, revealing two powerful hind legs and small front legs, each with long hooked claws.

"What is that thing?" Shawn asked, climbing up to stand beside me.

"It's a Croc Killer," Todd said, emerging from his pod with his bow across his back. "I thought they only hunted in water."

"A Croc Killer?" I repeated, confused. I stared back down at the dinosaur as it fanned out a massive fin that spanned the length of its back. Now that Todd had mentioned it, I did remember learning about a dinosaur that swam in the rivers. I couldn't remember its name. Todd's name for it was fitting, as it did resemble pictures I'd seen of crocodiles, except it was standing on two legs and its head alone was the length of a crocodile.

The Croc Killer propped its two front claws on the tree and turned its yellow eyes on us. It let out a screeching roar that had red-hot fear racing down my spine. A gush of hot, rancid air blew my hair back and I gagged. The creature's head was only about five feet below where Shawn's pod was hanging. A few more feet and it could have plucked him out of the tree and swallowed him in his sleep.

"We have to get higher!" Shawn yelled.

"Ya think?" Todd shouted back sarcastically. He rolled his eyes in exasperation as he reached for the branch above his head and pulled himself up. I was about to follow him when I realised that my journal was still in my pod, which was swinging alarmingly through the air, my backpack and bow rattling around inside. I hurtled myself back down the branch and dived into the pod when it swung my way. Everything in my backpack had fallen out, and I stuffed handfuls of clothing, food and my journal back inside. Shawn shouted at me, but I ignored him. There was no way I was losing my journal.

With my bow and pack over my shoulder, I crawled back down the trembling branch and followed Shawn and Todd higher. My feet fought to gain purchase as the Croc Killer switched from using its talons to rip chunks out of the base of our tree to banging on it, causing it to rock violently. *Don't fall, don't fall, don't fall*, I prayed silently, wishing we had picked a bigger tree. When Todd finally stopped on the last solid-looking branch, I knew we were in trouble. The tree was leaning way too far to the left. The dinosaur let out its screeching roar again and I cringed.

"It's almost like it knows!" Shawn called, his voice practically drowned out by the enraged growling below us.

"Knows what?" I asked.

"How to bring the tree down," he yelled back, directly into my ear. We held on to our branch a bit tighter as the dinosaur rammed the tree, causing it to shift a few more feet to the left.

"It does," Todd said grimly. "They're smart. Too smart."

"It's a spinosaurus!" I said triumphantly, having just remembered the name.

"Great," Shawn said. "Know how to kill it?"

"No." I frowned. "There wasn't a lot of research on them. Some of the only fossils were lost in World War One. To be honest, I didn't think anyone had succeeded in bringing one back."

"Somebody managed it," Shawn said through gritted teeth as he gripped the branch above him with white-knuckled hands.

"We have to shoot the exact centre of its eyes. Everywhere else is impenetrable," Todd said, handing his pack to Shawn, who slung it over his own shoulder.

Todd strung his bow and took aim at the bellowing spinosaurus. Reflexively, I shot a hand out to clutch the back of his trousers, terrified that one hard hit would send him careening to his death. Something looped around my middle, and I looked down to see Shawn expertly knotting a rope. He let out a few feet and tied it around Todd's waist, and then his own, before securing it to the tree. Todd waited until the spinosaurus looked back up at us to release his arrow. It was a close-range shot, but the creature's narrow eyes were set far back under its ridged brow bone. Todd's arrow hit right below its right eye and ricocheted off with a depressing ping.

Todd pulled out more arrows, but his next few shots clanged off the spinosaurus's scaly skin as ineffectively as the first. "A little help here!" Todd shouted as our tree lurched again.

With trembling hands, I reached back and clumsily untangled my own bow from the straps of my backpack. Shawn's rope tightened around my waist as I aimed my first shot. It went wide, not even hitting the spinosaurus. I grabbed my next arrow and tried to steady myself, but my second shot went even wider than the first. It was hopeless. The monster was moving and thrashing constantly, the tree was trembling and swaying, and I'd only ever hit a non-moving target.

Suddenly, we tilted hard to the left, and a sickening crack ripped through the air. The branch dropped out from under us, and we fell. Branches whipped by me and I screamed, snatching at them blindly. A second later, our tree's downward progress was brought to a crunching halt when it collided with something. I tumbled down a few more feet before Shawn's rope caught me around the middle, stopping my fall. I flailed in the air a moment before catching hold of a branch. Todd and Shawn perched above me, clinging desperately to their own branches.

Our tree had cracked off at the base, and the only thing that prevented it from crashing straight to the forest floor was the tree to our left that had mercifully caught ours between two large branches. My relief was short-lived when I saw Todd's shattered bow at the feet of the spinosaurus, which was now only three feet below me. Its hot breath tugged at my clothes as it snorted. The tree gave a sickening crunch and shifted another foot towards the ground.

"Sky, shoot!" Todd yelled. As though I were moving through water and not air, I pulled my bow into position. My fingers touched the arrows, but I couldn't seem to get them to work well enough to grab one. The tree cracked beneath me and dropped another foot. At this close a range, the creature's eyes were the size of setting suns as they stared up at me. A thin, translucent lid slid over the top of them, and the dinosaur's skin shimmered wetly in the dawn light.

"Shoot! Shoot now!" Todd bellowed. Someone's pack flew down to smack harmlessly against the creature's long, sharp snout. It let out a grinding growl and looked past me at Todd and Shawn. I had a full view of its left eye, and my fingers finally closed over an arrow. My arm drew the bow and released as if on its own, and I watched in stunned amazement as the arrow sank into the soft, unprotected centre of the spinosaurus's eye. It jerked and let out a high-pitched keening cry. Its body twitched. And then its breath whooshed past me as it collapsed.

"You did it!" Shawn was suddenly shaking me. "That was incredible!"

"No time for celebrating," Todd shouted as the tree groaned and shifted another few inches. "This thing isn't going to hold much longer." I shook myself, blinking at Shawn and Todd stupidly.

"I killed it?" I looked to Todd for verification. "You're sure?"

"It's not a possum," Todd called, already starting to climb down the tilted tree trunk, "they don't play dead. Now move it!" Shawn helped me untie the rope around my waist, and we hurried to follow. Todd dropped from the lowest limb on to the prone figure of the spinosaurus. He motioned impatiently at Shawn and me, and not really believing this was happening I dropped the last few feet on to the dinosaur's massive side. It barely gave as I landed, feeling more like rock than animal.

Todd made his way down the sloping side towards its tail, and Shawn and I were close behind. The creature had a pungent smell that reminded me of stale water or mould, and my eyes watered and stung. Its skin was damp, as though it had just come from the water, and I had to fight not to lose my balance on its slick scales. Before I realised what was happening, we were on the ground and running away at a dead sprint.

Moments later, all sound was drowned out by our tree falling on to the dead dinosaur with a sickening crunch. I whirled round to see it lying at a forty-degree angle, the spinosaurus's body crushed beneath its thick trunk.

"Well, it's definitely dead now," Todd huffed, quirking an eyebrow at me. Suddenly my knees went weak, and I sat down hard, unable to take my eyes off the dead dinosaur.

"You weren't sure before?" I asked, my voice sounding as shaky as I felt.

"Not one hundred per cent." Todd shrugged. "We didn't have a choice, though; it was get down or get dead."

"Well said," Shawn groaned.

"That was a nice shot, by the way." Todd grinned. "You must have hit brain for it to drop like that, and that's a pretty impressive feat considering how small those things' brains are."

"I thought you said it was smart enough to know how to knock down that tree," Shawn accused.

"Oh, it is," Todd said grimly. "It's my fault. I never even thought about a Croc Killer. They usually only hunt in the water. They're too slow to catch much on land. It must have tracked our scent from the pond."

Shawn's face went white. "The pond Sky went swimming in yesterday?"

I stared at him in horror. I'd gone for a swim in that thing's backyard? I squeezed my eyes shut as I saw my rash dip in the pond in a whole new light. My hand trembled as it went to the compass around my neck and I held it against my hammering heart. *Stupid mistake*, I thought angrily. Another one to add to the long list I'd accumulated since leaving the compound.

"I told you taking a bath was stupid," Shawn said. My eyes flashed open, and I glared at him.

"Don't you think I know that?" I snapped, and then immediately felt guilty for it. It wasn't Shawn's fault that I'd almost got us all killed. Again. He just shrugged and offered me his hand. I took it and stood up on shaky legs.

"Sorry," I muttered.

"Forgiven," he said simply. We'd been friends long enough that he knew exactly what I was apologising for.

"Nice work with that rope," Todd said to Shawn. "That was pretty slick. If you hadn't got it tied and untied so quickly, we'd all be dead right now."

"It was no big deal, just a simple timber hitch knot."

"If you say so," Todd said.

"Not so useless after all, are you?" I said quietly, so

only Shawn could hear. He didn't say anything, but I could tell he was trying not to smile.

"No time to chat," Todd said. "We need to get our gear." He headed back towards the fallen dinosaur at a run. Shawn and I followed.

"I can't believe I killed it," I said as we approached the dead animal, its size even more impressive from ground level.

"I know." Shawn shook his head. "You wouldn't even shoot at that raptor earlier."

"I must be a better teacher than I thought," Todd mused as he trotted briskly around to the creature's head. The spinosaurus's jaw hung open, revealing long, needle-like teeth the size of my forearm, and I held my breath as I followed Todd over the broken branches.

"Shouldn't we get out of here?" Shawn asked as he ducked underneath a low-hanging branch. "That wasn't exactly a quiet encounter. What if this guy had a wife or buddies close by that come looking for him?"

"This isn't compound life. We can't just order a new tree pod if we decide to leave ours behind. If we had been sleeping around that campfire instead of above it, we'd all be dead right now. So I think I'll get my pod back if it's all the same to you."

"Good point," Shawn agreed grudgingly. I looked at him in surprise. If Todd had talked like that to him at the beginning of the trip, he would have got angry. Maybe his trick with the rope had made him less self-conscious.

"Hurry it up," Todd said, looking nervous. "I'm less worried about this big guy's wife and more worried about scavengers." I began working at the knots in my tree pod.

"I can't believe I made such a rookie mistake." Todd frowned. "Now my bow's busted."

"I'm sorry, Todd," I said, remembering that it was his dad's bow. "I know how much it meant to you." He just nodded as he picked up the broken pieces, examining each of them before snorting in disgust and dropping them.

"Yeah, well," he said, "my mum means more. If we can find her, then this will all be worth it. You two had better hold up your end of the bargain."

"We will," I promised.

"How long do you think we have before scavengers show up?" Shawn asked, eyeing the carcass nervously as he rolled up my tree pod and handed it to me. No sooner had the words left his lips than an ear-splitting screech came from our left. It was our answer.

"Run!" Todd bellowed as the trees began to tremble with the sound of approaching feet. I threw my pack over my shoulder and ran after Todd. Another shriek, followed by growling and ripping sounds, came from behind us. The scavengers had found the spinosaurus and were making short work of him. They sounded big. Bile rose in my throat, but I forced it down, commanding my feet to fly as we zigzagged through rapidly thinning trees. I couldn't hear anything chasing us, but Todd didn't lessen his pace. When he finally slowed to a stop a few minutes later, I sank to my knees, my legs no longer functioning now that I was apparently not in any danger of being eaten.

"Scavengers," Todd panted, wiping the sweat from his forehead. "They will follow us as soon as they finish the Croc Killer."

"That will take hours!" Shawn gasped as he dug his canteen from his pack and handed it to me.

"Not hours, minutes," Todd corrected. "Scavengers can smell the blood for miles."

"Are they like sharks or piranhas?" I asked.

Todd brushed off my question. "Sure. Whatever. But the thing with scavengers is if there's one, there's twenty, fighting over that thing's bones as we speak."

"How did they get there so fast?" I asked as I pushed sweaty curls out of my eyes. "You shot that raptor yesterday and nothing showed up."

"It was a quiet kill yesterday," Todd explained. "Not a lot of noise, not a lot of blood. That Croc Killer made a racket loud enough to bring dinosaurs for miles."

"And when they finish with the spinosaurus, they'll follow?"

"If they can find our trail, they'll follow. I haven't spotted any streams to confuse our scent like we did yesterday after that allosaurus almost got you. How much further can you two run?"

"As far as we need to," I said as I shoved my canteen back in my pack. "But where are we running?"

"We need to find water. That will help us lose them. I don't know about you, but I don't want to get stuck up a tree again."

"Nuff said," Shawn grunted, and we were off and running. The pace was just as brisk as before, and it was a struggle to keep up. Todd was whipping his head back and forth in an attempt to see any would-be attackers, or maybe he was looking for a stream. I was too busy trying to suck air into my greedy lungs to tell which. The minutes dragged on, and the exhaustion of the previous day's hike and tumble with the allosaurus slowed me down. I gritted my teeth. I would keep up. Endangering my friends was not an option. A screech came from behind us, and I looked back.

A motley pack of dinosaurs in all shapes, sizes and colours were zigzagging through the trees, but they all had one thing in common: blood. Even from that distance, I could see the blood of the spinosaurus dripping off their pointed jaws and crusted on their talons. My heart lodged in my throat as the ground beneath my feet began to shake. We couldn't outrun them, and they were too close to risk climbing a tree. We were as good as dead. I hoped that it would be quick.

CHAPTER 21

"Shawn," Todd yelled over the deafening sound of pounding feet and screeching animals from behind us, "your bow."

"You want me to shoot them?" Shawn gasped, his face bright red as he fought to keep up with Todd's long strides.

"Hand me your bow!" Todd yelled again, and this time Shawn understood. He quickly unhooked it from its place on his back and handed it to Todd. Todd stopped running and spun around, his hand already drawing the bowstring back. He released it with a sharp twang and I heard a scream as one of the animals went down. I skidded to a stop and reached back for my own arrow, but in my exhaustion and panic, I dropped it. Todd released two more in rapid fire before I finally managed to get one to the string and released. It flew harmlessly into the trees, missing my target by a good five feet.

I grabbed for another, but before my fingers could close over it, there was a sharp twang from behind me and one of the dinosaurs dropped. Seconds later another fell, and then another. A few of the smaller ones stopped pursuing us altogether, choosing to rip into their fallen comrades instead. I didn't have time to turn around to see who our saviour was. I aimed and released and saw one of the medium-sized dinosaurs stagger, the shaft buried deep in its shoulder before another through the eye dropped it. A minute later it was over. I stood in shock between Todd and Shawn, my chest heaving as we took in the forest floor, littered with the bodies of dead and dying dinosaurs.

"Ivan?" Todd called, turning to scan the woods behind us. "Is that you?"

"Ivan?" I repeated, confused. "How do you know it's Ivan?"

Todd waved at me to be quiet, turning to squint into the surrounding trees. "It's Todd Birch," he called out. "The son of Jacob Birch of the Oaks? We met a few times when I was a kid."

"The Birch brat," came a voice from behind us. "Yes, I remember. And you're still a kid, although quite a bit taller than the last time I saw you. Never grew into that nose, though. Unfortunate." I whirled round and found myself face-to-face with a wiry old man. He peered up at us with cornflower-blue eyes set deep in a forest of wrinkles. His white hair was cropped close to his head, while his beard seemed to have a mind of its own and reached almost to his belly. Two massive bows were strapped across his back with thick leather belts. But the most striking thing about him was that he was missing part of his right arm. It ended only an inch or two after his elbow joint. Attached to the stump was a complicated knot of leather cording that held what looked like a bizarre metal fork on its end.

"Ivan!" Todd grinned as he thrust out his hand to shake the old man's. "It's been a long time. You just saved our lives!"

The old man shook Todd's hand as he inspected him before glancing over Todd's shoulder at us. His eyes met mine and an odd expression crossed his face. I looked behind myself, certain there must be a three-headed dinosaur or something equally strange creeping up on me to get that kind of look. But there was nothing there, and when I looked back, Ivan was still staring at me, his mouth open slightly in surprise. Not sure how exactly to handle this, I squirmed and looked down. He finally blinked and turned his attention back to Todd. I ran a hand self-consciously through the curls that had sprung loose from their ponytail to hang in a clumpy tangle around my shoulders. I'd known I was a mess, but I hadn't thought I was that bad.

Ivan frowned at Todd as he released his hand. "I am assuming that your father's absence means he's dead?" The bluntness of his question shocked me. I must have visibly winced, because Ivan's eyes flicked to me again, searching, before turning back to Todd.

Todd nodded. "Two years now. Died on a trading mission."

"Bloody shame. He was a good man."

"Thank you, sir," Todd said with a sad smile.

"I also assumed he'd trained you better. How did you end up with this nasty crew on your tail?" he asked. He strode over to inspect the closest fallen dinosaur. It was one of the smaller ones, roughly fifteen feet in length, with feathered, flightless wings that now stuck out at odd angles. Ivan walked right up to the creature and used his boot to untangle one of its legs. He pulled a knife out of a sheath on his arm and began sawing away at one of the thick curved claws on the creature's back foot. Faster than I would have thought possible, he'd cut all of the claws off, putting them into a leather pouch slung across his chest. He moved from dinosaur to dinosaur, sawing off a claw here or using massive pliers to pry out a tooth there. Twice he pulled out an arrow and shot straight into the eye or chest of one of the dinosaurs before approaching it. I realised that the metal fork attached to his bad arm was used to brace the bow so he could draw and fire the arrow with his good hand. It was ingenious, and obviously ridiculously effective. I watched in slack-jawed amazement until Todd elbowed me in the ribs, and I followed him to collect some of the usable arrows that lay scattered on the ground. Shawn came to, but he was too busy gaping at Ivan to pick anything up.

"What's he doing?" Shawn whispered as I pulled one of my arrows out of a nearby tree.

"His job," Todd said.

I looked over at Shawn and saw that he was a little green. I didn't blame him; Ivan was ruthless. Five minutes later, he rejoined us, his only remaining hand liberally coated in blood.

Before I could open my mouth to introduce myself and ask Ivan about my dad, we heard a long, whistling roar come from the forest behind us. Shawn jumped, but

Ivan simply glanced back at the trees before turning to us. He pulled a small bottle out of his bag and yanked the cork out with his mouth before pouring it over the blood on his hand. A sharp alcohol smell met my nose.

"I presume you are expecting hospitality and lodging for the night," he said grouchily as he recorked the bottle and put it back in his bag. The missing hand didn't seem to slow him down in the slightest. When we nodded, he huffed into his beard and, without another word, turned around and shuffled silently into the woods. I looked at Todd, but he just shrugged.

"Don't stand there like a bunch of slack-jawed idiots," Ivan called from the gloom of the trees. "Get the lead out. I don't feel like being eaten today."

"Why can he make jokes about being eaten?" Shawn whispered in my ear.

I shot him a look. "I don't think he's joking."

"No talking until we get out of this section of the woods," Ivan said sharply. "My house is a day's hike from here and this area is swarming with lizard beasties."

"Lizard beasties?" Shawn whispered sceptically as Ivan turned around and started walking. Todd just shook his head in warning and we dutifully jogged after Ivan's retreating figure. Ivan led us quickly through the trees to a small stream. Without ceremony, he stomped into the middle of it, and we followed, splashing up it for the next twenty minutes. My feet went numb in the icy water, and I couldn't decide if it was an improvement on the aching pain of blisters.

Hiking in silence was one of the hardest things I'd ever done. I had so many questions swarming around in my head, and the one-armed figure hurrying ahead of me might have the answers. But every time I opened my mouth to speak, Todd gave me a look that made it clear that would be a mistake. Ivan's walking pace was only slightly slower than Todd's brisk jog, and soon I found myself breathing too hard to talk, let alone start the conversation about my dad. Every now and then Ivan would look back at us. He seemed to be sizing me up, and it made me nervous. But then again, he might just be wondering why Shawn and I were huffing and puffing so loudly. I bit my lip and told myself to be patient. I contented myself with trying to figure out how in the world my dad would have met someone like Ivan. And then I had a thought that made my heart squeeze painfully. What if this wasn't the right Ivan? The more I thought about it, the more unlikely it seemed that my dad would have ever met the no-nonsense dinosaur hunter who killed with such deadly precision. If he *was* the wrong Ivan, than I'd wasted valuable time travelling to find him.

After endless hours of silent hiking, Todd broke the silence. "We appreciate you letting us stay with you tonight," he said conversationally. "This is Sky and Shawn, by the way."

"Sky," Ivan scoffed. "An idiotic compound name. They were always naming their children things like Grass or Seaweed or Daisy or some such nonsense. Like naming their children after the outside world would make up for the fact that they'd never see it." I'd never really thought about my name, but now that I did, his theory made sense. I'd had a boy named Leaf in my class and two girls named after flowers.

I was so preoccupied with my thoughts that I didn't notice the enormous concrete structure until we were almost inside it. I stopped to gape up at this giant relic of what used to be. It stood over ten storeys tall, with broken-out windows. Moss and vines covered almost every surface of the concrete-and-iron structure. It was called a skyscraper. Or was it? How tall did a building have to be to be considered a skyscraper? Either way, it was the biggest building I'd ever seen. There were pictures of whole skylines full of buildings like this in my history books. This one, however, sat alone.

Ivan stopped at the door and motioned at us impatiently to follow him into the crumbling wreck. I looked at it dubiously. It didn't seem exceptionally stable. Metal skeleton showed through where the brick and mortar had long ago crumbled away, and it was leaning to the left. The boys dutifully filed inside, but I hesitated. Moments later a roar and an animal scream came from the darkness behind me, and I scurried inside the musty-smelling building.

"Took you long enough," Ivan grumbled as he shut the door and slid a large board across to secure it.

"You think that will keep out a hungry dinosaur?" Shawn asked sceptically. I wanted to smack him for being rude, but truthfully I was thinking the same thing.

"No," Ivan said. "But it keeps the raccoons out. I hate those furry little buggers. Got to replace the blasted thing every other week because some oversized lizard decides he wants to come a-visiting."

"Well, that's just great," Shawn mumbled darkly as Ivan led us across the deserted first floor of the building to a large metal staircase in the middle of the room. I looked around with interest, taking in the tree roots that had worked their way up through the tile floor, and the mounds of dirt and debris piled haphazardly. A hundred and fifty years of nature being left to its own devices had practically erased all traces of the occupants that had once lived or worked here. I was snapped from my musings by the staircase Ivan was climbing. It seemed to disappear into the floor, and I stared at it in confusion.

"Escalator," he called from above us. "An old-fashioned transportation device to bring people from one floor to the next. Our ancestors were lazy. And probably fat." The staircase had a thick layer of dirt and debris everywhere except in the middle, where it was obvious that Ivan travelled frequently. I bent down to feel one of the treads and my fingers met ribbed metal. *Strange*, I thought, thinking of all the ways the compound could use metal like this. Shawn was obviously having the same thought, because I saw him stop at the second floor, where a large metal panel had fallen off the side of the staircase to reveal wires and gears.

Before I could stop him, he'd yanked two rusty

circles of metal out and thrust them in his bag.

"What are you doing?" I said, glancing nervously up to where Ivan climbed ahead of us.

"This is the kind of pulley Todd needs back at the tree house," Shawn said excitedly.

"This is Ivan's house," I pointed out. "Will you stop pulling it apart?"

"Right. Sorry," Shawn said as we hurried to catch up with Todd and Ivan, who were now an entire staircase ahead of us. I didn't have long to look at each of the floors as we passed, but I caught glimpses of rusted shelves and tipped-over metal racks covered in years' worth of dust and dirt. The higher we climbed, the less wrecked the floors were, and I saw Shawn eyeing some of the things we passed with interest. I grabbed his arm to stop him from digging at the different bits of old-world technology we glimpsed half-hidden under collapsed ceiling tiles.

"But that was a laptop," Shawn whined quietly so only I could hear as he gazed longingly back at the floor we'd just left. "Ivan obviously isn't using it."

"You are impossible sometimes," I muttered, not loosening my grip on his arm. I'd lost count of how many floors we'd climbed, and the blisters on my feet were screaming. "What floor do you live on?" I called ahead to Ivan, working hard to keep the whining tone out of my own voice.

"Top," he said. "I'd have to be dumb as a stump to live on the bottom." Breathing hard, the four of us finally scaled the final set of stairs. At the top, I discovered that the last ten steps had been removed. This forced us to pull ourselves on to the top floor of the building using a thick rope similar to the ones Todd had used at the tree house. I watched in amazement as Ivan managed the task with only one arm.

As my head emerged on to the top floor, I blinked in wonder at this strange little man's house. The space was cavernous, spanning the entire length of the building. Unlike the other floors, where inches of dust, broken ceiling panels and remnants of desks and machinery lay in haphazard piles, this floor was swept clean, revealing shiny white tiles. The only light came from the wall closest to me, and I gaped in amazement when I saw that it was made of unbroken glass. I stepped closer to look out over the treetops. We were much higher than we'd been the night before, and the forest seemed to go on and on in every direction.

Metal screeched behind me, and I jumped. Turning,

I saw Ivan, assisted by Todd, drop a thick metal plate down on the hole in the floor. The rope we'd used to climb was coiled neatly at their feet. Ivan walked around to all four corners, sliding metal bolts into place to lock the panel down.

"This," Ivan grunted as he forced the last bolt home, "is what keeps the lizard beasties from making us their dinner."

"Has one ever made it up this high?" Shawn asked.

"They've made it up," Ivan said sourly, waving his missing appendage. I swallowed hard and looked over at Todd. He shrugged and grinned. Finished with the bolts, Ivan hobbled around his home, lighting lanterns. As pools of flickering light flooded the space, it became clear that Ivan did all of his living in one corner, where a small bed, table and stove stood. The rest of the empty space was cast into impenetrable shadows by the fading light from outside. But even though Ivan's house was interesting, my eyes were drawn back to the spectacular view showcased through the floor-to-ceiling window. The sun, fat and red, dipped down and disappeared behind the trees, leaving waves of pink and orange in its wake. I just couldn't get over how beautiful things were up here, especially sunsets. And

I'd missed hundreds upon hundreds of them. I felt like something had been stolen from me. Brushing the thought away, I turned back to the rest of the group. While I'd been staring out of the window, they'd made themselves at home at Ivan's wooden table. I glanced behind me, into the shadowy darkness of the rest of the skyscraper, and shivered. After living in tunnels, all this echoing openness made me nervous.

"You're probably hungry," Ivan grumbled as he set a large pot on his stove and stoked the fire beneath it. Hungry was an understatement. My insides felt hollow and I realised I hadn't eaten since the night before.

"We have provisions," Todd said, and he produced the large hunks of leftover raptor meat and handed them to him. Ivan sniffed it before chopping it into chunks and tossing it into the pot.

"There is something oddly familiar about that guy," Shawn whispered to me. I raised an eyebrow at him.

"Really?" I asked. "I was just thinking that there was no way in the world my dad would ever know a guy like this."

"I'm amazed you haven't been grilling him about your dad," Shawn said. "Are you feeling OK?"

"I will." I frowned. "There just hasn't really been a

chance. And he's a little…" I trailed off as I watched Ivan scowling down at the stew he was stirring.

"Terrifying?" Shawn finished for me.

"I was going to say intimidating." Ivan's eyes flicked to me with that same penetrating look, and I gulped. "But terrifying works."

"So, Ivan, you are obviously still in the dinosaur trade," Todd said. "Why haven't you been by the Oaks in years?"

Ivan looked at Todd. "I'm semi-retired."

"What do you mean by semi-retired?" I asked tentatively as I sat down at the table. My eyes were growing accustomed to the darkness of the room, and I noticed large shadowed shapes against the far walls.

"It means I only trade when it suits me. I don't drag these old bones of mine around the woods any more from village to village. And I no longer have to deal with every idiot who thinks they know how to haggle."

"Oh," I said dumbly, looking to Todd for some guidance on how to communicate with this odd character.

"What have you and your mum been doing to get by without your father?" Ivan asked.

"We manage," Todd said stiffly, then frowned. "Well.

We did until these two came along."

I stared down at the rough wooden surface of Ivan's table and wished I could disappear.

"What do you mean?" Ivan asked sharply.

Todd glanced at me, and I saw that anger still sparkled in his eyes. "I found Sky and Shawn about two minutes before they were about to get eaten. After I saved them, I brought them back to the Oaks. Next thing you know, the Noah's guys showed up and took the entire village away in these big black flying machines called…" He trailed off, looking at Shawn.

"Helicopters," Shawn supplied.

"Right." Todd nodded. "Helicopters."

"We were followed," I jumped in. Todd was making us sound really bad. "I'm not sure how the marines tracked Shawn and me, but they did." When Ivan's head snapped to stare out of his window, as though he were expecting one of the Noah's black helicopters to come bursting through the glass, I quickly added, "We got rid of everything we'd brought from the compound. There is no way we have a tracker on us now." Ivan relaxed, but only a fraction.

"What I really want to know," he said, peering into his simmering pot, "is why the daughter of Jack

Mundy is sitting in my home." I jumped at the sound of my dad's name, my eyes snapping up to meet his twinkling blue ones.

"So you *are* the Ivan my dad mentioned in his note," I breathed, not daring to hope. "How did you know him? Have you seen him? Do you know why he left the compound?"

"What is your father doing sending you topside with nothing but this compound boy and the Birch brat?" Ivan asked as he began ladling food into bowls that he thrust into our hands unceremoniously.

"I prefer Todd, if it's all the same to you," Todd said.

Ivan raised an eyebrow at him.

"But Birch brat has a certain ring to it," Todd said meekly.

"He asked me to do something for him," I said. "Shawn came along to help me, and we met Todd."

"Why didn't he do this *something* he asked you to do himself?" Ivan asked.

"Because he disappeared five years ago," I said, my stomach sinking in disappointment. "So you don't know anything about my dad? He didn't come here?"

"Why would he come here?" Ivan asked.

I felt myself deflate. I'd been so excited about finding

Ivan, so sure he'd have answers.

Ivan sat down at the table across from me and leaned back, tugging at his beard. "Why don't you tell me how you came to be sitting at my kitchen table? Don't leave out any details, even if you think they are insignificant."

I took a deep breath, and nodded. "I was seven the night my dad disappeared," I began, telling him the same story I'd told Jett, Emily and Todd only two nights before. But this time, I didn't conveniently leave out what my compass contained. Ivan listened in stony silence, never taking his eyes off me. Getting looked at like that made me nervous, so I told most of the story staring at the worn table.

"So do you know anything about the note, or the plug, or the map?" I asked, finally looking up.

"No, I don't." Ivan shook his head, making his long beard swish like the hairy pendulum of a clock. "I haven't seen your father in eleven years."

I wrinkled my nose in confusion. Ivan wasn't making any sense. "Then how did you know I was his daughter?"

He looked up at me with level eyes. "Because you're a dead ringer for your mother."

I almost choked. "What?"

"Your mother," Ivan repeated as though I hadn't heard him. "I thought I was seeing a ghost walking through the woods this evening."

"Wait. You knew my mum too?" The hope that had died moments before flared back to life.

"I'd say so," Ivan said, taking a big bite of his stew. "Seeing as she was my daughter."

CHAPTER 22

"**Y**ou're Ivan the dinosaur hunter's granddaughter?" Todd said in awe as he looked at me with newfound respect.

"I am?" I felt stunned and disconnected, as though maybe Ivan was telling this to someone else. This couldn't possibly be real. Could it? My hands shook, sending the stew sloshing over the sides of my bowl. I set it down and pushed it aside.

"You are," Ivan confirmed. "My Clara had the same wild hair and birdlike build. Your eyes are your father's, though." He frowned. "A pity. Your mother's were prettier."

"How in the world," Shawn asked, "would your daughter, Sky's mum, have come to live in a compound?"

"What interest is it to you?" Ivan asked sharply.

"Sky's my friend," Shawn said stiffly. "What concerns her concerns me."

Ivan looked at me. "Do you trust the compound boy?"

"I'd trust Shawn with my life," I said automatically, my brain still trying to process everything.

Ivan harrumphed into his beard, looking unconvinced. "My daughter wanted a more formal education. She was into books, read everything she could get her hands on. When she turned eighteen, I helped her enter the East Compound, posing as a voluntary transfer from the South Compound so she could attend the university."

"But how——" Shawn began, but stopped when Ivan glared at him.

"I have my ways, and they do not concern you," Ivan said. "She was supposed to come back once she'd had her fill of formal schooling. She wanted to teach some of the children in the surrounding tree villages maths and science and that kind of rot." Ivan sniffed and took another bite of stew. "But she didn't come back. She fell in love with that idiot father of yours."

My jaw clenched defensively. "My father was brilliant."

"That's what Clara said. He might have been compound smart, but he had absolutely no common sense when it came to survival. I told your mother that, but she insisted on marrying him anyway. And then she died." He sniffed. "I always thought I'd die first, my line of work and all."

"But why didn't I know about you?" I asked. My dad would have mentioned if I had a grandfather. Wouldn't he? Maybe Ivan was mistaken.

"Because children are no good at keeping secrets from a government with eyes and ears everywhere," Ivan said. "I always assumed your father *would* tell you about me when you were old enough." He scrutinised me a moment, and I squirmed. "You do look like my Clara, though. Although she had the sense not to let her skin fry in the sun. Us redheaded folk must take extra precautions." Ivan's close-cropped hair and beard were white, but on closer inspection, I saw a few stray hairs that had retained their red colour. "Didn't they teach you anything useful in that compound school of yours?" he asked disapprovingly.

I frowned. "Not really."

"It wasn't completely useless," Shawn protested.

"Shawn, it was, and you know it," I snapped. "Stop pretending it wasn't."

"Hmmm," Ivan said. "You have Clara's temper too."

"Sorry," I muttered to Shawn, not feeling very sorry at all. Turning back to Ivan, I thrust my dad's note and map at him. "If you haven't seen my dad in years, why did he ask me to find you?" Ivan picked up the pieces of paper and read them before laying them down on his table. "These were hidden in Jack's compass?" he asked as he pulled another compass out of the front of his shirt.

"You have a direction whatchadinger too?" Todd asked.

"Whatchadinger?" Ivan snorted. "It's called a compass." He shook his head and mumbled something that sounded like "village kids these days" but I couldn't be sure.

"Can I see it?" I asked, not taking my eyes off the gleaming brass circle in his hand. When Ivan handed it to me, I held it up next to my father's. They were almost identical. "Why do you have this?"

"Every member of the secret society of the Colombe had one," Ivan said.

"What's the Colombe?" Shawn asked.

"Idiotic name, isn't it," Ivan said. "It was your father's idea, Sky. It's the word *dove* in Italian or French or some such nonsense."

"My dad loved languages," I murmured, remembering a long-ago life where languages were woven into the fabric of every day. "But why dove?"

Ivan ignored me as he reread the note from my dad. He set it down sharply on the table. "Your father was an idiot," he said after a moment. Before I could protest, Ivan went on, muttering more to himself than us as he scowled down at his bowl. "Sending you aboveground with no training and the barest of clues to go on. Jack Mundy, what were you thinking?"

I sat up, my spine straightening. "He was thinking that I could handle it." When Ivan didn't say anything, I scowled. "I'm still alive, aren't I?"

"You are," Shawn agreed.

"Of course she is," Ivan snapped. "She's my granddaughter, isn't she?" He frowned down at my untouched supper. "Eat the rest of that. I don't let food go to waste." I grimaced. My hunger from earlier had disappeared, but I picked up my spoon anyway and forced myself to take a bite.

"The Colombe." Ivan sighed. "I guess I'd better start at the beginning. I met your father fifteen years ago. I relocated east when Clara insisted on going to that compound university." I could tell by his expression that he hadn't agreed with her decision. Ivan took a big spoonful of stew and continued. "While she was at that university, she met a few other students who didn't buy into all the dinosaur dung the Noah was flinging about."

"What dinosaur dung?" I prompted.

"The dung about humans only being safe in underground bomb shelters," Ivan said. "Last I checked, there hasn't been any bomb. The dinosaurs haven't made our planet uninhabitable; people panicked after the pandemic when they realised they were outnumbered and *chose* not to inhabit it."

"Not all the humans," I pointed out with a glance at Todd.

"Correct," Ivan said. "There are thirty-five villages spread across North America that I know of, at least. I'd venture to say there are more than that, but the majority of humanity is still cowering under concrete. My daughter met others who believed that humans and dinosaurs can share this massive planet of ours. Of course," he said, turning to me, his eyes softening, "your mother knew that it was possible. I'd raised her to hunt and trap with the best of them." Ivan cleared his throat, and I saw a flash of pain in his eyes. I hated to admit it, but that look made me jealous. I would have given anything to have a memory of my mother.

Ivan cleared his throat and went on. "Once she felt like she could trust them, she told them about me, about life in the sunshine, about the villages in the trees. Your father named their little group the Colombe."

"I still don't get the dove reference," I frowned.

"Why does the Noah call himself the Noah?" Ivan prompted. "Why do they call the compound-living system his Ark Plan?"

"It's based on an ancient biblical story," Shawn said. "About a guy named Noah who brought a bunch of animals into a big boat called an ark to save them from a flood. So a hundred and fifty years ago, when William Brown saved the human race by bringing them underground, he called himself the Noah."

"Good to know they taught you something in that school," Ivan said begrudgingly. "But what about the rest of the story?"

"What do you mean?" Shawn asked. "That's it."

"No." Ivan shook his head. "The story didn't end with that Noah man stuck on the boat forever with all those animals. After forty days and nights, Noah sent out a dove to look for land. That dove came back with an olive branch, so Noah knew it was safe to come off the ark. So he parked that huge behemoth of a boat and let everybody out. Taking them into the boat didn't save them; it was letting them back off that did that."

"I get it," I said. "The dove symbolises that it's time to go topside again."

"Very good." Ivan nodded approvingly. "I was beginning to worry that you didn't have much in the way of brains. That is exactly right. The group consisted of your mother and father and a few other scientists and biologists that attended the university with them. I even snuck into the East Compound to meet with them a few times to discuss their ideas. Your mother was so happy," he said. "She believed that she was changing the world."

"Wasn't she?" I asked.

Ivan shook his head sadly. "She never got the chance. Shortly after she had you, the Noah caught wind of the group. We aren't sure how, but I have my suspicions that one of the group members got nervous and turned on them."

"I bet that didn't go well," Todd said.

"It did not," Ivan agreed. "The Noah was unsure who exactly was involved. This created a problem, as he couldn't very well execute every student in the university. So he came up with another solution. He scattered the entire university population to the four compounds, cutting off any opportunity they had to communicate. Your father was sent to North Compound. A few, including your mother, tried to escape into the wild before the transfer." Ivan's face clouded over. "Some got away, but your mother was killed."

"Killed?" I repeated, stunned.

"But the Noah values human life too much to kill anyone," Shawn spluttered.

"Were you not at my village yesterday?" Todd asked.

"I just don't understand," Shawn said, putting his head in his hands. "How can everything we learned be a lie?"

"It wasn't all a lie," Ivan said gently. "The man we are talking about believes wholeheartedly in what he preached to you. He believes that what he does, he does to save the human race. History has shown us over and over again that there is nothing more dangerous than a man who believes so completely in his own convictions that he can't see the truth, even when it's right in front of him."

"Lies," I repeated, feeling numb. "My dad always said my mum died giving birth to me. That was a lie too?"

"It was." Ivan nodded. "I can't think of anything more dangerous than telling his young daughter a secret that could get them both killed." I shut my eyes, trying to make myself understand what Ivan was telling me. My mum had been murdered? I waited to feel pain, sorrow, or horror, but instead I felt betrayed. I thought back to those fuzzy years when my dad and I lived in our little apartment. How much of our life had been a lie? There was nothing solid I could hold on to, nothing true to keep me balanced in all of this. Willing myself not to cry, I opened my eyes to find Ivan watching me. I swallowed. He wasn't just Ivan, though, was he? If what he said was true, he was my grandfather. I couldn't think about that right now, though. It was too much on top of everything else.

"Why didn't she take me with her?" I asked him, feeling the sting of abandonment. What kind of mother left her baby behind?

"I can only assume it was because she thought you'd be safer underground," Ivan said.

"You still haven't explained the whatcha, um, compass things," Todd corrected himself, his face flushing red.

Ivan waved his hand dismissively. "I provided those. I'd found a box of the things during one of my trapping trips, buried in the rubble. Clara wanted the group to have some kind of unifying symbol, and I liked to make Clara happy."

"You loved her," I said, knowing it was true. He had the same warm gleam in his eyes my dad used to have. I'd forgotten what that look was like until just now.

"She was my sun, moon and stars," Ivan said, "and if I'd known her daughter, my granddaughter, was living as an orphan in one of those horrid compounds, you better believe I would have come for you."

I didn't say anything for a minute as I studied him. It was obvious in his tanned and wrinkled face that he felt guilty for leaving me in the compound. I looked away and out of the window as tears threatened again. I swallowed hard and blinked them away. No one except Shawn had cared about what happened to me ever since my dad left. I glanced back at those steady blue eyes and nodded. "Thank you," I said. I knew it wasn't much, but it was all I had at the moment.

"So mission accomplished, right?" Shawn asked, clapping his hands together, his voice forcefully cheerful. "You brought the plug to Ivan. You succeeded!"

I looked at Ivan. "Do you know what's on the plug? What my dad found out?"

"I haven't the foggiest," Ivan said.

"Do you have a port screen?" Shawn asked. "One that will fit the plug?"

"I did have one of those infernal contraptions," Ivan said. "Your dad gave it to me, but it was ruined when my pack fell into a pond about two years ago."

"So this isn't over," I breathed. "We still need to get to Lake Michigan."

Shawn groaned and flopped his head down on the wooden table dramatically.

"Sure looks that way," Ivan agreed. "And we need to get there fast."

CHAPTER 23

I'd got answers, but somehow they'd left me with even more questions than I'd had before. All of the new information swirled around in my head and I tried to think through each fact, rationalise it and categorize it, just like I had in my dinosaur research.

Fact one: my mum and dad had been part of a secret society. OK, I could imagine that. I thought back to my memories of my dad, seeing them in a new light. My dad had never spoken against the Noah, but he'd never praised the Noah like everyone else in the compound had.

Fact two: my mum had been murdered. This one was harder to wrap my head around and I pushed the whole matter aside to think about later.

Fact three: Ivan was my grandfather. That last bit was the hardest piece of information to believe. Was I happy about it? I decided I was. It was nice to have a relative who cared about me. It made me feel like a kid, something I hadn't really felt like in a long time. He definitely wasn't the warm and fuzzy grandfather type, but that was OK too. His prickly demeanour seemed to hide a kind heart, at least when it came to my mother. Maybe, given time, he'd feel that way about me too.

Our meal finished, Ivan pulled a lantern off its bracket on the wall and gave us each a hard look. "Do you want a tour?" he asked reluctantly. Shawn cocked an eyebrow at me and I shrugged. I had too much on my mind to care about touring the abandoned guts of an old skyscraper. Todd, on the other hand, bounded to his feet like his chair had been set on fire, a look of eager anticipation on his face. Ivan chuckled as he slung his leather bag back over his shoulder and motioned with his stump arm for us to follow him.

As Ivan lit the wall-mounted lanterns, the warm golden light flooded into the dark corners of the enormous room and I gasped in wonder. Pile after pile of gigantic dinosaur hides lay on every available surface. They were stacked three feet high and stretched on large metal frames to dry. Barrels of claws and teeth stood in neat rows against the back wall next to orderly stacks of bones taller than me. A few dinosaur heads were even stuffed and hung on the wall. Their shiny glass eyes winked at me as I stood in the middle of the space and spun around slowly.

"This is ten times the inventory you used to have," Todd said in awe as he flipped the corner of a huge scaly pelt over to inspect the underside.

"Did you kill all of these?" I asked. Ivan grunted as he watched Todd hold up claws to the light and inspect teeth with a small magnifying lens he'd picked up off Ivan's worktable.

"Some I killed," Ivan clarified as he took a seat at the large wooden worktable and spread out the gory claws and teeth that he had collected earlier, "others died naturally, and I just showed up to pull off the pelt before the scavengers arrived. A few made the mistake of trying to kill me and didn't live to regret it." Ivan unscrewed a fat glass jar and poured clear liquid into a large dented metal bowl. He dropped the teeth and claws in one by one, and the contents fizzed. When the fizzing stopped, he removed the teeth and claws using thin metal tongs and laid them out in a neat row on his table. All traces of blood and flesh were gone, leaving them gleaming and clean. He then poured the contents of the bowl back into the jar, setting the liquid aside. The process was fascinating, to say the least.

"But what do you do with it all?" I asked, my head spinning.

"Sell it. Trade it. Eat it."

We all turned to watch Todd crow happily as he discovered an entire dinosaur skull hidden under a tarp.

"That boy is his father reincarnated," Ivan said. "I've never seen anyone get so excited over old bones. He'll make a good trader if he can live long enough to grow up. Most traders don't." I was surprised to hear a warm affection in his voice as he talked about Todd. From the way he'd treated him earlier, I'd thought Ivan didn't like him. I'd been wrong.

"You don't look retired!" Todd exclaimed with a grin as he bounded up to us. He gestured to the two large claws he was holding in each hand. "You have enough stock here to keep the outlying villages supplied for years."

"Hobby," Ivan shrugged.

"I wish I knew how to kill this efficiently," Shawn said. "I'd wipe the dinosaurs off the planet. One monster at a time."

"Not so fast," Ivan cautioned. "It's too late for that. The dinosaurs have embedded themselves in our world, and we must adapt and evolve accordingly or risk going extinct ourselves."

"Really?" Shawn asked, disbelief etched across his face.

"But wouldn't things just go back to the way they were before if all the dinosaurs were killed?" I asked, feeling just as confused as Shawn.

Ivan shook his head gravely. "Too much has changed since they arrived. The creatures of the past have disappeared to make way for the dinosaurs' hierarchy of prey and predators."

"But if they all died, we'd be able to live topside again." Shawn said.

"Evolution doesn't work in reverse, compound boy," Ivan said sharply. He looked around, as though searching for inspiration. He stood up from his worktable and pointed to one of its legs. Only then did I notice that while three of the legs were made of solid wood, the remaining leg seemed to be supported by a thick dinosaur bone.

"That table leg started to rot some years back," Ivan said. "I used that bone to prop it up, and over time the original leg has become weaker and weaker. Now, young Shawn, picture that bone to be the dinosaur population, and the table is the rest of the world we live in – the animals, the plants, the people." Ivan gave the dinosaur bone a swift kick, and as it fell, the entire table collapsed in on itself, the piles of dinosaur teeth and claws that had been perched on it skittering across the floor. "Get it now?" he asked.

Shawn frowned down at the table. Ivan didn't realise it, but he couldn't have used a better metaphor to describe the problem if he'd tried. Shawn understood how things were put together, how points and counterpoints needed to balance, and I could see his brain churning as he thought over what Ivan had said.

Without another word, Ivan stood and blew out the nearest lantern. Our tour was officially over.

The next morning I woke up with a stiff neck, sore muscles and Todd drooling on my shoulder. Gross. The bright morning sun was streaming in, and the mounted head of a T. rex leered at me from across the room. All three of us had bunked down on Ivan's floor the night before. It hadn't exactly been comfortable. Shawn's blanket was crumpled in a forgotten lump and he was nowhere in sight. I looked over at the metal panel still bolted in the floor and let out a sigh of relief. He hadn't left, so he had to be around here somewhere.

Easing out of my blankets, I padded quietly over to the wall of windows. The forest below us seemed to go on forever, and in the distance I could just make out Lake Michigan.

"It's hard to believe it's crawling with scaled beasties from up here, isn't it," said a gruff voice behind me. I jumped and turned to find Ivan already dressed in his rough brown tunic, two bows and a gun slung over one shoulder.

"Good morning," I mumbled, brushing my tangle of curls back from my face. I glanced nervously at his gun. It was huge and black; a long rifle style rather than a pistol like the marines carried. I wondered where in the world he'd got it from.

Seeing my gaze, Ivan looked down. "I prefer the bow," he explained. "But I believe in always having a plan B."

"Where did you get it?" I asked, awed and a little frightened at the sight of the lethal-looking weapon.

"I found it years ago. It was a corroded and rusted mess, but I managed to rebuild it with the help of a man in the Maples."

I looked up. "The Maples?"

"A village about fifty miles south of the Oaks," Ivan

explained. "There is a collector there who specialises in old-world weapons parts."

I nodded, feeling a tug of guilt as I thought about the only collector I'd ever met, Roderick. Because of me, he was dead.

"Your friend Shawn has been busy this morning," Ivan said, interrupting my train of thought.

"Where is he?"

Ivan jerked his head to the left, and I looked over to see Shawn on his hands and knees, reconstructing the table that Ivan had knocked over the night before. He'd used bits of the dinosaur bone and teeth to cleverly support the weathered wood. I smiled as he checked to see if the table was level with a small round bone.

"He's always been good at fixing things," I said, feeling proud. Shawn brushed off his hands and looked up to see us watching him. He smiled sheepishly.

"Good." Ivan nodded. "Wake up, you lazy bum," he roared in Todd's direction, causing him to sit up with a start as he looked around in bleary-eyed confusion. "Breakfast is in five, and I don't eat with people who smell like a stegosaurus's bum. The washbasin is over there." Ivan motioned with his good arm, and Todd stumbled in that direction, still half asleep. Shawn and

I joined him, splashing our faces and rubbing our arms with the water.

"The table looks good," I said to Shawn as we walked back towards Ivan's kitchen. He shrugged in response. Ivan sliced up some coarse brown bread and handed us each a slice. He plunked a jar of something bright red on the table and sat down, smearing the stuff liberally on his bread. Todd followed suit, but Ivan noticed Shawn's hesitation.

"What's the matter? Haven't you ever had jam before?" he asked.

"No," Shawn said, "what is it?"

"What do you mean what is it? What kind of question is that? It's a fruit preserve. This one's raspberry," Ivan said. "I can it myself." I took the knife Ivan offered me and coated my own piece of bread and took a bite. I grinned, the flavour exploding in my mouth, sweet and just the slightest bit tart. I imagined it was what sunshine tasted like.

"That's better," Ivan said, and I could tell he was pleased. "Eat it all; you have a big day ahead of you."

"We do?" I asked.

"Are we going to Lake Michigan?" Shawn asked.

"Are we going to go save my mum?" Todd asked.

"I will be accompanying you to the lake," Ivan said. "A lot of the bigger beasts roam the area around the lake, and I don't fancy my granddaughter stomping through the woods with you two as her protectors." Hearing him say the word *granddaughter* had me pausing mid-bite. The term still felt so foreign, but despite its strangeness, it sent a warm happiness flooding through me. Then I registered what Ivan had actually said.

"Wait a minute." I sat up straight, feeling that warm feeling fizzle a little. "They aren't my protectors. I can take care of myself." Ivan didn't say anything, but I thought I saw a slight smile cross his face as he cut himself another slice of bread.

"You aren't going to help me get my mum and the rest of the Oaks back?" Todd asked.

"I will," Ivan said. "But not until after we have delivered Jack's plug." Todd sagged in disappointment. I thought over what he'd just said again. Protectors. He was acting like I was this helpless little girl getting taken care of by Shawn and Todd. If anything, the opposite was true – at least for Shawn.

"I have a backbone," I snapped, glaring at Ivan. "And before you ask if I have guts, I have those too."

"Very good," Ivan said, nodding approvingly. "Compound life can make you soft and dependent. It's good to see you're neither of those things." He seemed amused rather than offended, his blue eyes sparkling with humour. I had a feeling I'd just been tested. "Back to Jack's plug," he went on, his face serious again. "I'm worried. Your father, despite his numerous faults, loved you. He would never have put you in danger. I'm anxious to find out what is on that plug that was worth risking your life for."

"Do you think my dad might be at Lake Michigan?" I asked hopefully.

"No," Ivan said, shaking his head. "My best guess is that your father's dead." His words fell like lead weights into my stomach and I felt myself visibly sag in despair. When he saw my expression, he raised an eyebrow. "Don't look so defeated, child. It is only a guess. If you want to keep your hope alive, don't let me take it away from you."

"Do you know what's in the middle of Lake Michigan?" Shawn asked.

"I can only assume one of the surviving members of the Colombe," Ivan said. "But we won't know until we get there, will we?"

"How soon do we leave?" I asked, anxious impatience shooting through my nerves again.

"This afternoon," Ivan said. "I want to work on your shooting skills first."

"I taught her the basics yesterday," Todd said. "And she hit that Croc Killer dead in the eye."

"She needs more than the basics," Ivan said, "and I would like to work on your shooting skills as well."

"Mine?" Todd said. "Why?"

"You were a decent shot yesterday, but you could be better. You only hit two of the four dinosaurs you were shooting at."

"They were moving," Todd objected. "It wasn't exactly an easy shot."

Ivan raised an eyebrow. "They will always be moving." I covered my mouth to hide a smile as Todd frowned and stared down moodily at his plate. Ivan sure was good at putting people in their place. Todd had been so confident in his shooting skills from the moment we'd met him. Now he was being told that they needed some work. I had a feeling his ego was more than a little bruised.

"I wasn't shooting with my bow," Todd muttered. "I'm a better shot with mine, but it busted when it fell out of the tree."

"I can fix that," Ivan said, and he pushed himself away from the table and stomped across the length of the skyscraper to a back corner. Moments later he was back, a bow almost identical to the one Todd had lost held in his hand. "Stand up," he said, and when Todd did, he held the bow up to him, squinting with one eye. "It'll work," he said. "It's a tad large for you, but you'll grow into it."

"This looks exactly like my dad's," Todd said, running an appreciative hand down its gleaming length.

"It should," Ivan grunted. "I made it from a rib of the same beastie."

"I didn't know you made my dad's bow," Todd said, and I thought I saw tears shining in his eyes for a moment before he looked down and ran a hand roughly across his face. "Thanks," he said, his voice hoarse.

"You're welcome," Ivan said, clapping him on the shoulder. He turned to us. "Don't just stand there staring; go get your bows and packs. We won't be coming back here." We did, and I helped him to unhinge the heavy metal plate. He jumped down the ten-foot gap to land on the dilapidated escalator in a crouch, bow drawn. He scanned the room below and then motioned for us to follow him. Moments later we were in the sunlight.

Ivan headed for the woods at a brisk trot. He never looked back, and he never said a word. After I'd shared a 'here we go again' look with Shawn, we followed. Ivan was quick, zigzagging through the woods with a grace and stealth I wouldn't have thought possible at his age. When he finally stopped thirty minutes later, it was in a small meadow surrounded by thick trees. Shawn and I were breathing hard and even Todd looked a little winded. Ivan didn't look like he'd been running.

"First things first," he said, "you never carry your arrows at the centre of your back; too hard to reach." He adjusted my quiver so the opening sat at my left shoulder. "I saw you drop your arrows yesterday," Ivan admonished, and my face heated in embarrassment. How had he had time to study me while simultaneously killing a pack of rampaging dinosaurs?

"I was scared," I said, and even to my own ears I sounded pathetic.

"Learn to function scared," Ivan instructed. "I want you to shut your eyes and practise grabbing arrows."

"That's it?" I asked. "Just grabbing them?"

"Grab one, notch it, draw and then do it again, until you could do it in your sleep," Ivan said. "I'll let you know when to stop." So I did. Ivan spent the next three hours working each of us in turn. First with the bows and then, when he saw that our arms were getting tired, he switched to knife throwing. I was surprisingly good at it, better even than Todd, a fact I could tell bugged him. I was wondering how I was going to hack an entire day of hiking after all of this training when Ivan finally held up a hand to signal we were done. I let my arm drop, sending a ripple of pain through my exhausted muscles. Despite the throbbing ache, I was excited. For the first time since coming topside, I felt like I might have a chance if I was attacked by a dinosaur.

"That's enough for now," Ivan said. "We need to get going. From the way you and Shawn were huffing and puffing, it may take us longer to get to the lake than I originally thought." He froze then, his head cocked to the side, listening. I froze too, but all I could hear was the tittering of birds and the low buzz of insects. My skin prickled as goose bumps broke out on my skin.

"What is it?" Shawn whispered, but Ivan held up a hand to silence him. I strained my ears, and I heard it: footsteps. A moment later, the world erupted in noise and gunfire as the ground around our feet was peppered with bullets. They seemed to be coming from every direction as dirt shot up and hit our shins and legs. I shrieked, throwing my hands up to protect my face and head. Ivan and Todd dived behind a nearby outcropping of rocks, but I stood frozen in panic for a half second longer before I shoved my terror aside, seized a petrified Shawn, and followed. I hit the hard-packed dirt with a painful thump that knocked the wind out of me. I wheezed, trying to force air back into stubborn lungs as my brain fought to process what was happening. Guns could mean only one thing. Had we really been tracked again? Shawn pounded me on the back until I took a few gasping breaths. With air in my lungs again, I manoeuvred myself carefully next to Shawn. The rock we crouched behind would have fitted two of us comfortably; four was tight. Ivan had the big black gun I'd seen earlier in his hands.

"You've been followed," Ivan growled. "I should have heard them. Getting old. Hearing isn't what it once was. We were sitting ducks waiting for them to take some target practice on us." He looked over at us, concern in his bright eyes. "None of you were hit, were you?" We shook our heads, staying low as bullets continued to ricochet off the rocks. My mind flashed back to when the marines had shown up at the Oaks. This was what the villagers had felt like, trapped in the trees, outgunned and outmatched. And just like the people of the Oaks, I didn't see any way out. I swallowed hard. We would have heard a plane or a helicopter, which meant we'd been followed on foot. The thought had me scanning the thick woods behind us, worried that a marine in body armour was about to emerge any second.

"Bows up," Ivan said, jerking his head at the trees as though he'd read my mind. "If you see movement of any kind, shoot first and ask questions later." A cold trickle of sweat ran into my eyes, but I didn't take my hand off my bow to wipe it away.

"You aren't using your bow?" Shawn asked, his voice shrill. His shoulder was pressed against mine, and I could feel him trembling. Although it might have been me. It was hard to tell. Shawn leaned forward and got a look at Ivan's gun for the first time, and his eyes went wide.

"I only use bows on innocent beasts," Ivan said. "It puts us on even footing." He popped his head above the rock for a second to look, quickly ducking back down as another flurry of bullets pinged off the hard stone. He glanced over at Shawn. "With humans, I use bullets."

"They have body armour," Todd said, his face strained as he scanned the woods. "They were wearing it when they attacked the Oaks. Our arrows won't penetrate it."

"That's nice," Ivan said. "I have a Winchester Model 70."

"What's the plan?" Shawn whispered.

"You need to get to the lake," Ivan said, his words rushed and clipped. "I will do my best to deal with this lot, and I'll catch up with you as soon as I can."

"But, Ivan," I protested, letting go of my bow to clutch at his arm. "You'll never survive this alone. There has to be twenty of them. Come with us. We can outrun them."

"Twenty," snorted Ivan. "They should have sent fifty."

"It's too dangerous," I objected, but Ivan just shook his head at me.

"Don't worry, granddaughter. I didn't find you just to lose you again. Get to the lake as quickly as you can." He looked at Shawn and Todd. "You keep her safe, or I will skin both of you and use your sorry hides as a rug." Ivan turned back to me. "Look out for those two knuckleheads. You have more brains in your pinkie finger than either of them combined. Wait for me to distract the marines and then run." And before I could protest, Ivan pressed a whiskery kiss to my forehead and rolled out from behind the rock and into the woods, heading swiftly towards the sounds of men's voices and gunfire.

"Sky, which way are we running? Which way is north?" Shawn asked, his voice high and panicked, and I ripped my gaze away from the spot where Ivan had disappeared to look at Shawn's dirty sweat-streaked face.

"We can't just leave Ivan to do this alone," I cried.

"We have to," Todd said. "And don't worry; if anyone can survive this, it's Ivan. That guy's a living legend."

I pulled out my compass and found north, but instead of tucking it back inside my shirt, I held it for a second. The warm metal pressed into my palm and I wondered what would happen if I just ran out into the open and gave it to the marines. Would it save my friends from being killed? My dad had asked me to risk everything to deliver the plug to Lake Michigan, but was it really worth dying for? I wasn't so sure any more. Just then, a loud bellow came from behind us, followed by a man's terrified scream and gunfire.

"Go," Todd cried, and we scrambled to our feet, careful to stay low to the ground as we sprinted into the woods.

CHAPTER 24

The woods were eerily quiet, the sounds of the gunfire quickly muffled by the thick trees that surrounded us. Tree branches whipped past us as we ran with nothing but the sound of our footsteps and laboured breathing thrumming in our ears. I was in the lead, with Todd running behind me on my right and Shawn on my left.

I wondered if Ivan was still alive. I hoped so, but I was worried. We had no idea how many marines were hiding in those woods with weapons and he was just a little old man with only one arm to work with. Not that any of those factors seemed to slow him down in the slightest, but I still couldn't shake the sick feeling of dread in my stomach.

As we ran, a prickly wariness started poking at the edge of my consciousness. Something felt off, and I wasn't sure what it could be. A quick scan of the woods didn't do anything to ease the feeling. They were too silent. Too still. I skidded to a stop, my bow drawn. Todd and Shawn ran on a few more steps before they realised I was no longer with them. They both turned to face me, questions on their lips, but I held up a hand to stop them.

"Something's wrong," I whispered. "Listen."

"I don't hear anything," Shawn said.

"I know." I frowned. "That's the problem. The birds aren't singing; the bugs aren't chattering. Why?"

The hairs on the back of my neck went up, and I strained my ears for a sound as my heart thudded in my chest.

The bullet buzzed so close to my ear that at first I thought it was a mosquito or a bee until it thumped into the tree behind me, sending a spray of splintered wood over my shoulders and head.

"Get down," Todd yelled, diving to the ground. I spun behind the tree that had taken the bullet meant for me. More bullets pelted the ground and the surrounding trees for another few seconds and then stopped.

"Sky Mundy, I know you're there," General Kennedy called out. I sucked in a breath as fear, hard and hot, burned in my chest. "Come out, and I won't shoot your little friend Shawn." Peeking around the tree, I saw Kennedy standing fifteen feet away, a gun trained on my best friend. Shawn glanced my way and shook his head ever so slightly, his eyes panicked and pleading. I ducked back behind the tree and squeezed my eyes shut for a second, willing myself to think. There had to be a way out of this. I looked around for Todd, but he must have hidden further into the woods. I prayed he hadn't been shot.

"I'm not a patient person, Sky," Kennedy warned. "One. Two."

I threw myself out from behind the tree before he could make it to three, my hands in the air. "Don't shoot him," I said. "Please don't shoot."

"Very good, Sky," Kennedy said, turning to face me, his gun still pointed at Shawn. "Now hand over the plug."

"What's on it?" I asked. "Why does the Noah want it so badly?" Kennedy stared at me a second in shock, and then he burst out laughing. But his laugh wasn't genuine; it had a hard, angry edge to it that frightened me almost as much as the gun he clutched in his hand.

"You mean to tell me," Kennedy gasped, "that we've been tramping through these dinosaur-infested woods, chasing a little girl who doesn't even know what she's carrying?" He broke into another peal of laughter. I didn't say anything. I was calculating in my head just how far it was from me to Kennedy. Was I fast enough to get my bow up to shoot him? And what if I missed? Could he get a shot off at Shawn before my arrow reached him?

"Why are you chasing me?" I asked, desperate for more time to think.

"We shouldn't be," Kennedy said, anger dripping off every word. "I've lost three good men trying to bring you to justice. Men I grew up with and trained with lost their lives for a girl that we should have killed five years ago. The Noah was too kind, granting you a pardon due to your age. He didn't think a child presented a danger, especially if we kept you under the strictest surveillance." He shook his head. "Wasting precious resources to search the room and port-screen data of an orphan girl who was nothing but a burden on our society. And how do you repay his kindness? By stealing vital compound supplies to take your father's secrets to the very people who could undo the Noah's entire plan."

"What plan?" I asked.

"I am out of patience," Kennedy said. "Hand it over, or Shawn dies and then you do. I have no problem taking the plug off your corpse. I would have shot you already if I wasn't worried about accidentally hitting the plug."

"How do I know you won't shoot him as soon as I give it to you?" I asked. I didn't look at Shawn. I couldn't. If I saw the fear on his face, my own terror would overwhelm me. Every muscle in my body was tense, and I worried I might snap from the pressure.

"Don't do it," Todd said, stepping out from the woods, his bow trained on Kennedy. "Your dad wouldn't want you to hand it over."

Kennedy sneered at Todd's bow. "That bow doesn't scare me, boy. Put it down before you hurt yourself."

"My dad would say to save Shawn," I said, not taking my eyes off the gun in Kennedy's hand.

"Dead men don't say much, last time I checked," Kennedy drawled, a smirk on his face that made my blood run cold.

"What did you just say?" I asked, feeling like I'd been punched.

"Don't worry." Kennedy smiled. "Your father will never know that you were a failure. Just like him."

"You killed him?" I asked. "He's dead?" It couldn't be true. I'd have known if he'd been dead all this time. I would have felt it. Wouldn't I?

"We found him a day's travel from the compound," Kennedy sneered. "He didn't know that we'd implanted tracker chips into all of our high-risk technology specialists." Kennedy smirked at Shawn.

"You're a liar," I said, my fists clenched. "If my father was dead, you would have broadcast it across the entire compound."

"I'm a liar, am I?" Kennedy said. "Maybe I just have to show you that I mean what I say." He turned back to Shawn, aiming the gun right between his eyes.

"Don't give him the plug," Shawn said through gritted teeth. "You can't trust one word he says."

"She'll do what I say," Kennedy said, enjoying the moment and my pain. "She wants to save your sorry life, just like her father thought that he could save hers by leaving her behind. Had we known that the plug we pried out of his cold dead hand wasn't the only one, she wouldn't have been treated so kindly."

"Kindly?" I spat, anger overcoming the fear and making my entire body hot. "You call how I was treated for the last five years kind? You made everyone in that compound hate me. I was seven. Seven! You assigned me work detail after work detail. I would have gone insane if it wasn't for Shawn."

"That Shawn," Kennedy said, shaking his head slowly. "Quite the friend you have. It's going to be a shame when he gets killed because you wouldn't hand over the plug. A plug you don't even know the value of."

"Don't give it to him," Todd said again.

"One," Kennedy said, and I saw his grip tighten on the gun. "Two."

Out of the corner of my eye, I saw Todd raise his bow and draw back an arrow, but I saw something else as well. Five feet away from Kennedy, shiny yellow eyes peered out of the brush. A long, arrow-shaped head poked up moments later, and I saw Kennedy glance at it dismissively. The tiny dinosaur only came to just above his knees. Raising its head, it sniffed the air curiously. I realised with a start that I knew what kind of dinosaur it was. It was a saltopus, and it was a scavenger. An idea took shape, and I bit my lip. My plan was a long shot, but it was worth a try.

"Three," Kennedy said, and he fired. I saw Shawn dive for cover, yanked my knife out of its sheath and charged. Covering the ground between Kennedy and myself in the blink of an eye, I collided with the hard body armour of his chest. He shouted in surprise, and we both fell backwards. I pulled back my knife, but he grabbed my wrist in his iron grip. Instead of driving into his shoulder like I'd intended, it sliced into his cheek, opening a long three-inch gash that immediately started bleeding. I hoped it was enough. With a jerk, I threw myself backwards, landing in the brush and rolling behind the closest tree. I stood up on trembling legs. My father's compass lay cool and hard on my heart, and I realised that my bow was lying fifteen feet away, useless. My plan suddenly seemed incredibly stupid.

"That was a mistake," Kennedy said, and I looked cautiously around the tree to see him wiping at the blood covering his face and wetting the neck of his body armour. I saw something move in the bushes behind him, and I prayed it was what I thought it was.

"You can't hide from me," Kennedy called, and I heard his footsteps coming closer to the tree where I was hiding. "I will find you, Sky Mundy. You have something that belongs to the Noah. One little girl will not ruin the human race's chances of survival.'

I held my breath as his feet crunched loudly in the leaves. About ten feet away, I heard Todd yell, followed by the sound of breaking branches, and Shawn yelped. Seconds later I heard deep male voices – two more marines calling out orders and attempting to capture my friends. Kennedy's backup had arrived, and any hope I'd had of Todd or Shawn shooting Kennedy before he got to me evaporated.

"Why, hello there," Kennedy said, suddenly coming around one side of my tree, his gun pointed at my head.

This was it.

I was going to die, just like my mum, just like my dad. I was going to let them both down. The plug would be taken, and I was going to be a failure, like Kennedy said I would be. Suddenly Kennedy screamed, and the gun jerked away from my head. The tiny saltopus had latched its razor-sharp teeth into Kennedy's calf. He turned his gun on the creature, firing three quick blasts. My would-be saviour went slack, blood pouring out of three neat bullet holes. Kennedy turned his gun back to me, and I kicked myself for not running in that second of distraction. He limped towards me, but before he could take more than a couple of steps, three more of the tiny dinosaurs came scurrying out of the woods, their noses raised. Two of them fell on their fallen comrade, ripping apart the poor animal. The third turned an inquiring nose towards Kennedy's blood-soaked calf. Kennedy turned and shot it point-blank in the head. It fell backwards, but three more of the creatures had emerged from the woods, and I could see the fear on Kennedy's face. One of them launched itself at Kennedy, and he yelled, his gun firing. I took my chance, and I ran, grabbing my bow as I sprinted past it.

Kennedy's shriek of fear echoed behind me, followed by more gunshots. Three more saltopus hurried past me as they scurried towards Kennedy and the smell of blood.

"Sky," Shawn yelled. "This way!" I whipped my head around to see him and Todd standing ten feet away, their bows drawn.

"Where were you?" I asked. "Are you OK?"

"We got caught up," Todd said, and I glanced behind him to see two marines tied expertly to a tree.

"We have to run," I said, as Kennedy's scream ripped through the forest behind us.

CHAPTER 25

"Do you think Kennedy's dead?" Shawn asked. I sat with my back against the trunk of the massive tree we'd climbed to hang our tree pods in for the night, trying to drink in the sunset. The surrounding forest was dazzling, painted in pinks and oranges as the thrum of insects started their nightly concert. My mind and my heart were full. I was alive to see this sunset and the next, but my parents were not. I imagined my mum at my age, soaking up sunsets, and I hoped that my dad had seen at least one before Kennedy had caught up with him. They were one of my favourite things about this dangerous topside world.

"I don't know," I said, shaking my head. We'd had this same debate several times that day as we'd fled Kennedy and the marines. "There were a lot of dinosaurs coming at him, but he had a gun, and they weren't very big."

"The more he killed, the more he intensified the

smell of the blood." Todd shook his head. "Making him bleed like that was smart. Really smart."

"It was a hunch," I said. "I spotted that saltopus and it gave me an idea. I'd read that they usually won't go after prey larger than themselves, but there were theories that they hunted in cooperative packs."

Shawn shuddered. "I'd say the theory was correct."

"Yeah," Todd agreed. "Ankle Biters are usually just a nuisance, but if they smell blood, watch out. We always just wring their necks if they start causing problems. No blood that way."

"And it was no hunch, Sky," Shawn said. "You've researched dinosaurs for the last five years. It paid off."

"I guess it did," I laughed, and winced when the movement sent a twinge of pain through my muscles. I was stiff and sore from the hours and hours of running we'd done that day. The first half hour we'd run in the wrong direction. It had taken that long for the panic and fear clouding my brain to part enough for me to remember my compass. I'd finally checked it and redirected our course.

"I was planning on helping you out," Todd said, shaking his head ruefully, "but those other compound guys came out of nowhere. It took everything Shawn and I had to bring them down."

"I'm impressed that you got them tied to that tree," I said.

"I wanted to kill them," Todd admitted. "But Shawn pointed out that if we did that, we weren't any better than they were."

"I knew both of them." Shawn shrugged. "They are both good guys with families back at North Compound. They were just following orders. I didn't think they deserved to die for that."

"Do you think they'll follow us?" I asked.

"I don't think the Noah is going to give up just because a few of his marines got mauled."

"What I still don't understand is how they followed us," I said. "We ditched everything that could have possibly contained a tracker." I glanced up at Shawn, but his face was clouded with the same worry as my own.

"I have a theory," Todd said. "I don't know much about those tracker things, but I do know a lot of people that can track in the woods without any fancy bits of technology."

"What do you mean?" Shawn asked.

"I mean, we didn't really try to hide our trail after we

left the Oaks," Todd said. "If one of your marine guys was good at tracking, they could have just followed us on foot."

"I don't know," I said, thinking about the compound's marines. "The marines rarely go topside. I doubt anyone knows how to do that."

"Then maybe they found someone who does," Todd suggested. "Most of the men of the Oaks could have done it for them. Not that they would have," he added quickly.

"Maybe," I said, rolling the idea around in my mind. It was possible, I guessed, but it just didn't seem to fit. I sighed. All I could do now was get to Lake Michigan as fast as possible, and pray we'd seen the last of General Kennedy and his marines.

"It sounded like that plug of yours is pretty important," Todd said, pulling me from my thoughts.

I opened my compass to stare at the tiny piece of metal. "It did, didn't it?" I turned to Shawn, who was sitting a few branches higher than me, brooding while watching the spectacular sunset. "What plan do you think he was talking about?" I asked.

He shrugged, pulling his eyes away from the horizon to glance down at where I sat. "A week ago,

I would have said the plan was probably something to protect the human race, but the Noah isn't who I always thought he was."

"Took you long enough," Todd quipped, and I kicked him in the shin when Shawn looked away. Todd flinched, and I scowled at him. Couldn't he see that Shawn was upset? He had believed in the compound way of life, in the Noah and his plan to save the human race, with his whole heart. Now everything he'd ever known or believed in was being called into question. I was struggling with it myself, and I'd never been a believer like Shawn.

"Do either of you have a knife?" Shawn asked abruptly.

I shook my head. "I dropped mine when I went after Kennedy. What happened to yours?"

"Todd and I lost ours when we were wrestling those marines," Shawn said, looking disappointed.

"It's OK," Todd said. "We can get by without a knife until Ivan catches up with us." Shawn didn't look reassured.

"You really think Ivan will be able to find us?" I asked. I knew I'd asked the same question five times already that day, but I needed the reassurance.

"His tracking skills are epic," Todd said. "He'll find us if…" He paused. "If he's alive."

"He is," I said. I had to believe it. Fate wouldn't be so cruel as to give me a family just to rip it away from me again. I hoped. Without Ivan, I truly was an orphan, just like Shawn had said all those years ago when we'd first met in the Guardian Wing. Shutting my eyes, I tried to picture my dad's face, but the years had made the memory hazy. I wondered if what Kennedy had said was true, that my dad had been dead for the last five years. Just like Todd's tracker theory, I found it hard to believe. If Kennedy really had captured and killed my dad within days of his escape, wouldn't it have been compound-wide news? The marines would have liked nothing more than to gloat about the death of a traitor. Unless, I frowned, they'd wanted to keep his death a secret once they discovered what he'd stolen.

I glanced down at the compass around my neck and the mystery it contained. *What did you steal, Dad?* I wondered silently. *And would you do it all again despite how things turned out?* A sigh escaped me, and Shawn gave me a questioning look. I just shook my head. I wasn't ready to talk about my dad. Not yet. I'd been carrying his disappearance around on my shoulders for the last five years. It had defined me and dictated almost every decision I made.

Now, somehow, that weight was gone. Maybe it was what Kennedy had said, or finding Ivan, or everything that had happened since I left the compound, but I felt free for the first time in a long time. I was still going to follow through and get the plug to Lake Michigan. The need to find out its secret still pulled at me, making it almost uncomfortable to sit still. But after that, I was going to go back to the Oaks, and I was going to start over. Well... I frowned. I had to help Todd save the people of the Oaks first. But after that, I would start my life as a girl who lived in a tree, breathed fresh air every day, and never missed a sunset. I stared out at the swiftly darkening forest. Far in the distance a dinosaur bugled and another answered its call.

"Are you sure you're OK coming with us to the lake?" I asked Todd. "This is taking longer than our original deal. I'd understand if you wanted to go after your mum and the rest of the Oaks villagers. Shawn and I can make it to the lake on our own." I felt another uncomfortable twinge of guilt as I thought about everything that had happened since I'd left the

363

compound. "We've already put you in enough danger for one lifetime."

"Are you kidding?" Todd asked. "My mother raised me better than that. She'd be furious if I left you now to go after her. She believes in independence and a life free of the Noah's tyranny. I have a chance to help ruin whatever plan he's cooking up. I'm going with you."

"Still…" I said, feeling guilty.

"Plus," Todd said, "you heard Ivan. Shawn and I have to look out for you or he's going to make us into a rug. I wouldn't put it past him either."

"You'd make an ugly rug," Shawn said from above us.

Todd snorted. "So would you, compound boy."

"Birch brat," Shawn retorted, and grinned.

"Well, thanks," I said. "You're a good friend." And I realised it was true. This strange boy who lived in trees and outmanoeuvred dinosaurs was my friend. I'd never had anyone besides Shawn; it was nice to know there was someone else on my side. My mind slipped back to Ivan, but I pushed the painful worry aside. Todd was right; Ivan would find us.

"I promise that as soon as we get this plug mess

figured out, we'll help you get your mum and the rest of your village back."

"I know you will," Todd said.

"So we head to the lake in the morning?" Shawn asked, sounding resigned.

"We head to the lake," I agreed. I opened up my compass again in the dimming light and watched as the dial spun and then pointed north. Hope uncurled in my stomach, stretching itself like a cat in the sun. I was going to finish my dad's mission. I was the daughter of parents who had died in the fight for freedom and independence. I was the granddaughter of one of the greatest dinosaur hunters of all time. I had friends by my side willing to put their lives on the line for me. I had everything I needed.

"I'm going to call it a night." Todd yawned. "I'll see you guys in the morning."

"We aren't going to have the kind of wake-up we had last time we slept in one of these, are we?" Shawn asked, looking nervously down at the ground.

"Man, I hope not," Todd said, quickly assessing the surrounding branches. "This tree is a lot bigger than the one we were in before, and we aren't near water. But –" he shrugged – "it's a risk you just have to take.

It's part of the territory of living aboveground."

"Don't remind me," Shawn groaned, and I smiled.

"Good night, Todd," I said as he crawled into his pod. Less than five minutes later, we heard the sound of his soft snore.

"That kid is unbelievable," Shawn said. "I don't know if I'm going to be able to sleep tonight. I just keep thinking about the last time. That Croc Killer isn't something I'm going to forget any time soon."

"We'll be OK," I said. "You should really try to sleep. We have another long day in front of us."

"Has there been any other kind since we left the compound?" He turned and climbed up the tree another ten feet to where his own pod was tied and climbed in.

I was alone. I took a second to enjoy the clicking chirps of the insects before pulling out my journal. With the last of the fading light, I sketched out Ivan's house, added information about the saltopus – or Ankle Biters, as Todd had called them – and jotted down the archery pointers Ivan had given me, before I forgot them. I was going to wake up early the next morning to practise. It was doubtful that I'd ever have Todd's skill or Ivan's uncanny ability, but I wanted to get confident enough that if I was ever in a situation like

I'd been in earlier that day with Kennedy, I wouldn't hesitate to shoot.

I looked up as the echoing call of a dinosaur floated through the evening air. In the distance, a herd of long-necked brontosaurus moved slowly across an open meadow, and I smiled. The topside world was more beautiful and dangerous than anything I could have imagined. With one last long look across the horizon, I turned and crawled into my own tree pod for the night, because I hadn't been lying to Shawn: tomorrow would be another long day, full of its own adventures and dangers and dinosaurs.

Look out for the next

EDGE OF EXTINCTION

adventure.

Coming soon . . .